All But the Blood

Book One of the
Blood Promises Legacy

Tracy Prater

This is a work of fiction. Any references to historical events, real people, or real places are used fictitiously. Other names, characters, places, and events are products of the author's imagination, and any resemblance to actual events or places or persons, living or dead, is entirely coincidental. Portions of this book are based on historical references and documentation. Certain names and identifying characteristics have been changed.

copyright © 2023 Tracy Prater

ISBN: 978-1-959700-18-0

Victoria Fletcher
hootbookspublishing.biz
vfletcher56@gmail.com

Dedication

For my mama and granny… I miss you.

Acknowledgments

Deep appreciation goes to the Washington County Historical Society of Abingdon, Virginia. It was the first stop of my many research trips. In one afternoon they helped me pull together maps, documents, and resources of all sorts.

Thank you to Ryan Comer, my attorney, who read the first draft and made sure that I was on track with the facts for this historical fiction of mine.

I want to thank my Alpha Reader and our town librarian Kris Sheets. Kris, your insights from research to final edits have been a blessing. To my Beta Readers, Kristie Allison and Allyson Green, thank you for sharing the parts of the story you loved and giving me the heads up on what was needed to make the story flow.

Thank you to the owners of Lafitte's Blacksmith Shop Bar for taking such good care of a historical icon and keeping the "spirits" alive. Special thanks to Jamie Gourgues, assistant manager at Lafitte Hotel, for her help in getting some details just right.

Thank you to Bloom Post and my little tribe in North Carolina. You never let me stop saying my "I am's". You believed I could do this before I did.

Long ago though, someone else believed I could be a writer: Mrs. Lorraine Heath, my high school English teacher. I will never forget your faith in me. I wish you were here to see that I finally did it. Thank you also to my high school typing teacher, Mrs. Betty Fawley. Mrs.

Fawley, you gave me the one skill that has served me in every area of my life.

As the writing process drew to a close, I was fortunate to come into contact with Lynn Adreozzi, the cover artist for this book. Your work absolutely captivates me. Thank you for working so closely with me to achieve my vision.

Victoria Fletcher, my friend at Appalachian Authors Guild and my editor/proofreader/formatter etc. at Hoot Books Publishing, thank you for your patience and guidance. Your words of encouragement have meant the world to me.

Heather Edwards, there are no words to describe our friendship. You have stuck by me through this entire process. From the first dream that started the story through a million brainstorming sessions on our way to gather research. The Lincolnton, Natchez, New Orleans, and Mt. Pleasant areas may never be the same. I look forward to many more road trips for research.

Tamba Elliot, the "daughter" of my heart. I hope you will be able to clearly see my intentions with this story. I truly want to honor the lives of those who have gone before. They deserve their truths to be shared and the whole story to be told.

Last but not least and most of all, my love and gratitude to my husband and son. Tom and Matt, thank you for your patience and support while this book was being written and prepared for publication. Two more are coming along so I will still need all of your positive energy to see me through. In the meantime, it is time for us to travel.

Character Lists

Meg Hurley's circle

Granny Del: Meg's grandmother

Mother: Maggie

Father: Lee

Granny Roberts: childhood neighbor

Ma Barker: childhood neighbor

Ben Roberts: friend from childhood

Jessica Roberts: wife of Ben

John Peabody: Meg's former professor/current colleague

Gabby LeBlanc Peabody: wife of John

Wavery Parker's Circle

Granny Bea- Wavery's grandmother

Mother: Caroline

Father: William

Brother: Calvin

Sister: Penny

Sister: Kate

Ann Rossi's Circle

Nona: Ann's grandmother

Nana Grace: Ann's honorary grandmother

Tony Rossi: Ann's grandfather

Sam Coffey: Grace's husband

Father: Joe

Mother: Elizabeth

Brother: Gray

Brother: Luke

Brother: Jack

Historical Figures

Samson's Family from Graystone Plantation

Nelson, father

Sarah, mother

Moses, brother

Twin siblings: Henry & Louisa

Baby sister: Deborah (Dibby)

Salt Works

Pastor Daniel Hughes

Emil Planter: Daniel's friend

Nelly Planter: Emil's wife

Reston House & Sugar Plantation

Hiram: overseer

Tassy: Kitchen worker

Hazzie: Tassy's granddaughter

Present Day New Orleans

Jimmy: bartender friend of Wavery

Dr. Gallo: professor at Tulane

Glen & Conrad: Wavery's neighbors

Matthew: owner of sandwich shop

Mr. & Mrs. LeBlanc: Gabby's parents

Amelie: owner of metaphysical shop

Contents

THE BLOOD OF THE PAST
FOREVER MARKS THE FUTURE

Preface

The young girl sat on a hard wooden chair in the corner of the room listening intently. For sounds. For signs. She closed her eyes tightly, trying to block out anything that would get in her way. Her ears picked up the softy pelting rain against the beveled glass of the window. The rain's echo tapped a much slower rhythm than the blood beat of her heart. The rapid staccato pounded in her ears, and she prayed that the woman would not be able to hear it as well.

Madame stood at the top of the stairs leading down into the lower room of the small cottage she kept at the side of the main house for certain purposes. Madame pulled her basket of supplies close. She was keenly aware of who awaited her at the bottom of the stairs. She knew exactly who the young girl was and what she wanted. Purposely creaking the steps on her descent, she alerted the young girl of her presence. The girl rose from her chair just as the older woman stepped from the last stair. The two of them, chins held high, looked at each other without speaking. After a moment, the older woman signaled for the young girl to remain silent and follow her outside where a carriage stood waiting.

The rain had come and gone in quick succession when the girl found herself riding in a carriage beside Madame. As the wheels rumbled over the rough roadway, the girl remembered the night she had managed to steal away from the plantation with only a small bundle of her belongings. Not that she had all that much that belonged solely to her. But it seemed that Madame had insisted the bundle be recovered from the abandoned outbuilding the young girl had been hiding in since first arriving to the city. The girl had overheard the older woman telling the driver what they were about before boarding the carriage, saying.

"We all know the importance of having something, no matter how small, that belongs only to you."

Once her belongings were retrieved, the woman and younger girl returned to the cottage. Madame instructed the girl to take her things to a room at the top left of the stairs. It was a small but bright room with a window facing the street and a side window facing the main house. The furnishings were minimal. A single chair and table sat beneath the street side window and a small bed was placed against the back wall.

The young girl had spent days practicing what she would say to finally convince the woman to take her on, not only as a servant but as a student. She hurriedly placed her bundle on the bed and turned to go back down the stairs. Surely, this was the sign she had been hoping for all along.

As the girl returned to the lower room, Madame pointed a long, graceful arm giving direction to stand in the center. The older woman circled around her, first from the left and then from the right. The girl half expected to hear the demand to open her mouth for inspection there as well. For a moment, it felt as if she were up on the Natchez block once again being made ready for the selling.

The woman shook her head up and down slowly. Then she moved within inches of the girl. She was so close the girl could feel a penetrating heat from the older woman's body. The young girl tried to keep from trembling. She had only experienced such emotional turned physical heat when she had been on the wrong end of anger.

The young girl grounded herself and began to use her other senses. This did not smell like anger. It was different. She looked into the woman's eyes to see flickers of a blue flame. The burning within the older woman came from an age-old knowledge. A knowledge the girl could only hope to experience one day.

The older woman veiled her eyes and spoke in an eerily quiet voice,

"Do you trust me?"

The girl knew the question itself was a test. She knew without a doubt that if she did not answer in the right way, all was done. The girl swallowed hard before stating in as strong a voice as she could muster.

"Not at all."

The older woman did not dare show her pleasure in the answer but replied,

"Good. I have no trust in you either— yet. Trust must be earned. You have come here to ask me to take you into my world. To teach you things that you will use to your own advantage. Trust this, I see you for who you are, for what you are. I see *and* I know things in ways that you may never be able to understand or imagine."

The older woman pushed her lacy shawl from her shoulders and tossed it over to the chair in the corner. She handed her basket to the girl telling her to take everything from inside to place on the table by the fireplace. The girl pulled back a woven cotton cloth and peered inside the basket. One by one she pulled out each item. Three amber bottles and three cork stoppers came out first. Then she found a blue bottle filled with liquid, a leather pouch tied tightly so as to not spill its contents, and lastly a small very sharp knife. After placing all the contents on the table, she felt herself begin to tremble in anticipation. She heard the woman whisper in a matter-of-fact voice,

"Now for your first lesson."

The girl watched as Madame lit a candle on the table and passed each of the three bottles through the flame. Then she watched as the blue bottle was opened and the older woman poured out something oily into the palm of her hand. The woman rubbed her hands together and then rubbed her hands over each of the bottles. Next, she loosened the cord on the leather pouch and reached inside to pinch out a powdery concoction which she sprinkled on each of the bottles. As she was sprinkling, she began whispering words unfamiliar to the young girl.

Madame sat the bottles down in a straight row on the rickety table, picking up the knife. The girl watched as the flames from the fireplace and candle appeared to send shafts of blinding light towards the blade of the knife. The girl continued to watch in awe as Madame raised the small knife above her head, turned in a circle three times before walking to three different parts of the room with her back to the young girl. At each direction, the older woman appeared to be speaking to someone that the girl could not see. Once this had been completed the woman returned to stand within inches of the young girl once again.

"Now let us see if you trust yourself. You will take this knife and prick the middle finger of your left hand. Make the piercing deep enough to obtain three drops of blood for each bottle. Your blood must be sealed inside each bottle with the cork and wax from the candle."

The older woman watched expressionlessly as the young woman reached out reverently for the knife. The girl took the knife and walked closer to the table with her back to the older woman. The woman held her breath in silent admiration as she watched the young woman hold the knife against her heart while standing motionless with her eyes closed. She tilted her head as if she herself were listening to unheard voices.

The girl held the knife steadily as she pricked the middle finger of her left hand. She saw to it that three heavy drops of blood went into each of the amber bottles. She then placed the corks tightly into each bottle before using the candle from the table to seal a part of herself inside. She turned to the old woman, meeting her eyes without flinching.

The woman returned the look and spoke quietly.

"Remember this lesson. Healing is found in the plants, but the magic is in the blood. Always."

She stopped in thought and then placed both hands on the girl's shoulders.

"If you choose correctly, you will find both the healing and the magic…the strongest of magic…your magic."

The older woman took the bottles and put them back into the basket, knowing that one day far away, the magic of the blood would return to this place.

Part One
First Blood

We all know that every bloodline appears to have one beginning— that is until we put it all together in what seems to be the end. Some would say this was the beginning.

Chapter 1
Meg's Beginning

In-between times are magical. They allow the mind and the heart to slip effortlessly into another place. A place where your soul can reach out to touch the past or imagine a dream for the future. Meg loved the in-between times. She especially loved the ones that appeared like charmed doorways at dawn and dusk each day.

Dusk was closing in as Meg sat at the old oak table in front of her study windows. The table had been refurbished into a desk that was perfect for working and gazing northward toward the rocky red point of the mountain standing guard over her little hometown. Meg felt "her" mountain could rival any peak, especially when it was covered with fall foliage, snow, or greenery. For now, however, it was bare and appeared forlorn and aching for springtime growth. She sympathized with the mountain, underscoring her own yearning for spring. It was the season of hope and possibilities, always seeming to tease of a new adventure.

 Meg closed her laptop and gazed out into the dusky light of evening. The glow of the sun was lasting a little longer each day but for now, the light of this evening was fading into night. The magic door of time was opening. Meg leaned back into her softly upholstered chair. She could feel herself sinking into the dwindling pool of light. Her body stilled, her eyes fluttered closed, and she walked through the door into a springtime long ago.

The sensations of becoming smaller and smaller overtook Meg's body and mind. She looked around and found she was no longer in her study. No longer surrounded by her beloved books and artifacts. She was standing in a field. It was the field across the road from her house. The house where she had spent her youngest years living with her parents and grandmother.

Meg looked down toward the ground and saw her 6-year-old feet smudged with rich black dirt. She could feel the fertile loam sifting between her tiny toes sticking out from her sandals. She looked up ahead to see how far her grandmother, mother, and the neighbor ladies had gotten on their sojourn. Their long legs could certainly outwalk her even if they were so much older.

She watched as each of the women carried small iron shovels and coal buckets usually kept by their wood and coal stoves. The women would use the shovels to easily scoop up and empty the rich field dirt into the buckets. Every bucket would be filled to the top and taken back across the road. The rich black dirt would be used to sew new seeds and to re-pot plants that had been wintering inside Granny Robert's sunken dairy building.

Meg's house sat snuggled between Ma Barker and Granny Roberts' houses. In between each house, there was a long row of tilled dirt. Each spring the three elders came together to help each other plant a variety of flowers and herbs. They worked in unison to sow the seeds, tend the plants, and share the harvest.

Meg looked toward the field. She couldn't ever remember coming here before, but the women must have because they didn't hesitate at all in pushing down the barbed wire of the fence and climbing over into the field. Meg's mama pulled the lowest strand of the wire up so that

Meg could scoot under to follow the women down the worn path. Meg knew the big boys from up and down the row of houses always came across the road to play ball. They must have been the ones to keep the path open through the field.

Looking back over her shoulder, Meg could see the main road that ran in front of the row houses and into town. It was a busy road early in the morning and again around four o'clock in the afternoon. During those bustling times, workers traveled back and forth to the plants, big trucks made deliveries and picked up goods to go out of town, and long yellow buses ferried children back and forth to school.

Meg looked ahead to see the ground dropping down to the gurgling creek that could be heard from her front porch. Meg remembered hearing the sweet sound of peepers at the creek a while back. She remembered holding the sound close to her heart knowing this was one of the first signs of spring.

Further over, Meg could see the train track that wound its way into town. The trains brought supplies into the plant and took away products for delivery. The big black engines that pulled the cars chugged along the valley filling the air with smoke from their stacks. Their whistles always sounding sad to Meg. Not at all like the happy tootles of the noon day and quitting time whistles that signaled from the plant just a mile up from Meg's house. Meg often pondered if the train whistle would have sounded happier had there been passenger cars attached to the big smokey engine. She imagined cars full of people going on grand adventures like in the old black and white movies she watched with her mother.

Just a few hundred feet from the railroad tracks, the foremost boundary hill sat waiting for the green grass to start growing again. Soon cattle would be turned out and they would munch away at the young spring grass on their way up the boundary hill. In no time at all they would make a smooth path to the top. The big boys always talked about going up and over that hill. They loved that no one from the houses below could watch while they played fox and hound. Meg wasn't sure what happened during the game, but the boys sure did seem to have fun with it.

Looking back, Meg realized that she was jealous of the adventures and freedom the boys seemed to enjoy. Her mother had so wanted her to be the little girl who wore poofy little dresses, played with dolls, and had imaginary tea parties. But Meg's heart yearned for adventures and discovery. All she needed were jeans, books, and a backpack for gathering treasure.

Meg remembered hearing Ben, Granny Roberts' grandson, talking about going past the hill for a small distance to camp out with his friends. She wished she were old enough to tag along but she knew it wasn't just her age that kept her from going. The boys would never allow a girl to tag along. Not long after hearing Ben brag about the fun he and his friends were going to have camping just behind the boundary hill, he came home singing a different song.

It was just after dark on a Friday night when Ben came running back full throttle from the much bragged about camping trip. The late spring night was warm with a tease of what summer might bring to the valley. Meg was sitting on the porch steps watching the sun fade into twilight. Her mama and daddy sat on the porch swing drinking the last sips of their evening coffee. Her grandmother and Granny Roberts were sitting in the old green glider on the opposite end of the porch swishing it back and forth with a slow creaky rhythm. Meg loved this feeling of being surrounded by the familiar smells of coffee and spring air. She loved listening to the cadence of frogs over at the creek and the gentle sounds of the swing creaking and the glider moving slowly back and forth.

Meg glanced around dreamily but was startled by her daddy suddenly putting his coffee cup down on the wide porch banister with a thump. He stood up tall and straight, squinting toward the field across the road. Meg followed her daddy's intense gaze to see Ben running as fast as he could through the field toward their house. Luckily, there was no evening traffic on the road because he certainly wasn't looking for cars coming his way. He bolted across the cooling pavement toward the folks gathered on the porch.

Meg sat wide-eyed as Ben began to explain why he had left the camp out. Meg's daddy must have understood how frightened Ben was because he immediately opened the screen door and reached inside to turn on the porch light. Meg could see the light reflected off Ben's glasses and the beads of sweat on his forehead. She saw his hands trembling as he held on to the porch banister. His voice shook as he described the incident that had sent him and the other boys fleeing home with no thought for the gear they left behind.

Ben took in a gulp of air before explaining how the boys were gathering wood to start a campfire when they began to hear voices in the distance. At first, they thought it might be other friends coming to join them. It didn't take long to realize the tones weren't the familiar laughs of their friends. The sounds they were hearing had nothing to do with laughter. The closer the sounds got, the more distinct they became. Ben described their horror at hearing the echoes of wailing and crying throughout the hollow behind the boundary hill.

Meg's inquisitive instincts were alerted. She instantly wanted to know why anyone would be crying like that and how they could be helped. She also wondered yet again why it seemed the boys always got to have all the adventures. Granny Del looked over to Meg and saw the wide-eyed look on her tiny face. Her grandmother had no idea that the story didn't frighten her in the least. Granny Del took Meg by the hand to lead her into the house. Just as she was telling Meg to pay no attention to Ben, she saw a strange look pass between her grandmother and Granny Roberts. She heard her father whisper to her mother that perhaps the boys would think twice about going back to "slave holler" after dark. Oh, how Meg had wanted to stay on the porch to hear the whole story. Little had she known that night she would soon have an adventure of her own across the road.

It was a few weeks later when Meg's wish for an adventure was granted. Here she was looking over to the green mounded hill that stood like a guardian to the place her daddy had called "slave holler." Meg had not really known what a "holler" referred to except for maybe the sounds that Ben had described when he came running back home in a panic.

Meg could feel a familiar itch rise inside her little body all the way up to her throat. It was the same feeling she got whenever she wanted to question or explore something unknown. Meg was an inquisitive child to say the least, but her family was patient with her unending questions. Now that she could read, her mama often found special books or magazines for her to help her find her own answers.

Her mama loved learning as well and tried to help Meg with all her questions and explorations. However, her mama drew the line at her venturing off on her own to explore. Meg remembered quite well having to go and pick a switch off the backyard bush the day she went through the garden patch and up the hill behind their house on her own little adventure. The hill was filled with cows and blackberry bushes which was tempting enough but the real pull for Meg was the road that wound around to the top. She so wanted to find where that road led. She hadn't thought she would be gone long enough to be missed. She was wrong. The switch on top of the refrigerator was now there to remind her of how wrong she had been.

Meg brought herself back to the present and watched the women walking on the path ahead of her. She wished they were going farther for the dirt they needed for planting. It would have been exciting to climb over the hill and find themselves in the holler. Meg really wanted to find out if what the boys had claimed to hear was real.

Most children her age would have been frightened to hear the story Ben had told, much less to attempt to discover if it were true. Meg wasn't like most young children. She also had her grandmother and mother nearby as their little group gathered near the over the hill place and the railroad tracks.

The women had stopped on the path ahead. Meg could see they were going no further. The group of women had walked only a few yards beyond where fallen logs were gathered around what looked to be an old campfire. They sat their galvanized buckets down and began to prod away at the rich dirt talking jovially among themselves as they scooped up the fruitful soil. She had heard the women talking about the fire site as they walked up, laughing, and wondering how many fires had been built here over the years. The women told her that a lot of times, travelers would jump off the train before it got to town. They would camp here thinking no one was any wiser before "catching" the next train out.

Meg looked around at the campfire area. Old worn logs provided seating and in the center of the logs was a circle of stones used to keep the flames from escaping. Meg felt her feet begin to tingle and a spark of energy rose into her legs the closer she got to the fire circle. This place felt different, almost magical. Meg recognized it as an in-between place just like the in-between when she woke up early in the morning or when the sun was going down just before dark.

Meg sat herself down on one of the logs pretending to be at the fire. The sounds of the women talking and digging began to fade away as if they were going through a tunnel. The sights and sounds of the day were moving further and further away from Meg. She blinked her eyes hard. She could almost see the fuzzy images of people sitting on the logs, but they couldn't see her. She wanted to ask them so many questions. What was it like to travel from town to town? Where had they been? Where were they going?

The sound of the distant rumbling of trucks going up and down the nearby road quickly brought Meg back from her imaginary trip. She could once again hear the women quite plainly and wondered if she had enough time to explore away from the circle. She remembered the switch perched above the refrigerator and changed her mind. Instead, she bent over and picked up a stick that someone had once used to stir the burning fire. She began to dig into the dirt. She poked and she prodded hoping that some of the travelers or even the big boys had left a bit of treasure behind. Maybe she would find some marbles or even some coins that she could use to buy a candy bar or a bottle of pop.

Meg dug as deeply as she could into the dirt at her feet but came back with nothing. Still determined, she popped up to go over to the next log seat. There she plopped down and shoved the stick deep into the dirt. She felt a thud. Meg began digging as fast as she could but all that she came up with was an old tin can of snuff. Out of the corner of her eye she could see the women moving a bit further away. Her heart jumped. She knew she was supposed to keep in sight of her mother and grandmother. She quickly dropped the stick, jumping up to run over closer to the women. Her legs had a different idea. Meg hadn't judged the distance needed to make it up and over the log. She now found herself on the other side of the log with her hands and knees immersed in the loamy dirt. Meg pulled herself up to shake the dirt from her hands and legs. She looked down to see if she needed to brush dirt from her clothes and surprisingly found blood running down her two small hands.

Strangely enough, there was no blood on her knees. No pain in her hands. Not even where they were bleeding. No pain, no stinging, just lots and lots of blood. And a small piece of amber glass stuck into the middle finger of her left hand. Meg didn't understand why she did it, but she quickly pulled the glass out of the cut and put it in her pocket. Meg was more afraid of having to pick another switch for not minding the women and staying close, than the fact that her blood was dripping all around her on the ground. She carefully held her hands to her sides trying to not let the droplets touch her clothes. She watched closely to see if the ladies would glance her way so she could quickly hide her hands behind her back.

The bleeding slowed but hadn't quite stopped as the ladies finished up and started their way back towards the main road to their houses. The dirt they had gathered would be kept on their back porches until the May 10th cold spell had passed. After that, everything could be planted safely. The group retraced their steps back home chatting about what supper was to be that evening. Meg was relieved that none of them seemed to be paying much attention to her except for a quick glance around to see that she was in tow.

On the way back, Meg dashed ahead to scurry under the fence on her own, hoping the barbed wire wouldn't catch on her shirt and cause her back to be as bloody as her hands. All she wanted to do was to run to the bathroom and wash before anyone noticed.

That was not to be. Just as they reached the back screen door of their own house, Meg's mother called out,

"Meg Hurley, what in the world has happened to your hands?"

Time seemed to stand still. Meg thought to herself, "here comes the switching," but that never happened. She recalled her mother sweeping her up into her arms and holding her hands over the sink. Her mother held her hands under the cold, cold water until what little blood was left seemed pink rather than red. Meg watched the rivulets of life edging down the white ceramic basin and into the silver capped drain. She remembered her mother asking if she had fallen into a pile of broken glass that none of them had noticed. Most of all she remembered the sweet kiss her mama placed on the top of her head.

While her mama had been running the cold water over her hands, her grandmother had gone into her bedroom at the front of the house. There she had pulled her healing box out of her big wooden hope chest. Inside the box were strips of white cotton that her granny had made from torn sheets each spring. Her grandmother called them clooties. Her granny brought the white cotton strips back to the kitchen and took a bottle down from the pantry. The bottle held a tincture that was made from the herbs gathered from the shared garden. Before she began applying the tincture, she asked Meg about the cuts.

"Did you cut yourself on whatever you were jabbing that stick with at the first log, or when you fell at the second log?"

Meg looked up to answer her grandmother. She saw her granny wink and smile. Meg realized her grandmother already knew the answer. Meg's grandmother never missed a thing. Granny Del gently dabbed the healing tincture on the cuts and wrapped each finger with a thin cotton strip.

Once both hands were wrapped just right, her grandmother took the small hands into her own. She stared at them for a time before bending her head over them. She blew her sweet warm breath over the back and then the front of both hands while she whispered words that Meg couldn't quite hear. When Granny Del was finished, Meg questioned her about the lack of sting and pain.

"Granny, I don't understand. The cuts never hurt. Not when they were bleeding and not when mama was washing them under the cold water. Not even when you put the tincture on. That stuff has always stung my scrapes before."

Granny Del looked over to Meg's mother and then turned to look Meg straight in the eye.

"This time the pain wasn't yours, but the gift will be."

Meg didn't understand how getting your hands all cut up could be a gift. Granny Del was always saying things that Meg didn't quite understand but always remembered.

Meg's mother told her to go to her room to change her clothes so she could throw the dirty ones in the wash. Both women were amazed that Meg's clothes were only spattered with dirt. They both wondered how in the world she had avoided getting the blood from her hands on her outfit.

Meg did as she was told, but before bringing her dirty clothes back to her mother, she reached into the pocket where she had placed the piece of glass that had been stuck in her finger. She carefully removed the shard and tucked it into the treasure box she kept under her bed.

For two long days, Meg begged to have the clooties removed from her fingers. Multiple times each day she held her hands up to show her mother and grandmother that she could easily bend her fingers without pain. Meg watched carefully as she flexed her fingers looking for any signs of blood staining the cotton strips. Luckily, there was no evidence of the cuts re-opening, and she was even more sure the bandages should come off now. Her grandmother was just as persistent in reminding her to be patient and wait.

"You know three is the magic number. On the third day, we will take off the bandages."

Finally, on the third day, Granny Del called Meg in from where she was sitting under the grape arbor in the late afternoon sun. True to her word, her grandmother led Meg into the kitchen to sit in a chair by the table. Her grandmother began slowly unwrapping the cotton strips from Meg's tiny little hands. Meg's mother was busy putting the supper meal together on the other side of the kitchen, but she occasionally glanced over to watch Granny Del work gently with Meg's small hands.

After the last of the cotton strips had been removed, Granny Del turned Meg's hands over and back inspecting them carefully. Meg looked down and saw that every cut had healed. In fact, her hands had healed so well and so swiftly, it was as if they had never been cut at all. No marks were left except for one. Meg looked down at her left hand. There she saw a tiny mark slightly below the fingernail of her middle finger. This scar was what her grandmother called a healing mark. This healing mark was exactly where the sliver of amber glass had been lodged into her finger.

"Look granny. I have a healing mark. It looks like the moon."

Granny Del pulled her eyeglasses down to the front of her nose. She placed Meg's small hand in her own to peer more closely at the crescent shaped scar. She studied the curved white tissue closely and then briefly shut her wise brown eyes for a moment. She bent her graying head down and gave a kiss to the little mark and whispered,

"Good. This is good. It will bring the gifts that belong to you."

Granny Del nodded to her daughter, who had stopped the meal preparation to watch the interaction between her mother and her daughter. Meg's mother intercepted Granny Del's nod and proceeded to walk to the front of the house and up the stairs. When Meg's mother returned to the kitchen, she was carrying a small linen bag. She handed the bag to Meg. At the time, Meg thought this must be the gift her grandmother had been talking about all along. Curious as ever, Meg excitedly pulled on the drawstring of the pouch to open it. The opening was just wide enough for her small hand to reach inside. Reaching in, she could feel the cool touch of metal at the bottom of the pouch.

Meg gently grasped the metal object and pulled it
from the bag. She looked down and saw a delicate silver
chain with an attached heart locket. She knew the locket
had once belonged to her grandmother. It had been a
Christmas present from her grandfather, whom Meg had
never met. Her grandmother had given it to Meg's mother
when Meg was born. Meg had watched her mother put the
beautiful necklace on when going to church or out for
something special with her daddy. Meg had secretly hoped
that when she was all grown up her mother might let her
wear it. Meg's mother spoke quietly,

"Meg, your Granny and I think you should have this
locket now, but you must be very careful with it. You
should only wear it to special places until you are older.
After that you can wear it all the time if you want. We want
you to keep it with you always or until the time comes to
pass it on to one of your own children."

Meg could hardly believe it. The locket was hers
now. She didn't have to wait to grow up to wear it. Every
time she had looked at it around her mother's delicate neck,
she had been mesmerized. It was so beautiful. Meg was a
bit worried that something might happen to it so she
decided right then and there that the locket would go back
into the linen bag, and she would tuck it away in her
treasure box. She would not bring it out unless her mother
or grandmother told her it was the right time to wear it.

Meg had a slight pang of guilt in her heart when
she thought of her treasure box. She looked up quickly to
see if either of the women had noticed a change on her
face. The guilty thought left her mind as she watched her
mother reach over and open the locket. Meg peered over
her mother's hands to look at the open locket thinking she

would find a special picture tucked inside. The locket was empty. She looked up at her mother and grandmother. Granny Del smiled a very knowing smile, winked at Meg's mother.

"Meggie, go into your bedroom and get the little piece of amber glass you tucked away in your treasure box."

Meg's thoughts went immediately back to the day she had returned from the dirt gathering trip with the women. She had anxiously waited for her mother and grandmother to doctor and bandage her hands thinking all the while about the piece of glass in her pocket. She didn't understand why but she desperately wanted to add that little treasure to the wooden box under her bed. Of course, mama, daddy and granny knew about the box where she kept things that were important to her. Sometimes it was a rock or a feather she found in the yard. Sometimes it was a bit of ribbon left over from a special present. Meg had never placed anything broken in her box before. But on that day the little sliver of amber seemed to ask to be included in her treasure collection.

Meg should have been surprised that Granny Del seemed to know that she had secretly slipped the piece of glass out of her pocket and into her treasure box, but she wasn't. Her grandmother, and even at times her mother, seemed to just know things.

Meg dashed up the curving stairs to her room. She plopped down on her knees and reached past the dust bunnies under her bed. She pulled at the wooden box trying to bring it toward her without getting a splinter from its rough exterior. When Meg had the box clear of the bed, she pulled off the lid and gazed inside. There was the tiny sliver of amber; the same color of the old pint size medicine bottles her grandmother used as a sprinkle bottle when she was ironing. The piece of glass was a thousand times smaller than any other item in her treasure box and yet it seemed to take up a space all to itself in the very center. Meg carefully picked up the sharp glass and carried it in such a manner as to not get cut again.

Returning to the sitting room, Meg handed the glass over to her grandmother. She half expected to be chastised for her deed. Instead, her mother's eyes were glistening and her Granny Del seemed to have a look of pride shining out of her face.

Granny Del looked at the perplexed look on the child's face.

"You may not understand now how important this sliver of glass will be for you, but it will all come about. Deep in your heart you knew to keep this piece of amber. At that very moment, you trusted yourself to act and you kept the piece of glass. You didn't question how or why. You just knew it was the right thing to do. "

Her grandmother sat down in the chair by the table and gently pulled Meg onto her lap holding her in a loving embrace.

"You are indeed a wise old soul my little girl. You have gifts inside you that you can't fathom for now. One day you will understand what your gifts are and how they can help you and others. There may also be a day that will come when you have to decide whether you want to continue to accept your gifts or turn away from them. The decision will be yours. No one will be able to make it for you. Until then, trust your mother. Trust me. We will help you until you are old enough to make those decisions on your own. "

Her grandmother's arms tightened ever so slightly as she whispered,

"I will always be with you. Always. Promise me you will never stop believing in what you have inside of the locket or inside of yourself. Keep it close always."

Chapter 2
Wavery's Beginning

Wavery Parker sank into the thick green kudzu on the side of the hill. This was the best time of year. The grass was growing taller, the kudzu was turning a rich shade of green, and the creek was tumbling with cold, clean water; but most importantly, school was almost over. Wavery held her breath in anticipation of the freedom she believed would come with graduation. Freedom from having to attempt to sit still all day under the probing eyes of her teachers and most of her classmates.

She didn't think they meant to be cruel, at least she hoped they didn't. They were curious though. They wondered why she was so different. True, she was taller than most of the boys in her class, at least for now. She had long, thin limbs and piercing blue eyes. It was what her eyes could do that really made her different. Her closest friends had known all along that those eyes could see things that were invisible to most people. Now others were starting to figure her secret out, too. Her friends and family had always called it her special gift but there were times that it felt more like a curse. Especially when it made her feel all alone.

Whenever Wavery felt lonely, she ran to the woods. Everything there, everything in nature, was reliable and trustworthy. There was no pretense in nature. No lies. She trusted nature and she especially trusted her place in the kudzu. The long lithe vines seemed to wrap their arms around her and hold her until she felt safe. Safe from prying eyes and wondering minds.

Even her sisters and brother who understood her best couldn't quite comprehend the gift she had been given. Her mama did to some extent; but it was her grandmother on her mama's side who knew exactly what the gift meant. She understood all the ways it could affect a young child who needed to grow into it.

Granny Bea knew all manner of things. She could whip up a poultice, tincture, or salve to heal most any ailment for humans or animals. People came from all over the mountain and valley below to barter for her special services. No one, young or old, gave any thought to Granny Bea being strange in any way. While she didn't "see" the way in which Wavery could, she was good at reading "the signs." She was also a self-taught painter. Her paintings of the area were so realistic you felt as if you could step right into them. Wavery could remember being around seven years old the first time she told her grandmother about how the paintings made her feel. Granny Bea laughed a tinkly little laugh when Wavery told her this and replied,

"Pshaw girl, I may be magic in some ways, but I don't think I have painted a portal… yet."

Granny Bea winked and turned back to the work at hand.

Once when times were tough, Granny Bea allowed a neighbor from down in the valley to buy one of her paintings. That neighbor worked up in Asheville and took the painting to his office. It was so admired by his co-workers that the neighbor returned trying to talk Granny Bea into selling more of her work.

Wavery remembered Granny Bea feeling embarrassed and flustered. She overheard Granny Bea telling the man that while she appreciated his offer, she wasn't taking money or charity. Things were just fine with her family. The man kept coming back over and over again trying to reason with Granny Bea. Finally, the man brought his own mother with him for one last attempt. The two women sat on Granny Bea's porch and talked a long time while the man walked the property. The man's mother was finally able to convince Granny Bea that no one was feeling sorry for her and that her paintings were truly beautiful and needed to be shared.

Granny Bea agreed to sell a few more and was in awe when the man asked for even more to be displayed in the local community center down in Foothills. Granny Bea never made a fortune, but the extra money did come in handy for her family. It was the simple act of creating that really made Granny Bea happy.

Wavery thought back to the time when she was very small and had gone walking down to the mountain town with Granny Bea. They traversed through the kudzu and to the path leading them by the place where the railroad cut ran past their little town. Granny Bea needed supplies to make her tinctures and that included a trip to the poke store for alcohol. Granny had explained to Wavery that long ago the men up on the mountain made their own alcohol that could be bought or traded for with eggs or butter or whatever the need of the seller. Those times had changed.

Granny Bea explained,

"In those days, neighbors could take care of each other, and the business stayed between them. Then the state had to come in and get what they said was due to them. Back then we also used to be able to go by the side of the tracks where the travelers would hop off the trains to camp. They would leave behind empty bottles we could clean and use to hold our tinctures. Now that travelers are kept off the freight trains, I have to go to the drug store or Five & Dime to buy bottles if I run out. Used to be all I had to buy were stoppers and wax to seal my found bottles."

As they passed by the railroad tracks, Granny Bea pointed out the spot where the travelers could find a safe spot to jump from the train and the spot where they would set up a camp until the next train they needed came through. Wavery looked over and saw that someone had brought in machinery to clean out the area. One piece of the digging equipment was still parked beside what had been the old campsite area. The workers had left a hole about ten feet wide and four feet deep. Granny Bea looked at the hole and snorted,

"If that hole was any deeper and a little shorter, you would think they were digging a grave."

Granny Bea, for all her old ways, was pretty much what folks back her younger days would have called a "tom boy." Even now, she was wearing dark blue dungarees and a light green shirt tucked in at the waist. Wavery looked at her Granny from top to bottom. Wavery didn't know how but the woman never seemed to age much. Maybe it was all the work outside in the fresh air or maybe it was the herbs that she ate and used as medicine. Even now Granny Bea's hair was a burnished brown with only a spare amount of white woven through.

Wavery watched as her grandmother sat down on the edge of the freshly dug hole and peered into its shallow depth. Wavery walked closer and squinted her eyes at her grandmother. It was as if Granny Bea had transformed into a young teenager before her eyes. She had moved back to a time long before the mind of Alma Beatrice Blue had turned to marriage and babies. Wavery focused her eyes on her grandmother. The image before her eyes was that of a young teenager yearning for adventure. She sensed the fleeting thought of the teenager wondering what would happen if she jumped into that hole. Would she come out on the other side in a totally different time and place? Just as quickly as the image was there, it was gone. Wavery could hear Granny Bea calling clearly to her. Wavery shook her head slightly, silently questioning if the thoughts had come from the young Bea or the one sitting here on this day.

"Wavery, come here. I want you to jump down in there and fetch me those bottles."

Wavery walked closer to the edge of the hole to see where her grandmother was pointing. Sure enough, at the center of the hole were the open heads of two amber bottles jutting out of the red dirt. Granny Bea warned,

"Be careful. They might be broken. You may not want to cut yourself."

Wavery was more like her grandmother than any of the other grandkids. She was always up for an adventure. Wavery grabbed a stick from the broken branch of a nearby tree and jumped into the hole. As her feet hit the bottom, she felt a strange jolt shoot up her legs. Wavery was sure the feeling wasn't from landing hard. It felt more like the earth had given her a boost of electricity in her legs. Wavery took the stick and began pushing the red clay from around the bottles. Usually, the dry clay would be hard to scrape away but the bottles seemed to have a mind of their own. Today, the bottles cleanly erupted from where they had been half buried in the dirt. It took barely a minute for the bottles to be free and for Wavery to see they were whole and intact. The bottles certainly didn't look like the long necks that her teenage brother and his friends hid in their bags when they went out on a Friday night. Wavery knew instantly these bottles were very old.

Wavery said as much to her grandmother who agreed.

"Yes, I know. They are just like the ones we used to pick up here long ago. No telling how long they have been here."

Wavery handed the bottles to her grandmother and pulled herself back to the top edge of the hole. Her grandmother wiped the bottles off with a rag she kept in the pocket of her dungarees, gave them a quick look over, then placed them in her pack before they continued the walk to town.

Later, when they had returned to Granny Bea's house, they sat on her front porch looking at the treasure they had found. Wavery held up one of the bottles to the sun and commented,

"The sun makes it even brighter in color. It reminds me of your glass puzzle pieces."

Granny Bea laughed gently at the term Wavery gave to her little bag of broken glass. The bag held amber pieces that Granny Bea would throw out on a cloth to read the signs for people.

"Well, honey, that is because these bottles are most likely from the same kind that my puzzle pieces came from way back when."

Granny Bea sat back in the old wooden swing, gently pushing it back and forth.

"Long ago, when I was a teenager, I cut through that very campsite on my way to a picnic with my beau, your granddaddy. I found one of those bottles broken on the ground. I worried that some critter might get hurt on them, so I gathered the broken bits up and put them in my bag. As I gathered up the broken glass, I felt my hands get all tingly. I looked down to see if I had cut myself, but I was fine."

"Later that evening, when I got back home and I was in my room, I pulled the glass out onto a cloth that was spread out on a table under the window. The moon was almost full, and I could see it shining down on each little piece. I left the pieces lying there under the moonlight and went to sleep. The next morning, I woke up early and started to pick up the glass to throw away, but I stopped. When I looked down at them, I could see a picture start to form. It was a picture of your grandaddy down on bended knee. A month later in June, that boy asked me to marry him."

Granny Bea hesitated and smiled a secret little smile before going on,

"Life just continued to get sweeter with him and more interesting for me."

Granny Bea stopped talking and just sat swinging for what felt like the longest time to Wavery.

Suddenly, Granny Bea jutted her foot against the splintering floorboards of the porch and reminded Wavery it was time for her to head back down the hill to the house she shared with her mama, daddy, and siblings. Granny Bea reached over to the porch banister where the amber bottles were resting. She picked up one of the bottles, wrapped both her hands around it. She bent her head slightly and blew a soft breath on the bottle before handing it to Wavery saying quietly,

"This one is for you; you will need it."

Wavery knew better than to question her grandmother and simply said thank you and gave her a big hug before heading home.

Wavery came home to the room she shared with her older sisters and placed her coveted bottle safely on the shelf by her bed. Every morning thereafter, she would hold the bottle up to the streaming sunlight and wonder about the traveler who had left the bottle. Every evening when the moon was sharing itself with the world below, she would peer through the bottle as the moon changed its phase. She wondered when her grandmother would tell her to take the bottle from the shelf and bring it back up the hill to be filled with some wonderful something they would stir up together.

The night before her fifteenth birthday, Granny Bea walked down the hill to bring her family a basket of freshly made bread. As Granny Bea was turning to go back to her own house, she called out,

"Wavery, come to the house tomorrow after school is finished for the day. Bring your amber bottle and we will work up a little birthday gift for you."

43

All the next day, Wavery could barely contain her excitement. She was more fidgety than usual. Her teachers noticed but put it down to it being her birthday. Wavery imagined that the adults thought this made her like the other girls: excited by parties, new clothes, and dances. Little did they know that her anticipation of what was to come ran much deeper. When the last bell of the day rang for dismissal, Wavery made a beeline for the door and broke into a run for her house. Once there, she stopped long enough to drop her books on her bed, change clothes and grab the amber bottle. With the bottle in hand, she began her way up the hill to her grandmother's house.

Wavery held the bottle tightly against her chest much like she did when she first brought the bottle home. Her grandmother was on the porch swing watching as Wavery approached.

The closer Wavery got to her grandmother's porch the stranger she felt. An off-putting buzzing had started ringing in her ears. She watched as her grandmother tilted her head to the side and then smiled a knowing little smile. The buzzing in Wavery's ears continued to grow louder and it felt as if she were walking into a clearly lit tunnel. Time seemed to slow down to a near stop. Wavery could feel herself and everything around slip into slow motion. She could feel her body brace itself as if trying to slow down enough to melt into her surroundings. These were the oddest sensations Wavery had ever felt. It was as if she were aware and unaware of all her senses in the same instant.

Later, she would think back on this moment and realize that she knew with the next step she took she was falling. The ground before her was a mixture of grass and dirt. There were no rocks or sticks to cause her to fall, yet she was falling and could do nothing to stop it from happening.

The sound of glass breaking echoed as loudly as if she had purposely thrown the tightly held amber bottle against a boulder. The echoing sound of the bottle breaking signaled the end of the buzzing in her ears. Wavery looked down with a sharp intake of breath. She looked sadly at the broken pieces of the amber bottle. Wavery was crushed that she had not been more careful. Now the time with her grandmother to complete the workings of her birthday gift was ruined.

Wavery looked at her grandmother with tears beginning to form in her eyes and tried to find her voice to apologize for her carelessness. The tears certainly did not come from the pain of the fall for there was no physical pain. The pain came from her heart. The loss of the amber bottle that Wavery had treasured felt as deep as the loss of this special time with her grandmother.

Granny Bea sprung off the swing and hurried to Wavery. She looked Wavery over carefully and saw that there was blood on her hands but nowhere else. Granny Bea shook her head and tried to reassure Wavery,

"Girl, I see a lot, but I didn't see it happening that way."

Wavery looked at her grandmother with questioning eyes. Granny answered the unasked question,

"I know you thought we were going to mix something up to put in your bottle but that wasn't why I wanted you here. You haven't ruined a thing and you know why? Because we were going to break that bottle anyway, on purpose, or so I thought. Hmph, guess they wanted you to break it by yourself since you put all your energy into it the day you first took it home."

Wavery was confused. She wasn't sure who "they" were, and she wasn't quite sure what her grandmother's plans had been exactly.

"I don't understand, why were we going to break it? What good would a broken bottle be?"

Granny Bea bent over and saw the broken bottle lying on the ground in twelve pieces. She reached into her apron pocket and pulled out a homemade muslin bag with a drawstring. Wavery watched intently as her grandmother handed her the bag and instructed her to pick up only eleven pieces and put them gently into the muslin bag. Wavery did as she was told and then handed the bag back to her grandmother. Granny Bea smiled and looked back at Wavery,

"You just gonna leave that last one laying there?"

Wavery bent over and picked up the last piece. It was tiny in comparison to the other pieces. She slid it into her pocket.

Granny Bea waved the young girl into the house and through to the kitchen. There she began to gently wash Wavery's hands and applied one of her homemade healing salves. As Granny Bea doctored Wavery's hands, she said,

"You only have one deep cut that may leave a scar."

Wavery looked down at her left hand to the deepest wound that uncannily held no pain. Wavery smiled a smile of understanding which she seemed to have inherited from her grandmother. In that moment, Wavery soundly knew the scar would end up being there for life.

Wavery looked over to her grandmother to see her pull the muslin bag out of her apron pocket and place it in the center of the kitchen table. Granny Bea spoke quietly,

"Now for your birthday gift. I'm going to start you with your lessons of reading the signs of the glass. I have my "puzzle pieces" as you call them and now you have your very own."

Later, when they were both ready to head back down the hill for Wavery's birthday supper and cake with the family, Granny Bea asked Wavery to wait while she fetched something out of her bedroom. The older woman returned to Wavery. She was holding a small bottle that had a wire loop inserted into the cap. Wavery watched as her grandmother let the bottle drop from her hand and was relieved that it was attached by the loop to a silver chain. Granny Bea stood there gently letting the bottle swing back and forth by the silver chain and explained,

"This is a bottle that ladies of old used to carry around with smelling salts or perfume inside. Your grandfather found it in a box at an estate auction and gave it to me. I had the loop made and attached to the cap down in Asheville so I could wear it on a chain."

Granny Bea asked Wavery for the small piece of glass she had in her pocket and then she uncapped the clear glass perfume bottle and dropped it inside. Wavery watched as Granny Bea blew her breath into the bottle and whispered words that were inaudible even in such close proximity. Granny Bea then closed the bottle and placed the chain around Wavery's neck, kissing her on top of the head,

"Now let's go eat cake."

Chapter 3
Ann's Beginning

Ann Rossi rested her head gently against the backrest of the oversized rocking chair. Her small stature made the white rocker appear to be even bigger. Ann looked to the side and saw seven more chairs sprawled across the wooden planked porch wrapping around the Rossi home. It felt so good to be back home sitting in the warm sun of late spring. College had been fun but Ann much preferred home.

The sounds of the birds chirping from the tall oaks and the laughter of Nona and Mrs. Coffey (affectionately known to the Rossi kids as "Nana Grace") melded together. Nona and Nana Grace were two of the strongest and most resilient women Ann had ever known. Ann could barely remember her Grandfather Tony or Mr. Sam Coffey. Her brothers were older though. They had a clearer memory of the two gentlemen who still had the capacity to make Nona and Nana Grace smile even after their passing. Ann's parents had told her and her brothers the story of how the two men had been friends since childhood and had become family to each other.

Tony Rossi Sr. and Sam Coffey had known each other since they were in bibs. They had stuck together like glue from elementary school through high school. They did everything together including enlisting in the Air Force the day after their high school graduation. The Air Force tried to separate them through different assignments, but they refused to lose touch with each other.

A young Tony Rossi found himself stationed in Louisiana where he met the love of his life, Ann Renee Hebert. Shortly after they married, Tony brought Ann to Charleston on his next assignment. As much as Ann had loved her home in Louisiana, she found herself loving the Charleston area as well.

Around the same time the young Rossi couple settled in Charleston, Sam Coffey was also assigned back to Charleston. Sam was excited to be reunited with his old friend and wanted to welcome Ann to South Carolina. On the way over to their house, Sam sauntered into Sullivan's Sweets and Treats. He wanted to purchase a cake for the newlyweds to celebrate their marriage and new home in Charleston.

Inside the bakery, Sam found himself staring into the deep chocolate brown eyes of Grace Louisa Sullivan. Later, Sam would tell everyone how time stood still the moment he saw her. He knew right from that moment that he was going to marry the woman standing behind the counter. Sam was very sure of himself but that didn't mean that he didn't have to work a bit for Grace's heart.

Grace worked magic in the bakery and could be as sweet as any of the confections she whipped up daily. Grace was as smart as she was sweet. Savvy in business and sole owner of the bakery made her careful about who she trusted. Grace was not about to jump into a relationship. Sam knew he had his work cut out for himself but he also knew that Grace was worth the work and wait.

The Air Force had Sam going back and forth between Virginia and South Carolina during the year of their courtship. When Sam was away, Tony and Renee spent a lot of time with Grace and the women became fast friends. At the end of the year, Tony and Renee happily served as witnesses when Grace and Sam tied the knot at a small wedding in a beautiful white church in the old neighborhood of Charleston.

Whenever the military called their husbands away, the women came together to support each other, and their friendship grew even stronger. Renee would take Grace along when she traveled back to Louisiana to visit family and, in turn, Grace introduced Renee to all the wonderful places that made Charleston and the surrounding area so special. The women would often go off for a day and tell no one about their adventures. They would come back laughing and smiling secret smiles that only best friends can share.

Both women according to Ann's mother wanted children right away. However, they each seemed to be having some difficulty in getting their wish. One weekend before Grandpa Tony and Sam were to fly back to Charleston, the two women took a drive to visit Grace's great aunt who lived out near the marshes. The old woman was known for her work with plants and healing herbs. Again, the women returned with secretive smiles and eleven months later two children came into the world in Charleston. A son was born to Tony and Renee (Joseph Antonio, Jr.) and a daughter to Sam and Grace (Lucy).

The story of the friendship between the two couples continued over the years. After Joe was born, Grandpa Tony decided not to re-enlist and came home to start a contracting and restoration company that thrived in the area of historical homes and businesses. Joe became his little shadow and learned everything he could about both the physical work and the business side of preserving the history of the area.

Sam Coffey decided the best benefits for his family was to remain on a career path with the Air Force, but luckily, he was able to come home to Grace and Lucy on a regular basis. In his absence, Tony and Renee continued to look after Grace and Lucy, at least as much as the independent Grace would allow. The years passed quickly and soon Lucy, an independent woman like her mom, moved to Savannah to work in an art gallery. Joe remained in the Charleston area and worked for his father.

Ann and her brothers also liked hearing the story of how their parents met. One day while driving the company truck to pick up building supplies, Joe ran into a beautiful woman— literally. Elizabeth Gray was driving on her way to the school where she taught when she stopped abruptly to let a squirrel cross the road lined with tall oaks. According to Ann's mother, Elizabeth watched in the rear-view mirror as a blustery, dark-haired man jumped out of his truck to give her a piece of his mind.

The beguiling smile she threw his way had him giving her a piece of his heart instead. Ann's mom said it was like lightning had struck them both. They dated all of three months before eloping and settling down to have 3 sons in stair step ages: Gray, Luke, and Jack. Both Joe and Elizabeth thought after Jack was born, they were done, but a joyful surprise arrived 3 years later when Ann Louisa (namesake of Nona and Nana Grace) was born.

All three brothers weren't exactly happy to have a girl creature underfoot and the fact was not hidden from Ann. She realized it especially when they teased her and refused to call her Ann instead shortening her middle name to "Lou."

"Hey Lou, hand me my football."

"Lou, bring me a glass of milk."

"Lou, run and get dad his hammer."

Her mother and father soon caught on to what the boys were doing. Joe wanted to take the boys out and have a little talk with them. Elizabeth put her foot down. She convinced her husband that Ann, as young as she was, needed to stand up to her brothers on her own. In the meantime, Elizabeth coached her daughter on how to handle the boys and their teasing without losing her temper— a skill that would come in quite handy later in life. She modeled how to help the boys without becoming their servant and how to set her boundaries even if it meant just walking away without a word. Ann was wise beyond her years and a quick learner. It didn't take long for Ann to begin to "train" her brothers on the use of mutual respect.

Sadly, the sibling teasing took a backseat the winter Ann turned five. During January, a freak ice storm hit the east coast concentrating on the Carolinas and Georgia. Grandpa Tony and Mr. Sam had driven to Florida to meet up with buddies from the Air Force and were on their way back when the worst of the storm came upon them.

The state trooper would later share that both men died instantly when an 18-wheeler slid and struck their car. The true strength of both Nona and Nana Grace surfaced during this horrific time. Both women would smile, albeit sadly, and share their own belief that both Tony and Sam were probably laughing so hard at each other and the stories they would spin that neither realized what was happening. Both women agreed it was better that the two men they adored had left this earth happy to be together.

By spring, Ann's father had taken over Rossi Restoration and Construction. At first, he worked day and night trying to find his way through the grief of losing his father. Elizabeth knew it was something he needed but she soon reminded him that his children also needed time with their father. So, Joe started bringing the boys along to work with him when he could. He wanted to teach them about the business and ensure that he was spending time with them. He promised to bring Ann when she was older.

That same spring, Elizabeth and Joe decided to buy a big white house with a wraparound porch in the center of Mt. Pleasant. The property included a large front yard filled with trees and an even larger back yard with a guest cottage. Both buildings were old enough to be on the historic register and both needed the loving hands of Rossi Restoration and Construction.

Ann's mother was adamant that the cottage work had to be finished first because she wanted Nona to move in with them. The cottage was far enough from the house for privacy but close enough for comfort. Joe loved his wife for thinking of sharing their lives and home with his mother, but he also recognized the independent nature of his mother. His thoughts were wrapped around how he would talk his mother into the move as he drove over to see her at the family home. He didn't expect her to agree to the move and was a bit surprised when she readily accepted the idea. However, he was not shocked when she included a few stipulations.

The first condition was that a car entrance from the back alley to the cottage had to be established. Her reasoning was plain and simple. It would be no business of Joe or Elizabeth when she decided to come and go. Secondly, she would only move to the cottage if a second bedroom could be added on the opposite side of the cottage from her own bedroom. She wasn't moving in unless Sam's wife Grace joined her.

Joe knew the separate driveway and the second bedroom addition could be completed without a hitch. The real problem would be convincing Grace Coffey into moving in with them. Joe looked over to his mother with worried eyes, "Are you going to talk to Ms. Grace?"

Renee smiled slyly, said a quiet no, and walked away. Joe was perplexed as to what to do next when he left his mother's. He drove straight home to see his wife. When he arrived, he began to explain his mother's terms. Joe was hoping that perhaps Elizabeth would agree to talk to Grace using her gentle nature and beguiling smile to convince the very independent woman to join them.

Ann had just wandered through the kitchen door after a long afternoon of play under the big tree in the backyard. She was taking off her shoes and listening to her parents' discussion about Nana Grace moving in with Nona. She heard her mother tell her father that she honestly didn't believe that either of them could persuade Grace if she were not of a mind to accept. Ann, again wise beyond her years, recognized that adults made things more complicated than they had to be. She shook her head at their silliness. Ann watched from the corner as her mother began to prepare supper and her father reluctantly left to go and talk with Nana Grace.

Ann quietly turned and left the kitchen to go to the front hall of their big new house. She was only five years old, but her parents had already taught her how to call the emergency numbers kept by the phone on the antique table. Nana Grace's number was one of those numbers. She could remember her small fingers holding the phone as she waited for Nana Grace to answer at her own house. As soon as Ann heard Nana Grace's voice answer hello, she started a most direct and short conversation as a beguiling five-year-old can do.

"Hello Nana Grace, this is Ann. Nothing is wrong. This is not an emergency. My daddy is on the way over to ask you a very important question. He is very nervous, and I don't want him to worry anymore. He and mama want to fix up the cottage in our backyard so both you and Nona have your own room. Nona won't come to live here unless you come to live here, too. Nona needs you and you need Nona. I think Grandpa Tony and Mr. Sam would be smiling and laughing more if they knew you and Nona were together laughing and smiling too."

Ann took a big gulp of air and continued,

"I need Nona and I need you. I love you. Good-bye."

Ann quietly put the phone down and ran to her room to hide just in case she was going to get grounded like her daddy said he did to the boys. Ann wasn't quite sure what grounded meant but it didn't sound like fun.

Later that evening, her brother Gray came to her room to find her. Gray seemed to tease her less than the younger two brothers.

"You can come out now. I don't know what you did but Dad and Mama told me to tell you that you are not in trouble and that it worked."

Gray turned and headed toward the good smells coming from the kitchen. When the whole family was seated at the supper table, Joe looked over to Ann and spoke softly,

"Good job. I think you have inherited Grandpa Tony's negotiating skills. You may end up heading up Rossi Restoration with that talent of yours."

Ann never knew if her parents, Nona, or Nana Grace ever told the boys about the phone call but after that, the boys teased her less, stopped calling her Lou most of the time, and watched with admiration as she grew into her own role at Rossi Restoration.

A few weeks later when construction began on the old cottage, Ann was called to perform her first "job" at Rossi Restoration. While working on an existing wall, the male Rossi crew found they needed to pull a copper cable wire from the enclosure separating the bedroom and the gathering room. None of the boys or their dad were able to reach the wire, nor could they fit into the space. Ann, now a ripe old age of five, was volunteered by her two youngest brothers to slip inside the tight space. Their dad, Joe, was a bit reluctant but could see no other way around it unless they used a sledgehammer to break into the wall causing a huge rebuild of the entire section.

Gray had been in the main house helping Nona Renee with meal preparations when Nana Grace drove up and came inside to the kitchen. Nana Grace looked out the kitchen window toward the cottage with some concern. She looked over at Renee watching Gray bent over a large, filled stockpot. Nona had started coming over regularly and preparing supper while Elizabeth was working. Nana Grace looked pointedly at Renee. Renee recognized the intensity of the look.

"What's wrong, Grace?"

Nana Grace shrugged her shoulders and said,

"Probably nothing, but Gray, do me a favor please. Run to the cottage and check on …the progress."

Gray, like the rest of his family, had learned early on that Grace Coffey seemed intuitive about a lot of things. Gray sprinted to the cottage just as his father was driving away. He went inside to ask about their father's departure.

"Oh, he is going down to the hardware to pick up the final shipment we need to finish up the cottage," Luke answered.

Suddenly, Gray heard the muffled voice of his sister.

"Hey- hey, I think I have it, but I am kind of stuck in here."

Gray looked incredulously at his brothers,

"Where the heck is Ann?"

Luke laughed, "She is inside the wall."

Jack turned away when he saw the protective fire that came into Gray's eyes.

Gray peered into the opening between the two walls. "Ann, are you ok?"

Ann called back,

"Yeah, I'm okay. It is just a little tight in here, I must be growing. It's really cool though. Daddy gave me his flashlight before he left so I could see where to pull the wire."

Gray practically yelled,

"Pull the wire? Don't touch any wires. Mama will kill daddy if you get electrocuted."

Luke reminded them all that the electricity had been cut off to the cottage. Any electrical tools were being operated by the generator if they weren't rechargeable.

Ann kept wiggling around in the space. Gray and the other two boys could see the light from the battery-operated torch flip back and forth.

Ann half whispered, half shouted in her excitement,

"I can see old papers, ewee— maybe some mouse poop, and— what's this?"

The boys could hear their sister moving around inside the space between the walls. Ann was tugging at something that looked brown to her and the back-and-forth action caused her elbow to hit against the inside of the wall,

"OWWW!"

Gray shouted then,

"Are you okay? Ann Louisa Rossi come out of there right now."

Ann answered in a small voice,

"Yes, well, maybe. I think I broke it."

Gray was almost in a panic, "BROKE WHAT?"

By now the other two boys who had been giggling at their sister's escapade stopped cold in their tracks. As much as they had always teased Ann, they loved her and now they felt fear rise into their chests.

Ann reassured her three brothers as she was extricating herself from the wall space.

"It's okay. I'm okay. I just hit my funny bone. I'm not broke, but this is."

Ann held up an amber bottle with the short neck broken off. Ann didn't notice the blood, but Gray did, and he scooped up Ann with the bottle in hand and made breakneck speed back to the main house.

Nona and Nana Grace were ready and waiting as Gray bounded into the house with Ann. Nona calmed Gray and his two younger brothers who had followed behind. Nana Grace gave a nod towards the boys and Nona led them back out to the cottage.

Ann looked up at Nana Grace with loving, trusting eyes.

"You knew, didn't you? You are gonna fix me, right?"

Nana Grace laughed,

"Yes, baby. I knew but, in some ways, so did you. You were never afraid to go inside that wall, were you? Deep down, you knew there was something just for you."

Ann nodded affirmatively. She didn't really understand how or why, but sometimes she just knew things: how to act, what to say, and what not to say. She also knew that just like Nona had something to teach Gray, Nana Grace had something to teach her. She felt a bubble of excitement growing in her tummy. The same kind of excitement she felt when she was at the flea markets and antique stores with her mama. The same kind of excitement she felt when she rode in the truck with her daddy to see the really old houses he was about to restore. She knew the excitement came from all the old things, wanting their story to be told and she wanted to be their storyteller. That's what she wanted to be when she grew up, but she knew now that whatever Nana Grace had to teach her would be just as exciting.

Ann watched as Nana Grace took the broken amber bottle from her left hand. She watched the older woman wash her hand gently all the while speaking some words in a language that Ann didn't quite understand. Even though she didn't understand the words, they felt familiar. Nana Grace blew three breaths over the cut on her middle finger of her left hand. Ann still held a piece of broken glass from the neck of the bottle in her right hand and she slipped it into the pocket of her pink cotton shorts. She would put it in her special box that she kept hidden in her closet. Nana Grace took the broken bottle and rinsed it under the water in the sink, dried it off and handed it to Ann.

"You might as well keep this too, being as how you like old things. You know, old things like this bottle, your Nona, and me."

Ann sheepishly took the bottle and practically skipped up the stairs to her room.

Part Two
Blood Returns

What is for us will always return to us no matter how long the journey.

Chapter 4

Meg could feel herself stepping back into the room. Stepping back from her memories. She reluctantly opened her eyes to find the room bathed in long shadows from the disappearing sun. She pushed her chair back and stood, beginning her nightly habit of closing the drapes to block out the growing darkness. Meg moved around the room flipping on the switches of the lamps that were dotted around the room. Their warm glow replaced the earlier sunshine. Finally, she went to the table that stood to the side of the overstuffed rocker. She picked up the framed picture of her grandmother from the table and pulled it into her chest. She had been so very lucky to have been loved by this woman. Meg put the frame back on the table and lit the candle she always kept by the picture.

Meg decided that there was to be no more work for the evening. She ran downstairs to lock the doors, make a cup of hot cinnamon tea, and grab a book before returning to her study. Back in the study, she settled down in what had once been her grandmother's rocker and pulled a small quilt over her legs. There were so many things in this room that reminded Meg of her grandmother and they all brought a bittersweet smile to Meg's face.

Meg reached toward the silver chain around her neck and found the locket hanging from it. Meg twirled the silver heart between her fingers. The silver heart was a reminder of her grandmother, the old days, and the old ways. Ways that Meg had always respected but had allowed to fade away since her grandmother's passing. Once her grandmother was gone, things never felt quite the same.

Understandably, the pain of losing Granny Del had shaken the entire family. Meg's mother had lost the woman who had given birth to her and who had been a companion for all of her lifetime. Meg could see the pain in her father's eyes as well. Her grandmother had loved the man as if he was her own child and her father returned that deep love and respect. Truly, a piece of all their hearts had left them with Granny Del's passing.

It felt like the days that followed the funeral moved in a numbing stupor for Meg, yet the world around her continued in a sense of normalcy that angered her. Traffic still passed by on the road in front of the house. The newspaper still landed on the porch every morning like clockwork. The shift whistles from the plant still tootled out through the air. Didn't they know Granny wasn't there? She wasn't there to sit on the porch wondering where people were going. She wasn't there to ask mama to read the obituaries to her as they drank their morning coffee. She wasn't there to tell Meg the 4'oclock whistle had blown and it was time to start supper. Those first evenings at the supper table after her grandmother was laid to rest were almost too much to bear for the three left behind. The empty chair was just another reminder of what was going to be different forever.

Meg watched her parents help each other to deal with the grief they were feeling. She saw them grow closer than ever. They did their best to reach out to her, to help her feel better. Meg wanted to feel better but she wondered if she would ever feel like her old self again.

Meg just wanted the pain to stop. She reasoned the only way she could make that happen was to not talk about her granny at all. Meg found herself avoiding any conversations with her parents or friends when they began reminiscing about Granny Del. Meg didn't trust herself to not break down completely if she were made to talk about her granny. So, she didn't.

It was much harder to run away from the memories at night. Every time she tried to sleep, another recollection of her grandmother would flitter into her mind. Meg made the decision to fill her days with as many activities as she could. That way when it was time for bed, she would be able to go straight to sleep.

Meg joined the allotted number of school clubs, volunteered at the local animal shelter, and helped with charitable events throughout the county. Meg also immersed herself in her studies.

Meg felt it was important for her to latch onto as many educational opportunities as possible. She knew in her heart this was a way to honor her grandmother and all the Appalachian women who had come before her. Some of those women had never been able to attend high school, much less finish and go on to higher learning. Granny Del had been one of those women.

Granny Del had barely reached eighth grade before her parents had packed their family up and moved from the mountains of North Carolina into Virginia. By the age of fifteen, she was married and by the age of 16, she had borne her first child. There had been no time for schooling for Granny Del. Meg knew she could barely read or write. Her grandmother knew just enough to write a simple message on a card and sign her name.

Schooling for her children became very important to Granny Del and she passed that down to Meg's mom. It had become important to Meg as well. More than anything, she wanted to make her grandmother proud, no matter how much effort and energy it would take. Meg had learned education was the only way forward. Like a blink of an eye, her high school years passed quickly. Meg found herself leaving for college. Luckily, she didn't have far to go. She was accepted to Byars Creed about twenty minutes from her house.

The physical distance between her hometown and the college was trivial in comparison to the distance between her world as a small town and the world that was opened up through the college. Byars Creed was indeed a whole new world for Meg. She found herself surrounded by a measurably different group of people and Meg felt very far removed from them. The diversity of her small-town world had extended ten-fold. While there were a few students from the local region, most were from other states and even from other countries.

Oddly, the students from across the globe seemed to be more open and accepting of the students like Meg, who were local to the Appalachian Mountains. The other students were something quite different than Meg had been used to experiencing. A select group of students, basically those not from the region, appeared to treat those with a mountainous accent very differently.

Meg observed their actions. She watched as they seemed to purposely leave the regional students out of activities and gatherings. Meg heard the whispers about the "hillbillies" from the mountains. She heard them and thought about the irony. The students who were doing the whispering had chosen a college perched in the middle of the southern Appalachians to attend. What had they expected?

Meg's education during those four years went beyond the academic. She learned a lot about herself and the people around her. She found herself studying the behaviors of the students from all walks of life. She became an astute observer of human nature. Meg wondered that if she were to exist and thrive in a world beyond her small Appalachian town, would she have to adopt a whole new set of behaviors? If she changed herself that much to succeed out in the work world, what would it do to her? Would it slowly erode the teachings of her grandmother and the "gifts" she supposedly had within herself?

Meg decided it was time to let go of the past. She heaved an audible sigh and sunk more deeply into the rocking chair. She tucked one knee beneath her body and used the toe of her other foot to start a gentle rocking motion. Her shoulders and neck were tight from bending over the keyboard of her computer all day at work and again this evening. She leaned her aching body deep into the softness of the chair as if she were a little girl again leaning into the sweet softness of her granny's arms. She imagined her grandmother's voice lulling her to sleep. If she strained hard enough, would she be able to hear Granny Del once again?

Meg thought back to the time after Granny Del's passing when she had heard her voice. It had been almost two months to the day of her grandmother's passing and, ironically, on the very day of her grandmother's birth.

Meg had awakened on that snowy morning in February to the whispering of "Morning Glory, Evening

Star." Meg realized she must be dreaming, still she looked around the room for her grandmother. Growing up, Granny had always come to gently wake her up every morning of her entire life with those same whispered words. That felt like such a long time ago. She wished she had asked her grandmother for more details. Why in the world did she include "evening star" in a morning salutation? Granny was gone now, and Meg would likely never know the answer to the question.

"I'm just tired," Meg whispered to the walls.

A second voice beyond her rang out with a matter-of-fact tone.

"Of course you are tired. Not listening to your heart and mind will wear you out, body and soul. Especially if you have been doing it for years,"

Meg glanced toward the door, but she already knew that no one had entered. She already knew there would be nothing to see. Yet every time she heard that molasses rich voice, it still gave her hope. Hope that once again she would be able to look into Granny Del's brown eyes. Meg glanced around the nearly empty room for any shadow of her figure. Nothing. She was gone again.

It had been 10 years and not one glimpse. Meg had resigned herself to never actually "seeing" her grandmother again. But over the years, her grandmother's voice had come through more and more. Just a voice on random occasions. Sometimes the voice was in Meg's dreams and sometimes it was just floating through the house. No matter how the words arrived, Meg always tried to remain grateful for being able to hear that sweet, loving, yet sometimes stern voice.

Meg laughed out loud at her own silliness for thinking she had a way of controlling the situation. Clearly, even in death, Granny Del was still the queen of the family. Meg straightened up in the rocking chair and placed both feet on the floor. She was half expecting Granny Del to ask her what she thought was so funny.

Meg paused hesitantly but the stern voice held silent. Meg had never told anyone else but her mother about hearing her grandmother's voice in dreams or elsewhere. Was it because she was concerned that people might think she was insane? If Meg was being truthful with herself, it was more likely that she didn't want to share any small part of what was given to her by Granny Del.

Regardless of the answer, the voice she loved so very much only came through on the oddest of occasions. More often than not they held some message that Meg had a hard time understanding. Meg blamed her lack of understanding on her professional training. She had developed into an objective thinker often bordering on the literal. She trusted only what could be proven with facts. Sadly, in the end it meant that her mind took precedence over her heart. She had clearly lost touch with trusting in feelings, the possibilities of dreams, and the magic that had been so very real in her world.

Chapter 5

Meg decided it was time to close the door on her study for the evening. She walked downstairs and through the long hallway of the house to grab her hooded jacket, checking to see that her gloves were tucked in her pockets. Spring was on its way, but the evenings were still holding onto the chilliness of the fading winter. Meg hoped a brisk walk would clear away the cobweb of memories and thoughts running through her head. The sun had set and the stars were twinkling brightly in the sky as Meg stepped off the front porch. Her plan was to make a quick circuit through her neighborhood, past the bandstand in the middle of town, and back up the hill to her house. With any luck, she would return to the house ready to settle down for a peaceful sleep.

The cold air practically pushed her back home where she took a hot steamy shower and then set the alarm for the next morning. Once she was tucked in her bed, it didn't take long for Meg's eyes to flutter closed. Her body was at rest, but her subconscious mind remained active all throughout the night.

Meg had been gifted or perhaps cursed with a very active mind and there were times it seemed to have an agenda of its own. Tonight was one of those times her brain was going into overdrive leading her through dreamtime. All through the night, she could see herself floating in and out of the different stages of her life. It was like watching a movie as part of the audience and then also being able to think through what was happening as a participant.

Meg watched as her little girl self walked and wandered about exploring the world around her. She could hear her parents talking about how inquisitive she was, always wanting to know the "how" and "why" behind everything. She remembered knowing the right time to ask questions and to whom she should pose the questions. She could see herself sitting politely in a roomful of adults that included her family and Ma Barker from next door. They barely noticed her because she was so quiet.

In the dream, Meg could see herself sitting with her grandmother and her friends on the porch, lingering in the kitchen as her aunts and uncles came to play cards, or sitting hidden under the big square quilt frame next door at Granny Robert's house. All the while, Meg was listening to the older folks talk. She learned so much by watching the adults around her and listening to their stories. Listening to them and being with them made her feel safe and loved. She never wanted to leave them, and she never wanted them to leave her. She wanted to feel this way forever. As soon as that thought settled in her brain, she felt herself jerked away to another time.

Meg looked through the filmy surface of the dream and once again saw herself but now she was a teenager. She was filled with a type of energy that she couldn't quite name. It wasn't the childlike energy of discovery. It was more of a pushing energy. She wasn't sure if the energy was pushing her or she was pushing the energy. She tried to concentrate, to figure out what was going on in the dream. It had something to do with her studies. She felt a harried drive to excel at her schoolwork. She needed to be a standout in her work so she could go to college. She had to go to college. The energy became even more unbalanced.

Meg realized she was in a panic. She had no idea what she would study in college. She needed a plan. All her friends had a plan.

Her friends were already mapping out college and career paths and they were only sophomores. Why didn't she have a plan?

Meg felt herself dropping from the sky onto the campus. It was her first year at college and she was as confused as ever. She still had no plan and she felt so alone. She missed her childhood friends and she felt like no one here wanted her around. She could hear the whispers. Look at her, she doesn't know how to dress. Listen to her, she sounds like a hick. How did she even get into this place?

Meg told herself she was fine being on her own. She didn't need the others. They were too busy attending parties rather than being serious students. She heard herself say, "I am a serious student. I am going to make Granny Del proud."

In the dream, Meg turned in a circle and was suddenly sitting in a classroom. Which building was she in? Whose class was she in? She looked through the glass in the door and saw Dr. Peabody and his wife. Could they see her?

Meg could hear them talking about her and the rest of the class. Dr. Peabody was complaining about the rambunctious antics of freshman in the spring. He pointed out how different Meg was in comparison. Meg wasn't sure she really wanted to be that different. Being different could be so lonely.

Meg flashed into Dr. Peabody's office. His wife Gabby was there as well. They were showing her a map and a huge book. They told her these were the tools she needed to make her final decision. Meg finally felt calm. They had helped her find her way. Everything was there and coming together. Her passion for discovery and her love of history and people were the right answers. Gabby Peabody was handing something to her. It was her degree. Master of Arts in History and Research. Granny Del would be so proud. Meg felt so happy, but it didn't last long.

As Meg sank deeper into her dreams and moved from time frame to time frame, her body tossed back and forth beneath the cotton quilt. Subconsciously, she pushed back against the covers trying to move but felt she was trapped with nowhere to go.

Life in her dream began to feel stagnant. Meg woke up, went to work, returned home to sleep, and then started the same pattern over again. Day after day the slog of work began to chip away at Meg's soul. Meg felt like she was outside of her own body watching her life float by on an endless current of drudge.

Meg saw herself walking through the city to get to her work. She felt numb and suffocated by the immense gray towers of stone and lack of greenspace. The never-ending concrete sidewalks were swallowing her whole. She tried to look at the people passing by hoping to change her feelings of dread and loneliness. She saw nothing but a hollowness in their eyes. There expressions and actions were abrasive. In her dream she could see people talking incessantly. Strangely, their lips were moving but the sounds they emitted were non-intelligible. The dream had truly become a nightmare.

Meg floated from the city street into her workplace at the university. Meg felt like she was in two places at once. She was there standing with feet on the floor and at the same time floating above it all, watching the scene as if in a play.

She had been dropped into a huge library surrounded by books from floor to ceiling. There were no windows and only one door. She tried so hard to prove herself through her meticulous work with details. Each project she was assigned seemed to be on a less significant scale than the last. Every time she finished a project and turned in the results she would look at the door in the front of the library. Each time it became smaller. Meg worried that it would become so small she may never be able to get back out of the building.

Meg saw herself walking into meetings or into the break room and overheard whispering from colleagues. As soon as she entered the room, the voices stopped. Meg could feel herself enter and re-enter the room repeatedly. Each time the whisperings becoming louder. Louder but never coherent enough to understand. She could see herself, feel herself going in and out of the door and each time the door became smaller and smaller as if she were being shut out completely. Meg didn't want to be left out but finally the door became so small there was no way he could fit in and with that, she jerked awake with a tremor fiercely coursing through her body.

Meg sat straight up in bed trying to catch her breath. She remembered well what came next and it was no dream. Meg would soon find out that lack of experience was not the only factor in keeping her assignments simplified and shutting her out of the path she had worked so hard to travel. The memory evoked a surge of anger that heated her body and set a tone for her morning.

Chapter 6

It was a sunny Friday morning on campus. Students were ambling to their first classes in the history building; not quite ready to be awake but building excitement for their weekend to come. Meg was usually the friendly face they looked forward to seeing in the morning but today they noticed she walked with her head down and not at her usual brisk pace. Meg made her way into the offices that housed the research department. Her co-workers were as surprised as the students at seeing Meg not quite herself. Dr. Peabody breezed through with his extra-large cup of well-creamed and sugared coffee. He took one look at Meg and stated bluntly,

"You look like hell. You want to talk about it now or later?"

Meg whispered a reply,

"Thanks bushels. Not ever really but I know you, so let's say later. Much later."

John Peabody had been married for a very long time with two children of his own. He had learned early when to back off from a discussion. John and his wife had taken Meg under their wing when she was a student here at the college. They had helped to guide her toward her chosen path. Just like her parents, they had felt somewhat bereft when she decided to head north for work after graduating, but they all realized she had to make those decisions on her own. Selfishly, they were all equally glad when she returned home. John was especially thankful that her return coincided with an open position here in the research department.

He raised his coffee cup in a salute and left the offices to teach his first and last class of the day. He would peek in on Meg after class to see if she was ready to share. He had a feeling it might take the whole day for her to move into a headspace where she felt ready to divulge what seemed to be weighing her spirit down.

Meg closed herself off in her office. She was determined to dive into what she thought would be an absorbing rather than a thought-provoking task, specifically immersing herself in statistical data. Ironically, she realized she was doing the very thing which had kept her pigeonholed in her first job. She began to massage her aching temples remembering the agitated night she had spent going in and out of the dreams of the past.

Meg gazed out into the ether and let her thoughts return to the day at the university near D. C. when she had finally reached a breaking point. It was just a regular Tuesday afternoon spent addressing a rather mundane task. Meg left the research offices to head over to the auditorium in the education building. She had no idea that in just over an hour, she would make a life altering decision while barely taking a breath.

Meg had been requested to make a presentation to students in the education department. The topic of the address centered around the latest research tools her department had to offer to graduate students. The presentation was simplistic and straightforward. It consisted of a brief department issued PowerPoint presentation that literally could have been presented by the office secretary. Meg had hoped the department would let her enhance it a bit to include a work session for some hands-on exploration. Her wish had not been granted. She had been given firm direction on the format of her presentation with no leeway whatsoever.

Meg ended the very succinct presentation which lasted less than thirty minutes and the audience began to exit the small auditorium. Meg was packing up her materials to leave as well when a slightly older, well-coiffed woman approached and introduced herself.

"Good afternoon. I'm Dr. McNulty. I am the chair of the master programs in the education department."

Meg turned to smile as Dr. McNulty continued,

"I wanted to extend my thanks for the presentation. It will be a great... starting point for our students."

Meg wanted to say that it was a starting point and barely one at that, but she held her tongue. The bare minimum presentation would only leave the students with a brief synopsis of the tools they would need in the future. She knew from experience they needed more. Meg knew she needed to remain professional, so she chose not to share her true viewpoint. Inwardly, she reminded herself that it was important to remain discreet and respectful of her own supervisor and Dr. McNulty.

Meg smiled and said,

"Thank you. Please don't hesitate to give us a call if we can help you with anything further. I would be very happy to come and speak with the students in small groups and provide them with further information as well as a work session if that is deemed appropriate."

The woman before her seemed to hesitate. Meg wondered if her offer appeared to overstep. Perhaps such an endeavor, no matter how helpful, did indeed need to be cleared among department heads. Dr. McNulty appeared to overcome her hesitation and reached out to touch Meg on the arm. Meg looked down at the woman's finely manicured hands and a business card resting firmly between her fingers.

Meg felt a sudden jolt of excitement. Finally, someone wanting to network as colleagues. Meg was glad she had decided to tuck her own business cards in the outer pocket of her dress jacket before leaving her office. She was eager to share. Meg smiled broadly and took the proffered card.

Meg lowered her eyes and hastily read the information printed on the front. She slowly raised her head. Meg looked at the woman before her, a bit perplexed. The card listed the name of a speech therapist, not affiliated with the university. Precipitously, the woman answered without being asked,

"I wanted to share my niece's card with you. You did a wonderful job today with your first presentation for us. I feel sure you will be asked to do many more presentations with our department here at the university. Considering that, I thought perhaps… well, I just thought maybe you might want to get some help with …well, you understand."

The light clicked on in Meg's brain. No one would be needing or wanting Meg's services until she changed something about herself. She absolutely understood. The memory of her freshman year washed over her. History seemed to be repeating itself and that was never a good thing. At least not for Meg. Surprisingly, she felt neither disappointment nor anger this time. What she did feel was resolve and a confident spur of trust in what she was about to say and do.

Meg recognized exactly what the woman was trying to, not so eloquently, convey. She had overheard a few others on the staff mention her southern accent in what seemed to be off-hand remarks. She now wondered if the whisperings had actually been a more detailed discussion of Meg's perceived deficiencies. Meg squared her shoulders. She was done dealing with the unjustified opinion of others.

Meg knew with certainty that she always spoke with precisely correct grammar and had no qualms about her degree of intelligence. More importantly, she had never been ashamed of her lilting southern mountain accent. It was as much a part of her as was her eye color or the scar on her finger. The stranger before her had no idea about who Meg was nor what she had just ignited.

Meg smiled the sly smile she had inherited from her mother and grandmother as she looked the card over once more. Meg raised a defiant chin as she ever so slowly crumpled the card into a ball. Reaching out she gently took the shocked woman's hand. Meg dropped the crushed card into the flaccid palm of the less than gracious woman. Meg unconsciously lifted her left hand and touched the heart locket hanging from its silver chain. She looked straight into the woman's eyes, never flinching for even a second.

With a husky rasp, Meg replied in a purposely drawn-out affectatious voice. Every word that sashayed out of her mouth was as rich and thick as bitter-sweet molasses.

"My dear Doctor McNulty, I may speak slowly, but let me assure you, I am not slow on any level. I absolutely understand what you are saying to me. Let me be very clear so that you understand as well. I have no need to utilize the services of your niece for my manner of speaking but perhaps you should undertake some instructional services for your own comportment. Professional etiquette really does not appear to be your strength."

With that, Meg turned on her heel and left the building with a determined step and her head held high. Meg had been raised with a strength of perseverance, a never-give-up attitude, and a strong work ethic. She never envisioned herself as a quitter. Yet, Meg was wise enough to know that quitting was only a foible if it robbed you of your personal strength and self-worth.

A seemingly innocuous discussion had morphed into a breaking point for Meg. Perhaps the experience should have felt more painful and embarrassing, but it hadn't been that way at all. Much later, when Meg was able to sit still and reflect on that whole period of her life, she would finally recognize just how things had to build up before she could make a change. Everything happened for a reason her granny would have said. The experiences she had gone through brought her back to a path where she could recognize her own worth.

In that one pivotal moment when confronted by a total stranger she had spontaneously and inherently begun to trust herself once more. She finally recognized who she truly was and had always been.

Instead of going back to her office, Meg headed to her apartment. Once there, she typed a letter of resignation and begin packing for her move. Two weeks later, she was home.

Chapter 7

It was a Saturday, which meant no alarm clock for Meg. No hopping out of bed to run a hot shower. No making coffee to drink on the drive to work. It was a morning where she could be one with her bed until her parents' cats were ready for food or her own urge for food and drink took over.

It was also one of those mornings when the cold from the previous night wanted to hang on for dear life. This time of year, the old house held on to the chill long into the morning especially when the day dawned overcast and frosty. Old houses like this one were peculiar in so many ways. In the spring and autumn, they were always so much cooler inside than the temperature outside. In the summer they held heat like an oven and in the winter the cold penetrated every inch, making the wooden oak floors feel downright icy.

Meg thought about hopping up to turn the thermostat up a notch or two but the handsewn quilts held her snuggly in place. She decided lingering in bed was a much better idea. Meg snuggled back down into the homemade covers and began to dream of traveling to a place that didn't have snow or the bitter cold that was fighting the arrival of spring. Winter there would be short, and spring would be a much longer season filled with soft warm breezes. Meg had a secret wish to one day live in a warm southern climate during the winter, being able to come back to her mountains for late spring through fall. If only she could come up with a job that allowed her such a fantasy. Or she could win the lottery. That would work, too.

The temperature outside had its own influence on the old house's heating system and Meg heard the heater begin to rev up and run with a gentle hum. The purring fan of the system and the quiet of the early morning soothed her like a baby. She was lulled back into that dreamy in-between place where you never know if you are truly awake or just about asleep. Just as she had reached that magical space between here and there, the voice from yesterday rang clearly through her bedroom.

"You were right, you could have asked me about the evening star. Why don't you ask now?"

The voice wasn't jarring in volume, but it was certainly familiar enough to bring Meg away from her balmy dreams. She swiped her hand across her left ear where the words seemed to have landed. She tried to shake off the sleepiness and wake herself up. Her heart pounded a bit more fiercely as she realized that she wasn't asleep and again her grandmother's voice broke through.

"Well, why don't you ask? I'll answer. "

Meg shook her head again. What in the world was going on? She touched her hand to her forehead and found no fever, no bump from a fall.

"Youngin', nothing is wrong with you. You are as awake as can be. I always told you, 'Even if I go, I will never leave.' Remember now? I keep my promises… on both sides."

Meg glanced over at the old wind-up clock. She could hear the base sound of the methodical tick tock. She looked out the frosty window to see gray light peeking back at her, and heard her own voice huskily whispering,

"Is that you granny? Why can I only hear you and not see you if you are here with me?"

Meg looked across her bedroom into the milky glass mirror on the dresser. She wondered if she were going a bit crazy living alone here during the winter months, while her mother and father were traveling the west in their revamped van. Meg was keenly aware that she could not see the figure she associated with this re-occurring voice. Meg was a little worried about herself. Was it because she had never truly dealt with the grief of her grandmother's passing? Was she simply imagining this oh so familiar voice as a means for holding on to what was gone for good?

"Stop that right now. Stop thinking that way," her grandmother's voice admonished sternly.

"You are not losing your mind. You are not sick. You are not asleep. What you are is headstrong and stubborn. It's time to come out of that head of yours and find your heart. Find what you already know is deep inside you. You have the same gift as your Great -Aunt Retta. My sister knew how to use it wisely and well. If only you could have met her. Hmph. Maybe she could have convinced you to accept the gifts as they have been given."

Her grandmother's voice took on a poignant tone,

"Do you really have to see me to believe?"

A melancholy feeling passed through Meg. *Did* she want to see her grandmother, or would that be just more pain than she could endure? For now, "hearing" her grandmother was disquieting and maybe as much as Meg could handle.

Before Meg could answer, her grandmother's voice continued,

"You were always a worrier. Seems you still are. I know the gifts that run in our blood come with a lot of responsibility. They also come in really helpful at times. Helpful to yourself, surely, but helpful to others as well. I'm really proud of you and how you grew so book smart. But really, how much good does that do you if you only use it to feel safe? It helps you fit in and look to be like everybody else. But, little lady, you are not just like everybody else. You have a real knowing deep inside of you."

Meg was now sitting up straight in the bed covertly looking around the room just in case she could catch a glimpse of her granny as the stern, but loving, voice continued.

"That kind of deep knowing is truly a gift. It has come down to you from a long way back. I thought your mama was going to have it, but her gifts are different. I am telling you girl; it wouldn't be there for you unless you were the very one who needed it most. It wouldn't be yours unless possessing it meant you could help others. There's real responsibility attached to it for sure. For you, the responsibility is making sure that you use it wisely to help others. If you decide to accept the birthright of your blood, then you will be able to do more and hear more than just me."

Meg wasn't sure what moved her to continue speaking out loud to someone she couldn't see but she decided it was time to attempt a conversation.

"So, you are telling me that if I fully decide to accept this gift that I will be able to hear you and others that have passed on? Just how do I accept it? It's not like you have it in a pretty box tied with ribbons for me."

If Meg *could* have seen her grandmother, she would have seen the pride in the brown eyes shining toward her,

"Well, there you are. Finally. I see the spunk is back. Your mama always called it sass but I always thought you were just spunky like me and my sister Retta. Now as far as accepting, well, you may have just started by talking with me today. You see, it's all about trust. Trust in the things that you can't prove like you do with your book learning. It's trust in yourself. Anything else you want to know, smarty pants?"

Meg thought back to how her grandmother had awoken her and asked,

"So why *did* you always wake me with "morning glory and evening star?"

Her grandmothers' voice softened to an almost whisper,

"You were that little flower that held my day and the star that brightened my night."

Meg felt tears well up into her eyes and huskily replied,

"I love you, Granny. I miss you so much. Sometimes it makes me ache."

Her grandmother heartily responded,

"I love you, too, but there is no need to miss me. I am right here just like I told you I would be. Hmm, another thing…evening star might mean more to you eventually. They have always been used to guide, you know."

Meg's curiosity was piqued. Even as a child, her grandmother would make off-the-cuff remarks that she wouldn't explain at the time. Meg strongly felt this was one of those times and didn't push.

Granny Del continued their chat for a bit more,

"It seems you truly may be ready to take the next steps with your gift."

The older woman paused to laugh,

"Even though it's not wrapped and ribboned up."

"Just remember, none of the women in our family had the same gifts, so we all had to pull together like puzzle pieces to do the work. It's a shame you didn't have sisters to work with…but that makes no never mind. You are going to find the pieces of the puzzles in others as you go along in life. In fact, I have the knowing on this one. Finding others like yourself is coming sooner than you think."

Chapter 8

Monday morning found Meg back at the work she loved. The drive to the college was quick; so quick she barely had time to finish her coffee. The grass was starting to green up in a few of the fields and crocuses and daffodils were starting to push up through the ground even though the official date for spring was still weeks away. The students and staff she regularly passed as she entered her building noticed that she seemed to be in a much better mood today. She smiled and waved, moving swiftly toward her office.

Once inside, she jumped right into her work. It did not take long for her to become deeply entrenched in the mass of documents and artifacts involved in the college's latest study. After an hour or so of working, Meg reached up to rub the stiffness from the back of her neck. The white gloves covering her hands felt odd against the tendrils of hair hanging from the low messy bun.

"Damn, she said out loud, "another pair of gloves wasted."

She ripped the gloves from her hands and threw them in a wire trash basket. Meg reached up and rubbed the back of her neck once again. She moved her reading glasses to the top of her head, pushing her bangs back out of her eyes. She stood up to stretch and walked over to the window to gaze across the familiar campus of Byars Creed College.

She watched the students travel up and down the hilly sidewalks scurrying to their next class or over to the library. She remembered walking up and down that same campus as a freshman. Admittedly, she had been scared out of her mind and excited at the same time. The dichotomy of those feelings had filled her with such apprehension.

She had known at a very early age the importance and self-proclaimed responsibility of being the first of her family to not only graduate from high school but attend college. It was both a blessing and a challenge. Now she fully realized the challenge was something she had placed upon herself. No one had asked that she take on that obligation. She had decided on her own that she had a legacy to fulfill.

Byars Creed was a mere fifteen to twenty minutes from her hometown. For all intents and purposes, it could have been in another galaxy. Her first introduction to college academia made her feel unearthly but not in a good way. After all this time, Meg had finally accepted that her own lack of confidence was probably the greatest factor in her feeling of alienation. She also knew it wasn't the only factor.

There had been more than a few instances where she remembered non-local students purposely excluding or ignoring students from the region, especially those who had been labeled "off campus students." Even then a distinction was made between those who needed to live at home and those who had enough funds to live in their own nearby apartment.

When Meg finally returned to her alma mater to work with Dr. Peabody, she shared her feelings about what had happened in D.C. and how that event had mirrored some of the feelings of her undergraduate days. Dr. Peabody and his wife, Gabby, had gone to great lengths to assure her that the faculty was aware of such instances and work was continuously being done to ensure that everyone felt welcome and valued.

Meg hoped her work on the current research project would underscore the value of individual recognition and diversity as well. The study would certainly not change the past, but if done correctly, it would establish a level of transparency shining a light on the entirety of what had occurred long ago.

Meg wandered back over to the large mahogany table, put on a fresh pair of gloves, and began diligently sifting through the historical documents, diaries, and letters. Her current assignment centered on finding any additional factual documentation which discussed the college's historical use of enslaved peoples prior to and during the Civil War. All in all, it was actually an extenuation of work already begun. The college board was adamant in their quest for transparency.

Similar to other institutions of the same time period, the college had utilized local slave labor to build the physical location and to carry on the business of the school. Enslaved people had been used to cook, clean, and keep up the farm lots used for growing food for the college students and employees. Meg bristled when she read document after document stating the slaves had been "hired" as if they had a say in taking the job. Being "hired" in this instance meant that they had been leased from the local slave owner. Ironically, the earnings for their labor went directly back to the slave owner. The enslaved were clearly treated as chattel.

In the years leading up to the Civil War, the president of the college was a proclaimed supporter of slavery and southern nationalism. His documented words established his belief in the connection between his own religious belief of Christianity and loyalty to the newly founded Confederacy. It was not surprising that documentation supported the fact that many students were influenced by his indoctrination as they voluntarily left the college to fight with the Confederate army.

With so many students going to war, the college was temporarily closed and was utilized as a confederate hospital. The college president remained to serve as a chaplain to wounded Confederate soldiers brought in from near and far. Even as a professed Christian and chaplain, he refused to provide service to Union soldiers. None of these facts had been disputed. Meg had collected documentation outlining the actions of the college as an independent organization as well as the actions of its employees.

The recent "visit" by her grandmother had sparked something inside Meg. She was once again feeling that little itch of growth and trust in following her own instincts. She had recently begun assessing the possibility that there were deeper layers of connection between the enslaved workers and the college. If those connections proved to extend beyond the college, a broadening of the study might prove to be beneficial. If nothing else, Meg could envision initiating an additional study with a hypothesis of her own.

Meg had a growing theory based on the area's location and ability to move supplies to varied positions in the southern states. The very same locale and capability to move product southward could be used in reverse, thereby providing a prime method in supporting those who wanted to end slavery.

The Great Wagon Road, the railroad lines, and the riverways served as principal modes for the transportation of food, ammunition, and salt used before and during the war. Sadly enough, those same venues were also utilized to move the enslaved people from the north southward and down to Natchez, Mississippi. The pathway from Virginia down to Natchez was referred to as the Slave Trail of Tears. Once in Natchez, men, women, and children would be traded and sold before being dispersed among the southernmost plantations.

Meg wanted to explore the possibility that the very same routes could have been a reverse path to eventual freedom. The hypothesis offered the question of the possible connections between the region, the college, and the Underground Railroad. Being a supporter of the Underground Railroad was considered a clandestine and dangerous activity. Still, there had to have been some locals who saw the evils in slavery and who had the moral compass to attempt to end the abomination. It was a dangerous undertaking physically, emotionally, and financially and so the activities of those involved were well hidden. So well hidden, that Meg was finding very little documentation so far.

Strangely, while the acts of great human kindness were hidden, a more atrocious occurrence was well documented. During an autumn battle in her hometown, many Union soldiers, including troops from the U.S. Colored Calvary, had been wounded and killed. The wounded were transported as prisoners of war to the

Confederate hospital that had been established in the main hall of Byars Creed.

A Union surgeon that had been captured was assigned to their care. Meg had readily found the documentation the surgeon had left stating Confederate troops had entered the building with dire intentions. Upon entry, they began executing the transported troopers. In the end, five to twelve of the black troopers as well as a white lieutenant were murdered in their hospital beds.

The Confederate soldiers later defended their actions as righteous acts of war. Meg could see no defense of their actions. Cold and simple, this act was a massacre of fellow human beings unable to protect themselves. Meg was sure of one thing. The horrific event could and never should be erased from history.

The facts clearly existed that there were many institutions and individuals participating in the slave trade. Meg was trained to be objective and to ground her studies in fact, not feeling. Yet, there was something in her heart pushing her to find proof of locals who chose *not* to participate in the act of slavery and who attempted to help the enslaved reach freedom. Would it be possible?

Chapter 9

At work the next day, Meg found herself combing through a box of materials that had recently been donated to the college. The varied documents highlighted the names of people in the region who had purchased and traded in the local slave markets. Meg was grateful to the donor who had gathered a plethora of information from other researchers, authors, and newspaper resources. Still, she had the arduous task of piecing together many of the sources to ensure accuracy and validity.

Meg poured over the credentials and records listing how and where the enslaved were used for labor in the local area. A sour taste rose in her throat when she found documentation of the specific use of the slaves in the production of salt in her very own hometown. Meg thought back to the many events held in her hometown which celebrated the history of the town and the making of salt. Never did she remember any reference to the slave population.

As a young girl, she herself had participated in and enjoyed those celebrations. She had been enthralled to discover how people from a bygone area had lived day to day. She recalled walking among the restored cabins to observe volunteers cooking at the fireplace, quilting, and making apple butter in large kettles over an outside fire. On those special weekends, she had been transported to another time and place.

In her mind's eye, she could see the enjoyment of the older male volunteers as they gathered together to explain and demonstrate each step of the process for making salt. She had been amazed at the ingenuity of taking logs and hollowing out the centers to make wooden pipes for the salt brine to travel through to the large black kettles used for boiling. To this day, the town still had many huge iron kettles that were original to the process as well as the "pump logs" on display.

That particular event seemed so innocuously pleasant at the time, but not all parts of the celebratory weekends set right with Meg. There had been a portion of the festival that gave her a sick feeling in the pit of her stomach and had made Meg's skin crawl. At the time, she didn't understand why that feeling had washed over her, but as an adult, she now understood.

It centered around a gathering of mostly men who set up a re-enactment camp in the center of the town fields. The camp was filled predominantly with gray clad men and only a few participants dressed in blue. Many of the participants had driven in from out of town to participate, but not all. Meg remembered feeling sad to see people she knew from town, older men and their sons, joining in with the event.

Meg didn't think she would ever be able to forget the anxiety she felt when she entered the encampment. Even now she could feel her body reacting to the memory of fighting for her breath as she skittered through the pathways between the canvas tents. She had practically broken into a run, avoiding the eyes of the men and boys dressed in woolen gray uniforms. Her instinct was telling her to move as fast as she could up to the ridge overlooking the field. There she might be able to breath normally again.

Once Meg had climbed to the top of the hill, she sat down amongst the seeding Johnson grass and took a deep clean breath of air into her lungs. Meg propped her elbows on her knees and watched the spectacle before her. Sitting there high above the fields, she realized now why her body had rejected being in the field below.

These were the fields where men had been herded like cattle to work the salt day after day. They were the same fields where bullets and cannon balls had flown through the air in protection of that salt. Now that she had the full understanding, she had to wonder if that was really anything to celebrate.

Looking back, she could see herself sitting high on the ridge and becoming calmer. The events down in the field seemed far away. As the breeze swirled around her, she felt safer and more removed from the things she had no control over. She thought if she shut her eyes, she could pretend that none of what was going on in the field had ever existed.

To this day, Meg could recall shutting her eyes and hearing the quiet sounds of voices behind her on the ridge. She quickly opened her eyes and turned to look toward the direction of the voices. No one was there. Back then she had brushed the incident away as nothing, blaming the sound on the wind blowing across the ridge. But now, after the "visit" with her grandmother, she wondered if she indeed had been picking up on voices even as a young person.

When the time came for the "battle" to begin, Meg made sure she was already back at home. She had no desire to witness men portraying soldiers from either camp. She didn't want or need to watch them fall to the ground as voluntary dead. The August heat of their unconditioned house necessitated open windows throughout the house, but Meg had a plan for blocking out the sounds of the pretend battle that would echo off the boundary hills. She went to her bedroom, shut the windows, and pulled the curtains together. She stuffed torn up tissue in her ears and hid her head under a mound of pillows trying to block out the thunder of cannons and guns. Cannons and guns shooting blanks all for the sake of re-living history.

It was much later in high school and during her first years at college when Meg learned the deeper truths about her hometown. Truths that had not been voiced and facts that had been neglected. Meg clearly didn't understand why the details of enslavement in her little town had been glossed over. Shame? Guilt? She chastised herself for never have given the whole experience much thought until leaving home to study and work in a much more diverse world.

As the years passed, Meg purposefully schooled herself on the history lessons that she should have received. She continued to find writings by local authors whose superfluous works were highlighted on the shelves of local libraries and historical societies. Meg knew many of them and remembered many who had passed away years ago. They were nice people, but it appeared they didn't have the heart or the willpower to speak plainly about the role of slavery in the valley. Too many attempted to paint a rosy picture where blacks were always treated well. Local authors of a certain period of time viewed the past as if it were a southern utopia for all. Their penned stories were effused with a tender remembering. Only those who had never suffered the chains of slavery could imagine such a fond recalling of the past.

Meg would bet that their written stories had been passed down orally during gatherings on front porches. No one had bothered to look deeper into what was being shared. The youngest of listeners would have instinctively placed their trust in the adult rendition of the stories. It certainly didn't make the adults bad people, but it surely didn't make anyone wiser. Meg begged to question if any of those stories would have held the same fond remembrances told on the porches of black families?

Meg was now immersed in work that pushed truth forward and it was a truth that had no room for middle ground. Thank goodness the college recognized the moral obligation for taking ownership of its association with the acts of slavery. Meg questioned whether her hometown was ready to step forward and do the same. If the results of her work continued to reveal more detailed information about slavery in the salt works, how would that be received by her community?

Meg momentarily pushed away her unnerving thoughts and looked toward her office window. In the distance, she could hear a lone train whistle. She pushed back her chair, rose slowly, and walked to the window. She leaned her head against the cool pane. She could both hear and feel the rumble of the train as it click-clacked on the parallel path running along the main campus.

This same train line had established a spur into her hometown in the 1850s with the sole purpose of retrieving salt. This was the same line of tracks beside the field where, as a child, she and her beloved elders had gone to gather good rich soil for spring plantings. It was the same line by the clearing where she had fallen and was cut by the broken amber glass. She remembered the rivulets of blood pouring from her hands. Meg looked down at the crescent scar on her finger. A scar that had never faded. She found herself wondering about the people who had been forced to labor in the salt works. Had they carried scars that never faded?

Meg's thoughts went back to the celebrations in her hometown once again. It seemed as if everything had been done for the sake of re-living a romanticized time and to draw in tourists, hoping to keep the town alive. There had been no real blood, sweat, or tears shed during those recreations. But in hundreds of years past, the process was far more difficult and more time-consuming and completed on a much larger scale. And in the end with much larger consequences.

Back in the day, the entire production of salt was on a much larger scale. It had taken scores of workers to see the process through from beginning to end. The briny water had to be primed and pumped out of the ground before traveling through the log pipes to a multitude of huge black kettles. The fires under the kettles had to be kept at a constant temperature and the kettles themselves had to be tended. After the water boiled away, the wet salt had to be placed in baskets to begin the drying process.

The scale of the original salt making process had been slimmed down for the celebration weekends. The only men from her childhood memories of those times were the elder white men of her community. There was not one single black person taking any part in the event. Which was irony at its worst.

From the 1700s until the mid-1800s, the veins of salt running underneath her hometown had been worked by the same group of people forced to do the most physical and demanding portions of the process. This group had nothing in common with the white mine owners or overseers. This group of people had been purchased like cattle at the market. They were forced to work unendingly at a task ensuring more humans could be bought, sold, and held in bondage. Why would the descendants of those who had suffered these bondages want to take part in such a celebration?

Meg pushed herself back from the window and began pacing back and forth. The connection between the college and her hometown was unmistakable. The insight into the details of slavery and salt making seemed ambiguous at best. Were the details simply vague or were they purposely being hidden? Meg walked back to the chair at her desk and lowered herself slowly into the seat.

Meg laid her hand on her abdomen trying to assuage the sudden churning. Had she been making excuses for herself? Could she continue holding on to the thought that she had simply been a child, naïve about this period of history in her hometown? She was an adult now. She had to ask herself if she was continuing to subconsciously gloss over the truth, over the entirety of the story.

Without a doubt, her research had the possibility of leading her to answer her own questions. Answers that could turn out to be both embarrassing and painful, even for her own family. She knew of a family member whose gravestone proclaimed Confederate soldier status. This knowledge filled her with a sense of trepidation.

Meg had begun her assigned study with a clear objective set forth by the college. Should she simply stick to that task, or was there a moral obligation to dig deeper? Meg sat straight up in the leather chair. Clearly, she had professional obligation to the assigned study but now she felt a deeper responsibility in giving voice to that which had been silenced.

Her friends and neighbors might find fault with her actions, but her family would always support doing what she believed to be the right thing. It was a matter of principle. Principles her grandmother had lived by and attempted to instill in Meg. Her grandmother may not have had a formal education but the wisdom she carried about the ways of people was far more valuable than a degree. She watched a person's actions and measured those actions against their words. Granny Del said signs came in a lot of different ways. Meg could remember Granny Del saying,

"Some people will try to tell you who they are, but *all* people will show you who they are. Just give 'em time."

Meg thought back to a few days ago and the "conversation" with her grandmother. Her grandmother had been simply trying to remind Meg to read the signs, trust in herself, and value her own intuition.

Meg inhaled deeply. Her research up to this point had been based on dry facts and figures. She knew without a doubt those facts needed to be supported with narrative components illustrating the human connection. Combining the numbers and the qualitative data could lead to a more accurate presentation of the connections between slavery and the college, as well as slavery in the general locality. More importantly, it could reveal details of the lives and deaths of the people involved. The time had come to remove the mask of invisibility of the enslaved no matter what awful details might emerge.

Meg recognized how vital it would prove to be able to associate names with the people whose lives were not their own. The possible revelations could go a long way in helping a great number of people beyond the academic world to understand the very real experiences the enslaved had suffered. Meg already read much of the evidence of the horrid acts perpetrated on the enslaved across the south. Documents and factual accounts of these events were housed in various libraries and foundations where anyone could read about them if they chose to do so. Deep down, Meg felt that similar despicable acts were more than likely to have occurred within the salt works. Would she be able to find them?

Chapter 10

Another thing Meg remembered her grandmother saying was that a person would know where to go if they understood where they started. Granny's wisdom had always proven correct. Meg saw no reason to doubt it now. So, it only made sense for Meg to take her investigation back to the beginning. All the way back to a time before the battle that had brought the injured to the college hospital.

Questions about that time ran wildly through Meg's brain. When and how were the people held in slavery brought to her hometown? Who were they as individuals? What happened to the families they came from? Did they go on to have families of their own.

The first point of her research had to start with the arrival of slaves in the area and more specifically in her hometown. Meg would need to delve as deeply as possible to piece together the puzzle associated with her newly forming theory. Maybe then the treatment of the enslaved by the mine owners and the locals living in the surrounding valley and mountains could be discovered.

The research committee in the history department at Byars Creed had practically given her carte blanche with her time and methods for research so far. Meg was grateful for that, but she wanted more. Meg bit her bottom lip in worry. Documenting how the enslaved people were brought to the area as well as how they were treated while would be a fundamental to the project. Would it be possible to convince them to support enlarging the scope of her research?

In her gut, Meg knew that her theory regarding the entry and possible exit methods by the slaves had to be connected in some way. If only she had the opportunity to retrace the path of an individual or individuals. Meg felt a sudden tingling on her arms and knew in that instant someone was out there wanting her to find them, even in death. If Granny was right and she had the "knowing," this was her first step in trusting her own intuition.

Meg laughed to herself. It was almost ironic how this was all playing out before her. How in the world could she explain the theory she was contemplating was embedded in what most academics would describe as folklore? Meg could picture herself telling the committee about the gifts passed down through her family and how she wanted to trust those gifts to lead her to the right sources for the study. The prestigious group of academics wouldn't merely laugh at her, they just might have her carted off to an institution,

Meg made the decision to keep the fanciful notion of intuition to herself. She simply had to trust that she would succeed in securing the committee's approval. Her best bet would be providing additional documentation demonstrating the plausibility of her theory. Additionally, trusting her merit as a researcher should be enough to convince them. Informing the committee that her intuition would be a main guide was out of the question. Meg didn't even feel emotionally ready or professionally safe enough to explore her gut reasoning with her mentor, Dr. Peabody.

John Peabody, current chair of the history department, had been one of her favorite instructors when she was working on her undergrad. His reputation as an extraordinary academic and remarkable teacher was well

105

known. His expectations for students were high but reasonable. He tried to present as gruff and tough in the classroom, but Meg had caught on to his acting skills early on. She had seen through that strong exterior and right into the heart of the man.

What Meg had never realized was that John Peabody had also witnessed her own authenticity and vulnerability. He had quietly observed as she grew into a young woman who had the ability to step outside the safe walls of family and home to reach her goals. He also saw a young woman who was frightened of being ridiculed for even trying to be more. He watched as she navigated the current of classism propagated by a few of her fellow students from across the country. Students who suffered from an ego of "more and better than." Those students had only come to attend the mountain college because their parents insisted, or their academic backgrounds weren't up to snuff for the Ivy League setting they so wanted to be a part of. Instead, those few classist students feigned a persona they would never be able to carry off in the real world. Meg, on the other hand, did her best to not let their actions affect her. John Peabody witnessed a strength of character in Meg that would always set her apart from the pretenders.

Meg trusted John Peabody as much as she trusted her own father, but he didn't know everything about her family. She and Dr. Peabody had never really discussed the intimate details of her background especially her grandmother's heritage and gifts. For that reason, she didn't believe that Dr. Peabody would be able to understand Meg's use of that type of intuition in her work. Meg was sure, however, that he would be able to advise her on how widely she could expand her research. He would know what it would take to get the committee's approval. Meg leaned up in her chair and glanced out her office window once more. She shrugged her shoulders, grabbed her keys, and stood up to go out the door calling out to no one in particular,

"It's now or never."

A few minutes later, Meg settled herself on the stone bench under the second-floor window of the history building. Students were going in and out of the front entrance of the building as some classes ended and others began. She looked down at her watch. It was around 1:45 on a beautiful sunny Tuesday. Freshman history had been in session for about forty-five minutes. Within the next ten minutes, Dr. Peabody would have completed just enough instruction to allow students to finish the work on their own during the Wednesday Lyceum Day. Meg glanced up at the window just above the bench. She smiled wryly wondering how long it would take this semester's students to figure out John Peabody's somewhat eccentric pattern of behavior.

Meg took a second peek at her watch and saw that it was precisely 1:50. Time for the show, Meg thought to herself with a knowing smile. Without hesitation, the sash of the second-floor window flew up with a whoosh. Meg looked up to see the familiar sight of one long leg and then another pop through the opening of the wide window. This uncanny vision was followed by the strong thud of two feet ensconced in well-worn athletic shoes hitting solidly on the ground.

Meg knew from experience that not one student would move toward that window to see what John Peabody's next move might be. They would all be sitting in their seats, looking around in semi-shock, wondering what to do next. It would take them a few minutes before they realized he wasn't coming back. Then they would begin to slowly amble out of the classroom, free to enjoy the time they had been given.

Meg reached under the stone bench and pulled out a tennis racquet accompanied by a slender can of lime green tennis balls. She handed them off to John Peabody.

Dr. Peabody grinned sheepishly at Meg. She returned the smile and asked, "First time with this class?"

"Nope," said Dr. Peabody, "it's the second time. But I think it still shocks them. It is still hilarious to me that after all these years, no one ever warns the newbies. No one will even discuss it with them until they are officially sophomores. What is that about?"

Meg remembered well the first time she had witnessed John Peabody "jump" out the window on his way to play the game he was famous for on campus. To say she was shocked was an understatement. Even back then, everyone but the freshmen knew what would happen and they kept it close to the chest. Meg believed it was reasonable to believe that the secret was kept for two reasons. The first being that it was almost a rite of passage to listen to and watch the freshmen discuss the strange behavior of the otherwise brilliant history professor. The second was the love that students and colleagues had for John Peabody.

Everyone who knew John Peabody respected and cared for him as both a teacher and as a person. They also knew he loved three things above all else: his family, history, and tennis. Family first always. History and his beloved sport ran neck and neck in second place for his affection.

John had grown up locally. The young farm boy could bale hay and serve up some real stingers on the high school tennis court all in the same day. He had made quite a name for himself winning a vast number of county, regional, and state tournaments. His reputation on the court captured the attention of the local sports press. His superb tennis skills also helped him to acquire an athletic scholarship at Byars Creed where he went on to sweep all the conference championships during his undergrad days.

In all honesty, John Peabody had been good for Byars Creed and Byars Creed had been good for John Peabody. That was probably the reason that the powers above never said a word about the eccentric way he led a class or for that matter exited a class. His instructional methods and his theatrical exits were both colorful in language as well as in action. His exaggerated egresses through the second-floor window on a sunny afternoon to play tennis was just one more lovable thing about John Peabody. He didn't even realize it was lovable, he merely thought it was a way to keep those around him on their toes.

As an undergrad, Meg enjoyed Dr. Peabody's methods for teaching and leading the history department in the most creative ways. She had been enthralled by the way he was able to transport her and her fellow students back through the annals of history. He had made what could have been a dry memorization come to life in every class. His avid storytelling, underscored by his mesmerizing voice, seemed to hypnotize even the most reluctant fan of history. Meg remembered looking around in a daze as John Peabody ended his class with the same phrase each time. Quietly he would whisper, "Until next time." All the students in the class seemed to shake their heads as if waking up from a dream before filing slowly out of class.

Now Meg was considered one of John Peabody's colleagues. Yet, she still was in awe of the man and his methods no matter how eccentric even he had to admit they could be. John recognized that Meg was the very opposite of eccentric in her own professional life. He knew exactly how serious Meg could be about her work and research. If truth were told, Meg was just as serious in her personal life as well.

John often thought she was perhaps too serious in both areas and that worried him quite a bit. He hoped that one day she would find a way to step away from that core of solemnity weighing her down. But today wasn't the day. He saw the determined look in Meg's eyes. She hadn't come here today to see the show or have an idle chit chat.

As much as John was itching to get to the match waiting for him on the college courts, he found himself moving toward the bench. He started to take a seat beside Meg, but she motioned for him to remain standing. Meg stood up to walk with him down the hill to the tennis courts. As they made their way toward the area behind the library, John looked over to her and asked,

"What's on your mind, Meg?"

Meg thought for just a moment about telling Dr. Peabody *everything* that was on her mind but held back. If she shared everything, John Peabody might walk her straight to the infirmary instead of the tennis court. Instead, Meg concisely explained what she wanted to do with the research expansion as they sauntered down the sloping sidewalk. John listened intently and without interruption. As they made their way across campus, she finished up her verbal outline.

John never doubted that Meg would come to him unprepared in any manner. He wasn't surprised that she had quite the detailed proposal already thought out in her mind. Meg then began to try and explain the why behind her thinking. She wanted Dr. Peabody to unmistakably understand her heartfelt need to secure the support in order to carry out her research expansion. John Peabody reached out and gently touched her shoulder.

"Meg, slow down. Let me stop you there. I know without a doubt you are about to tell me every logical reason you can think of to convince me to help you. Let me be absolutely clear about this. I know you. The real you. The you that is a serious professional. The you that is a heart centered soul." John took a breath as he stepped from the sidewalk to the grass beside the courts and continued,

"Sometimes…hell, most of the time, you lean so far into the serious that you get stuck there. You need to know, really know, that leaning into your heart will serve you just as well. Recognizing what you know in your heart to be true only highlights the passion you have for your work. I trust your professionalism. I always have. I trust your heart. Without question. If only we could get you to trust yourself. I'll start the conversation with the others later this afternoon. You will have your answer by the end of the week."

Meg wasn't quite sure how to feel or what to say in reflection of John's genuine words. She quietly thanked him and made her way back to the office. Walking back, she felt a sense of relief wash over her. She had been able to avoid sharing the part of her reasoning connected to her personal intuitive abilities. For all his eccentricities, Dr. John Peabody might think she was nuts. Unless… well, he did say he knew her, the real her…could he possibly know *everything*?

John Peabody watched as Meg distanced herself from the tennis courts and from him. He wondered if she felt the presence of the protective shadow following her. The shadowed figure turned to look at John. John lifted his hand to his brow in a brief salute, not worrying a bit if anyone on the courts was watching. They already thought he was a bit nuts, but he didn't care. Meg, on the other hand, would feel it deeply if she thought folks ever thought of her as being unconventional in any form. Maybe that was the reason that she hid her gifts from the world.

Chapter 11

Dr. Peabody was true to his word. At the week's end, Meg had secured the approval of the committee to expand the parameters of the study. Three weeks following, Meg found herself closing in on possible connections between the less talked about Slave Trail of Tears and the Underground Railroad. Researching documents from the state, its various counties, and their historical societies was slow and tedious at best, but Meg was certain it would pay off in the end.

She meticulously sifted through every single document and artifact, often feeling like she was putting together a jigsaw puzzle. A puzzle whose pieces were all cut to almost the same size and shape. Anyone else might have been tempted to discard what appeared to be the more mundane examples in the collections. But experience had led Meg to understand the importance of finding even small similarities of information between documents. Cross referencing led to finding emerging patterns. Patterns that turned the seemingly obscure into important finds. One just had to be patient and persevere. A lot of coffee breaks didn't hurt either.

Interestingly, one set of records provided by the state archives along with the journals from a former plantation in eastern Virginia shared many of the same corroborating details. These details led Meg towards the identification of a young man who had been brought from Graystone Plantation and sold in nearby Abingdon, Virginia.

Abingdon was just over ten miles from the college and around 20 miles from the salt works. The purchasing documents for the young man indicated that the owners of the salt mines were connected to the buyer. Meg's curiosity peaked. She wondered how he and others would have been transported to the salt works. The trek there during the specific historic period in question would not have been so quickly undertaken as it would today. Meg made a note to contact the county historical society for information on the roads and trails that led from Abingdon to that specific area.

Meg hypothesized that if the young man had made it safely down the Slave Trail of Tears to Abingdon, he must have been in good enough health to have been considered worth purchasing. Considered worth purchasing? Meg felt her stomach roll. Bile rose in her throat. Where and when had she allowed the line between objective research and making unfeeling suppositions about another human being become blurred.

This young man had been treated like mere chattel during his lifetime. Now here, Meg was utilizing him as just another cold statistic for study. Was that the totality of the meaning of his life? Wasn't her careless thought just another example of the devaluation of the human experience of slavery? Meg leaned into her heart just as John Peabody had suggested and decided she could not allow that to happen.

The young man in question was not just another dry statistic for study. For God's sake, he had been someone's son. Just as she was someone's daughter. He had been part of a family at one time. He had been loved. He had been missed. Somewhere in time a mother's heart had ached to see him once more.

Meg knew without a doubt she wanted to learn his full story. She desperately wanted to share his story. If she didn't, she would consider herself no different than those people of long ago. People who had silenced his life by stripping him of his freedom.

Meg looked over the sale papers once again. Samson's age was listed as 16 years at the point of sale in Abingdon. Had the original slave owners, the LeGris family, chosen his birth name based on Biblical reference or in hopes for his physical stature and endurance? The latter would certainly have served their capitalistic purposes.

Meg set her intentions to go into a deeper dive to discover any information about Samson's life after being taken to the salt works. She realized finding artifacts from the company records hundreds of years later might prove to be difficult if not impossible. Would they even still exist? The first step on the path to discovery would be a search for a roster of workers at the salt mines. She felt sure such a document could provide a lead into Samson's story. She was about to receive a surprise. One that would give her a whole other trail to follow.

Actually, the beginning of the trail came to her in the form of an old friend she had known since childhood. Ben Roberts, famous for his escapades with the game of fox and hound and scary camping trips, had called and scheduled a meeting at her office for the next day. Byars Creed had an extensive relationship with the main church in her hometown. Ben just happened to be the current pastor of that church as well as a former student of John Peabody and a graduate of Byars Creed.

Meg was excited when Ben called and explained that Dr. Peabody had shared the topic of her project with him. Meg was even more excited when Ben explained he wanted to share some documents which might prove to be a help in her endeavors.

Ben arrived promptly at ten a. m. the next morning. Meg felt as giddy as a child receiving a present on their birthday. Her hands were visibly shaking as Ben passed over an old bank box to her. She placed the box gingerly on top of her desk. Carefully she removed the box lid to find a multitude of documents and letters. The yellowing of the paper indicated they had been stored in the church archives for quite some time. A small bundle wrapped in what appeared to be a piece of an old quilt rested on top of the documents. Ben gently reached in and took the bundle, laying it carefully to one side. He could see the anticipation in Meg's eyes and knew his friend couldn't wait to dig into the treasures before her.

Ben cleared his throat to get her attention.

"Meg, fair warning, my gut tells me you won't find too much there that you haven't already uncovered in the files from the local historical societies. If nothing else, the papers inside that box may only provide you with some confirmation but really nothing new."

Ben could see that Meg was trying to hide her disappointment. He felt a nip of guilt for leading with that information. Meg was looking down despairingly at the contents of the box and didn't notice Ben's mischievous grin.

"Forget all those papers for a moment, what you really need to see is what is wrapped in that piece of quilt."

Ben took the bundle from where he had placed it and began to judiciously remove the material. The softly colored and somewhat worn cloth fell away to reveal a very old and worn book.

"This beauty is not from the church archives. Jessica and I found it in the attic of the Hughes' house that we are renovating. My wife is as inquisitive as you have always been. She is determined that we will make lots of discoveries as we refurbish every room. Oddly enough, we found this the day after I spoke with John about your project. He doesn't know about this little gem yet."

Ben gently opened the book to show the inscription on the inside. This was a personal journal. Meg's heart quivered to think of all the possibilities that could be found in the pages that had aged from white to the hue of an old tea stain. Ben looked at the anticipation sparkling in Meg's eyes.

"This journal belonged to another man of the cloth decades ago. That man, Daniel Hughes, had left documents and journals encompassing the business of the church and those items had to remain in the custody of the church archives. It seems this journal, however, was his personal journal that had been destined to be passed down through our family. Of course, Jess and I had no idea of its existence until we began cleaning out the attic."

Meg did remember that there were some Hughes' relatives adjoined to the Roberts family. She remembered them coming to visit next door at Granny Roberts' house often. It just so happened that the Hughes' and Roberts' families had been joined a generation before Daniel, the author of the journal, was born. Ben and Jessica Roberts had recently purchased the Hughes house from family members wanting to make a permanent home for themselves. Ben smiled at Meg as she instinctively put on gloves before taking the book from Ben's hands. She gazed at the leather-bound work like a newborn, and she handled it just as delicately.

"Meg, when Dr. Peabody explained what you were doing with your project, I thought for sure that the church documents might be of some help. I had no idea that Jess and I would be able to share something like Daniel's personal journal with you."

Ben started to make his way toward the door, talking all the way.

I'm going to leave the documents and the journal with you, so you have plenty of time to go through them. Of course, you are more than welcome to photograph any of the church documents that you need as well as the journal."

"Ben, I can get the photos completed today, if you don't mind waiting for a bit. Surely you don't want to leave all this, especially the journal, for long."

"Meg Hurley, if it were anyone else working with these artifacts I might hesitate. I have known you all your life. I know exactly how careful you will be. I really do think the journal might be something you will want to take your time with and read all the way through-several times. I'm pretty sure you will find something of value in the turning of every page. Once you have read it, take the photos, and call me. I'm betting you are going have a few more questions for me by then."

Ben waved and went out the office door on his way to visit Dr. Peabody. Meg sat down at her desk to begin reading. She was usually a quick reader on the first run through but the combination of antiquated script and the need to be gentle with the pages slowed her down quite a bit. After a few hours, Meg found herself stopping to stare off in space. Her imagination was working overtime forming daunting pictures in her mind. The scenes from behind her eyes were at times unthinkably sad and terrifying. So much so that she had to stop halfway through the reading. She secured the journal in the office safe, grabbed her keys, and locked the office door. She needed a walk to sort through the feelings Daniel's words had evoked.

Meg found herself walking past Tobias Hall where she often wandered the building in attempts to catch a glimpse of those she referred to as visitors from the past. Others called ghosts. She had never told anyone that was what she was doing for fear of the strange looks she might receive. She even found it a strange thing to be doing. Not for the reasons other people might think. Meg never questioned the possibility of their presence, but she did question her ability to see and hear them. More so than not, Meg made these walks testing herself and the gift of knowing her grandmother had sworn she had within herself.

Oddly enough, she often ran into Dr. Peabody wandering around Tobias Hall as well. Many times, he would almost walk on top of her before recognizing she was even there. She wondered if he felt or saw the visitors, especially if she happened upon him when he seemed to be talking to himself. It seemed they had an unspoken understanding between them, and they never questioned each other about why they were in the building at the oddest times.

For now, Meg needed to clear her head and try to sift through the information she had read in Daniel Hughes' journal. With that task in mind, Meg did not enter Tobias Hall but continued to walk past as fast as possible without breaking into a run. The only visitors she could deal with today were the ones visiting through writing in the journal of Daniel Hughes.

It took Meg a full week to read the journal and examine the documents in the box. When she was complete with her task, she made a call and arranged to drop by the old Hughes' house to visit Ben and Jessica. When Meg arrived at their house, Jessica met her at the top of the steps of the wide front porch and took the old bank box from Meg's arms. Meg carefully took the bundle that held the journal to look over with the couple.

"Come on in and excuse the mess. We decided to just live here while we work on the remodeling. We stopped work for the day, so Ben is out back by the fire pit. Head on out and I'll bring us all some coffee. I can't wait to hear what you think about the journal."

Jessica pointed the way through the hallway past the kitchen and out to the backyard. Any other time, Meg would have been eager to stroll through the old house looking at the work the couple was doing, but this evening she was on a different mission. Ben was waiting and had placed some cushioned lounge chairs around the fire. Meg had wrapped the journal in tissue paper before putting the quilt around it. She handed the journal to Ben with a smile. Jessica came out of the house carrying a tray of goodies and placed some homemade cookies and coffee on each of their side tables. The three of them munched for a bit, sharing small talk before they settled into the story found inside Daniel Hughes's journal.

Ben began, "I am glad you could come by to visit. I feel like the old family home will be blessed by us looking into this together. Was I right? Did the information from the journal point you in a direction you want to follow?"

Meg answered immediately. "It surely has; in fact, it has opened up even more questions for me."

Ben nodded, "I thought maybe your first question might be why we hadn't shared this information before now. Honestly, we didn't know Daniel Hughes had personal journals until recently. Jess is the one who found them.

Meg was a bit startled at the mention of journals in the plural. Could there be more than the one she had been reading?

"I am sure you realize that this house didn't exist in Daniel Hughes's lifetime but lots of old family boxes from years and years past were stored in the attic of this house. Jess was up there digging around and came upon a small wooden box that held the journal that I brought by your office."

Jess interjected, "Yes, you know how much I love antiques. I've always had a fascination with old handmade boxes and chests. I wish I had opened it sooner, but we were in such a hurry to get to the renovations that I left it for later. The day Ben brought you the first journal, I went back up to the attic to clear and clean a bit more. I found a larger wooden box underneath a pile of old clothes and moth-eaten blankets." Jessica pushed her coffee cup away.

"I was excited to see David Hughes's name etched into the top inside lid of the box. What I saw inside, however, really didn't seem to have belonged to him. There were mostly old quilt pieces and cut up cloth. I simply thought that someone had used the box to sew old quilting materials, especially since an old quilting frame was lying against the wall behind it. I decided to just leave it there and go back to it later."

Jessica's eyes darkened a bit as she continued,

"That night, I began having some odd dreams about the quilt pieces. In my dream, an older lady was telling me to get them. She kept saying, 'You need to get them out.' After the third dream, I decided to go up in the attic and pull the quilt pieces out to see if any of them could still be used somehow or if they had all dry rotted. I wasn't sure how long they had been stored."

Jessica didn't appear at all anxious to share her dreams with Meg.

"Ben was out for the day doing hospital visits and church business," Jess continued," It was rainy and cozy up in the attic. So, after I pulled the material out of the box and checked it, I began to clean the box. I thought the handmade craftmanship deserved to be polished up and shared for folks to see. My thought was to display it in our family room. I had pulled out the quilt pieces and was trying to move it closer to the window to see better when I realized that it was exceptionally heavy. I opened the lid and was dusting inside when I hit a false bottom. I grabbed a screwdriver from Ben's toolbox in the corner. I jiggled as hard as I could, trying not to damage the wood. It took a minute or so, but finally what I originally thought was the bottom of box popped out. That's when I saw a couple of books lying snuggly in the bottom recess of the chest."

Meg wondered if she was sitting there in front of her friends with her mouth wide open, but they seemed to be excited to share this information as she was to hear it.

"Jess practically ran me over at the door when I got home. She took me by the hand and led me up to the attic. We sat there for hours looking through the books which turned out to be more personal journals belonging to Daniel Hughes. I had known he kept journals of church business that were archived as property of the church, but these were very different. He mentioned church activities in them to some extent, but there was so much more. I asked my siblings and my parents if they had ever known these journals existed. All of them were adamant they had no idea about the journals or any wooden boxes. My grandparents are gone now but none of the family can recall any of the older folks telling stories like this."

Ben picked up the journal Meg had brought back and removed the wrapping. He began looking through the pages. Meg tried to hide her wince as she glanced at his ungloved hands. The historical researcher in her had strict protocols but this was his family's journal. He could handle it as he wished.

"It seems that Pastor Daniel recognized that Samson's story would be invaluable in times to come, or he would have never taken the time to write it down. The journal entries at the beginning capture the weeks prior to their meeting. It is like he was setting the scene for what would then be written on a regular basis."

Ben suddenly hesitated and looked at Meg.

"As soon as we found the journals and read them, we wanted to share it with the college through you. Honestly, I never thought about it until now, but since the church records don't share any of the same information, could this journal simply be a made-up story by a would-be author? Could this long-ago grand uncle of mine have been a budding writer? Maybe he felt he had to hide his creative work because it wouldn't be approved by the church?"

Meg smiled broadly at the couple before her,

"No worries there. My research documentation supports that a young 16-year-old boy listed as Samson was auctioned off in Abingdon and brought to the salt works to labor. It also documents that a brother, Moses, was sold off on the same day. The very brother that Samson speaks about in Pastor Daniels' writings."

Ben and Jessica asked Meg to stay for the evening so they could continue their chat. Jessica stepped into the kitchen to check on a casserole she had in the oven. She returned with three pairs of new gloves from the laundry room. She smiled broadly at Meg and winked conspiratorially. Meg knew instantly that Jessica understood her.

"So," Jessica said, looking at Meg,

"Let's stop for a bit to have some food, and then we can dig into what's in the journals. I would love to hear what you have found out in the rest of your research as well, if you are allowed to share."

Part Three
Old Blood

Where old blood whispers, the truth is made known.

Chapter 12

Ben settled back against the cushions of the chair and began to recap what had been found:

In the beginning of the first journal, Uncle Daniel writes about the few weeks prior to meeting Samson. He talks of riding his horse around town going to visit the older people from the church and passing by the salt furnaces. He writes about growing up with several of the men who oversaw the work at the furnaces. I assume this actually meant those men oversaw the enslaved men doing the actual work.

Daniel Hughes had used his written words to produce a picture of what life was like in the year 1851 in the mountains of the southwestern corner of Virginia. He had been a man well versed in the politeness expected from the pulpit and in the discussions with his community, but he had not hidden the raw truth of what he witnessed in the small world around him.

Ben was correct in recognizing his grand uncle's writing abilities, but he didn't have to use them to fabricate a world filled with drama, pain, and tragedy. All of that and more had played out before his very eyes, touching his heart and soul in ways that a lesser human would never want to fathom.

Daniel wrote of dreams that came to him in the middle of the night for three months straight. In the dreams, he could see hands reaching out to him for help. Always hands but never faces. The hands came in all sizes and shapes but were always darker than his own. Daniel began to pay special attention to the activities he documented on the day before he had the dreams. In every instance, the dream came after a day in which he rode his horse or used the church carriage to pass by the salt works on his way to visit the sick and elderly.

Daniel had penned his memories of always looking straight ahead, never making eye contact, as he rode by the workers. At different points in his brief excursions, he could hear manual pumps being primed and worked to bring the brine out of the deep caverns of salt. He could smell the acrid scent of the fires being stoked under the huge kettles as huge wooden stirrers scraped against the side of the cast iron cauldrons.

Daniel recognized the consistent dream held a message for him. A message he couldn't seem to decipher on his own. He turned to prayer as he had been taught. He would lie in his bed once the tableside candle had been extinguished and silently ask for the significance of the dream to be revealed. Nothing came but the dreams continued.

Daniel wrote that his exasperation finally got the best of him. He had stayed up much longer than usual, sitting on the narrow steps leading up to the front porch of his cabin. He kept putting off going in to get ready for bed. He dreaded the thoughts of going to sleep and having the same dream return yet again. Finally, he pulled himself up and looked up to the starry sky. His prayer for an answer was no longer silent. His voice felt ragged as it rang out against the cool air of the night.

"Please, please, either tell me what you want me to know or let me be."

Daniel made his way into the dark cabin, not even bothering to light a candle. He sprawled across his bed fully clothed and fell into a dreamless sleep. A few hours before the sun rose, Daniel was awakened by a clear and present voice.

"Use your eyes to see and your heart to feel."

Daniel looked around but there was no one in the cabin with him. He hurriedly rose from the bed. The door was latched and the window closed. He peered through the window but saw nothing. He opened the door and walked to the edge of the porch looking up at the remaining stars in the sky and then across the land before home.

"Thank you," he whispered.

Daniel's words poured freely and pulled them all into another time and place. Meg found a tingling running through her as Ben continued to share details from the worn journal.

Daniel finally realized what he was being called to do. On his next rides by the salt works he began to see what was playing out before him. His attention was drawn to the many levels of work it took to produce the baskets of salt. He watched as wells were being dug to bring the brine water from more than two hundred feet below the surface of the ground. He rode past the sheds where the furnaces were kept ready for the constant process of boiling away the water leaving heaping amounts of salt.

Daniel often passed wagon load after wagon load of cut timber being brought from the nearby hills. Trees were being harvested for more than the wood that was unloaded and thrown into the fires beneath the kettles.

Daniel took the time to ride out to the "holler" where he watched as trees were felled and specifically cut and hewn to produce cored out logs. The logs would serve as pipes for the brine water to be pumped to the kettles.

Salt making was all encompassing from beginning to end. It followed a demanding schedule requiring that salt be taken from the kettles from the previous week's harvest before moving into the next round of production. Twenty-four hours a day, five to six days a week of back breaking, soul breaking work. A never-ending onslaught of work forced on men who had no choice to anything else or be anything else other than captive.

Daniel found himself looking at the worn, blistered hands responsible for manning the pumps and performing all the tasks needed to produce and bag the salt. He had not yet been able to muster the courage to look into the eyes of the men who carried on with the burdens of the grueling work, but the hands of old and young alike were forever etched into his memory.

His focused sojourns past each group of workers prodded his other senses as well. The closer Daniel was to each group, the more he could smell and almost taste the scent of the perspiration and something else he could not quite name. He wondered to himself,

"Could a person smell and taste the fear, the anguish, the hopelessness that settled deep within other human beings?"

Not long after that question had entered his mind, Daniel decided to make a visit to his childhood friend Emil Planter. Emil had tried to make a living for his family by farming but had found working for the salt company provided a more stable income. Emil had some education so his work was split between the salt works office and as an overseer of the labor used for salt production. Emil and his wife lived in a home provided by the salt company as befitting his position.

Daniel could understand the need to do your best by your family, but he was beginning to question how any man could justify the forced labor and captivity of other human beings. Perhaps he had always inwardly questioned it, but once the dreams had taken over his nights, the answers he sought were becoming more important to his own heart and soul.

Daniel wrote of the evening spent on his friend's porch chatting about the local news and family relations. It was almost time to take his leave before he found the courage to ask his friend questions about the workings of the salt company. Emil was surprised. Daniel had lived close to the salt workings all his life. Emil asked him why it was only now that Daniel was interested in learning the steps it took to get the salt from brine to bag.

Daniel recalled taking a deep breath, looking Emil straight in the eyes and explaining bluntly that he wanted to know about the people who worked for the company, not the process of the salt making itself. Emil nodded his head thinking that he understood the question. He began to recant the history of the company and the owners, the office workers, and the overseers when Daniel stopped him. Daniel told Emil he wanted to know about the real workers, the ones who actually did the sweltering back breaking work.

Once the words were out of his mouth, Daniel saw a flare in Emil's eyes. For the longest time, a cavernous silence hung between them. Daniel worried that he may have overstepped the bounds of their friendship.

Perhaps Emil remembered that Daniel was his oldest and most trusted friend. Perhaps he realized that Daniel being a man of the cloth was called to ponder many questions related to the congregation he served. Whatever the reasoning, Daniel was grateful when Emil began to answer his question without anger. Emil's words were delivered in a quiet matter-of-fact tone when he began speaking of the men brought in to do the manual labor. Most noticeable to Daniel was the fact that Emil never shared the names of any of the individuals. He simply referred to the workers as "they" or "them."

Emil explained how "they" were purchased either by the salt company or leased from businesses and farmers across the region. The leasing contract called for the company to provide minimal housing, clothing, and rations of food to the laborers while paying the owners a set sum. Solitary men were the ones usually leased. Men with wives and children for the most part were the property of the owners of the salt production. Small wooden quarters set aside for their housing was located deep in a hollow just over the boundary hills west of the salt mines.

Emil also explained the details of the shifts of work for the salt making. Monday through Saturday, a group of workers toiled during the day and a second group was brought in to work through the night. There were a number of overseers assigned to each shift. Men who were married with families were more often given the daylight hours to work. Single men were given the night shifts.

Emil was assigned to work eight to twelve hours during the daytime. One of Emil's duties was to account for each of "them" by daybreak when "they" were to be at their assigned task. Rarely did he or another overseer have to ride out to find a missing worker. It was rare that one of "them" did not show up on time. They knew the consequences if the absence was not due to being on their deathbed. When Emil heard those words come out of his own mouth, his head seemed to drop to his chest.

Emil held his hands tightly together in his lap, with his head lowered, never once looking Daniel in the eye. They sat in thoughtful silence for the longest time. Daniel didn't like leaving his friend looking so dejected, but he was wise enough to know that Emil had the reckoning of dealing with his own conscience and soul. Daniel prayed that his friend would find some kind of peace within his heart.

Daniel rode back to his own cabin reflecting on the decision he had made long ago to never marry and have a family. He couldn't see a way of making a living as a preacher and supporting a family in the way Emil was supporting his wife and children. Yet, Daniel was human and had at times felt jealous of Emil's station in life. This night had *not* been one of those nights. This night had brought an understanding that nothing was worth the gains gathered through the blood and sweat of a human being kept from a life of freedom and safety.

Daniel arose from another night filled with disturbing thoughts and dreams. His mind could not let go of everything that Emil had shared with him. It had taken him a long time to settle into sleep. When sleep did finally come, his dreams were filled with the images of hands reaching out. Daniel awoke in a cold sweat. The early morning hour brought a stark realization. Daniel did not have the right to find fault with his friend for not facing up to his actions. Daniel, in his own way, was guilty of a similar sin. There were no visitations to the sick or elderly scheduled for the day, but Daniel still saddled his horse and made his way to the salt works.

Usually, Daniel rode brusquely past each workstation. On this day, he purposely slowed the gait of the horse as he arrived first at the pumps, then at the furnaces, and finally at the loading station. His hands trembled ever so slightly each time he reigned the horse to a stop.

Daniel took in a breath for courage and made the conscious effort to look directly in the eyes of the working men. Most rarely stopped their work to return his gaze. A few that did momentarily halt their task would quickly avert their eyes, or hang their heads. A very few, however, straightened their spines and returned Daniel's gaze unflinchingly.

No words were ever spoken by the men or by Daniel. Daniel intuitively knew that the lowered eyes and hung heads signaled an aversion to the possibility that this was just another white man ready to beat them down. Daniel's stomach curdled at the thought.

The few workers who had met his gaze evoked an entirely different feeling in Daniel. He had seen a righteous anger in their eyes and a strength not yet beaten out of them. Those men had somehow retained their spirit. Daniel could sense a belief in some higher power through their stalwart gazes. Again, his intuition kicked in and he realized he had felt their belief in a power that offered comfort, relief, and maybe one day a final path to freedom. Hope was such a small word to assign to these unspoken ideas, but there it was. Daniel nodded in respect and pointed his horse toward home.

Once he had returned to the cabin, he completed the few chores needed and made his way back to the porch. The sun was setting as he planted himself into a rocking chair made by his grandfather. He rubbed his hands over the smooth curved armrests. He was thankful for the chair passed down from the gentle old man. He was equally as grateful for the woodworking skills passed down even though he rarely used them these days.

As the rocker swayed back and forth, Daniel thought back on the day he had spent riding through the salt works. The memory of the individuals at each of the workstations had him wondering about what their lives were like after a day's work was finished. What were those men doing now that the sun had set? Did they have a porch where they could sit and listen to the sounds of the mountains around them? Did they have a soft bed to rest upon?

Even though Daniel had never visited the places where the slaves slept, he felt he already knew the answer to those questions. He once again sent up prayers of gratitude for all that he had and asked for forgiveness for not seeing to the needs of *all* his fellow men and women. Daniel rose from his place on the porch and wearily moved inside the cabin ready for bed. Before retiring, Daniel made an entry into his journal. He described how much he looked forward to a restful sleep. A sleep without the dreams of hands reaching out in distress.

Daniel did not dream of hands again. Instead, this night brought Daniel a dream of a face. A young man's face. The face held bright brown eyes, wary like a deer in flight but with the strength of a bear. The face was darker than Daniels's, just like all the hands he had seen in his past dreams. Daniel tried speaking to the young man. No response. Fleetingly, the face came in and out of his dream. At times remaining close then fading away. Daniel awoke the next morning knowing he had received yet another sign.

The employees in the office of the salt company had been telling Emil of his friend's regular visits throughout the different work sites. This coupled with Daniel's visit to his cabin stirred Emil's curiosity. Emil had done a lot of thinking and soul searching since that visit. Now he had to wonder, just what was Daniel thinking and doing?

Emil made sure he was present the next time Daniel rode through the salt works. He was standing behind the brine pumps when Daniel first approached, sitting tall on his horse. Emil intently kept an eye on Daniel as he and a few of the workers exchanged long looks. Emil didn't understand exactly what was going on with the silent exchange, but he was ready to jump in.

Emil walked over to his friend and told him to dismount. The flat tone in Emil's voice had Daniel wondering if he had once again overstepped boundaries.

When Daniel had dismounted. Emil leaned over and whispered softly,

"I am not sure what you are doing, but if I can't do anything else about all this," quietly nodding to the men forced to labor over the salt making, "I can at least support you and what you feel you need to do here. They, I mean these men, might take you better if you stop staring at them and start talking."

Emil winked slyly at Daniel.

"You *are* a real good talker. Some say you might make a good preacher someday."

Daniel felt the smile before he saw it. The Emil of his childhood had returned. Daniel placed his hands on Emil's shoulders. They stood face to face. Daniel could see the heart and humor of his old friend shining through once more. Emil began to introduce Daniel to the men. From that day forward, Emil addressed each man individually and by name.

Daniel began coming by the salt works each week just to check on the workers who would speak with him. He knew the people in his congregation and the office of the salt company might wonder why he had undertaken this practice. Sometimes being a preacher and knowing the Bible came in handy. When asked, he would spout off a supporting scripture and speak of the dreams God gave him of hands reaching out. Honestly, Daniel still didn't know how these visits would evolve but he knew deep down there was more to come.

Chapter 13

The next visit between the two friends occurred at Daniel's cabin. Emil had brought food prepared by his wife Nelly. Nelly was a fine cook and a good woman. Daniel thanked Emil and put the food away for later. The men made their way outside to sit on a roughhewn bench under the oak tree. The two sat there in comfortable silence whittling on sticks just like when they were younger boys. Daniel sensed his friend had something on his mind, but he waited patiently for Emil to gather his thoughts. Finally, he heard Emil take a deep breath. Daniel turned to listen to his friend.

"I have been thinking on all manner of things since you were at my cabin the other night. Nelly and I had a long talk after you left. I've also told her about your visits to the salt works. You know, my sweet Nelly is as smart as she is pretty. She told me that you were trying to show us how God wanted all human beings treated. I think I finally understand more about your visits there."

Emil looked up from the wood and his knife and directly into Daniel's eyes.

"Almost all of the workers have come to us from… situations… situations of constant and repeated… mistreatment. That kind of mistreatment that happens over and over has trained them to work without ceasing or complaint. It has made them learn to not speak back and, under no circumstances, not run."

"Daniel, I swear on my life that I have never put hands on any of the men."

Emil took a vicious stroke of the knife against the stick in his hand before continuing.

"I can't tell you other employees haven't put their hands to them. After watching you with the men and talking with Nelly, I worry that even if I haven't touched them, just my being a part of the company makes me as guilty as those that have."

Emil placed the knife and stick on the bench and turned to look at Daniel square on.

"The more Nelly and I talked, the more I realized there had to be something I could do besides just praying for forgiveness. Maybe it will be one step at a time, one person at a time."

"Nelly and I have saved some money back. I am going to take that money with me when I ride down to Abingdon in the salt wagons next week. There will be supplies to bring back, but I am saving a spot in my wagon. I am saving a spot because I am going to the auction block."

Daniel was more confused than ever. How exactly did his friend think that purchasing yet another worker would absolve his guilt or change anything?

Emil saw the incredulous look in his friend's eyes and tried to explain more clearly.

"Hear me out. I swear I have good intentions. I have a plan. I am going to bring back someone who I will lease out to the salt company to work Monday through Thursday. I will make sure that he is working during the day so that I can take good care of him and the others."

I honestly can't tell you what goes on at night, but I hear that there may be things, not good things, happening. I want him to live with you. Our understanding will be that he helps you here and at the church on Fridays and Saturdays. Of course, he will rest on God's Day. You can take him to the salt works each morning. I will bring him back here each evening. The company is willing to provide clothing and food allotment for the work week if you will house him. Nelly and I will bring food for Fridays, Saturdays and Sundays for the both of you."

Daniel blurted out, "How does that help him? He will still be forced into hard labor for eight to twelve hours a day. He will still be a prisoner. It might be a safer captivity, but it is still captivity. He still won't have the God given freedom that every human deserves."

"Nelly said you would say that. She told me to tell you that at least it is a start. We have to start somewhere. We can all pray that God shows us the next step. Are you willing to help us take our next step? Are you willing to take whatever steps God shows us next?"

It was Daniel's turn to hang his head. He wasn't sure whether it was hung in sadness or prayer. Maybe one had to come before the other, at least before the next step could be taken.

The faint sound of the oven bell rang through the evening air breaking the magic of the story. Meg, Jessica, and Ben shook their heads simultaneously bringing themselves back to the present. A trip that neither of the three really wanted to take but the casserole was done, and they all admitted to being hungry. After the meal was complete and the dishes done, Ben built a fire in the firepit so the three could resume going over Daniel's journal. It didn't take long for Ben's voice to transport them once again.

Daniel wrote of a later conversation with Emil in which Emil had shared his experience of purchasing a young man from the auction block in Abingdon. Emil spent the morning unloading the bags of salt. He left his wagon and horse hitched at the livery and made his way through town. He passed quite a few well-dressed men heading toward the auction block. An increased number of buyers could possibly cause him to be outbid if there were few workers being offered. Instead, upon his arrival to the area where the auctions were conducted, Emil was told that a coffle of slaves had been brought down the Wagon Road heading toward Natchez.

The head agent in charge of the convoy had made the decision to sell some of slaves in Abingdon to fund more supplies. Emil felt the acidic taste of fury rise into his throat as he watched the hardened white man cull mostly older black men from the group. Emil reckoned that the overseer didn't think they would have the health and stamina to make it all the way down to Natchez. Only a few of the younger men were chosen to head to the block. Emil wondered what the overseer was thinking in choosing these young men who appeared both healthy and strong. Perhaps they were looked on as troublemakers. Perhaps the agent recognized they would bring a good price that would fund the continued excursion south.

Emil stood to the side and watched as two young men were taken from what appeared to be a family. He reasoned that they must be brothers. It seemed strange to see an entire family together in the coffle. Emil couldn't help but wonder about the story behind this. His curiosity was as strong as his determination to meet his goal. He made his way to the block. He had to at least try and take one of these young men back to the salt works. If only he had enough money, he would have taken both men so at least what he assumed to be two brothers could remain together.

As he moved closer to the block, Emil recognized the men working the auction. They were stalwart friends of the owners of the salt mines. One of them, Jackson Smyth, came to the salt works often. He had even attended church services preached by Daniel. Emil felt an unseen force pushing him toward Jackson Smyth. After greeting each other and shaking hands, Emil explained why he was there. Jackson Smyth listened as Emil spoke of a need for a worker for the salt production who would also be working for the preacher and the church.

Emil felt only a twinge of guilt at the half-truth but not enough to back down from trying to quickly make a purchase. The very mention of Daniel and the church must have been the deciding factor for Smyth. Smyth identified the two young men as Samson, the oldest brother, and Moses, the youngest. Emil found that he could not make the decision on which brother to choose and allowed Smyth to work out the details with the agent.

Within minutes, a deal had been set between Smyth and the agent of the coffle. Thankfully, Emil had been spared the act of calling out bids from the front of the auction block. When all of Emil's money had been handed over, the tallest and oldest of the two brothers became the property of Emil Planter.

Emil's trip to Abingdon had accomplished his goals, yet he still felt a hollowness in his core. Daniel was right. The ownership of another human brought him no pride. It filled him with overwhelming despondency like he had never felt before in his life. That sadness was compounded by the looks exchanged between the two young brothers as they were separated.

Samson stood behind Emil with chains locked around his ankles ensuring that he could not make a run for it. They both watched as the younger brother, Moses, was taken to the block. The chains around his legs made it difficult to climb up the steps. Emil watched as the agent smacked him with a stick, much like farmers would smack a bull trying to get it into a pen.

Bidders for Moses came to the block to inspect the merchandise. They poked and prodded almost every body part. They pried his mouth open for examination. Satisfied with the goods, the men left the block, and the bidding began.

The whole undertaking quickly evolved into a frenzy of sound that made Emil want to bend over and wretch what little he had on his stomach. More than anything, he wanted to leave all this behind. Emil straightened himself. He held on to the reminder that no matter what he saw and felt, it could be nothing as bad as what the men on the block were forced to live through.

For whatever reason, it felt important to remain and listen for the fate that was to befall Moses. When the bidding was over, Moses had been purchased for work on a farm about 10 miles outside of Abingdon just off the Wagon Road. It gave Emil some relief that the brothers would not be that far from each other. Perhaps one day Emil could bring them back together. The young men had remained silent throughout the entire ordeal. Once both brothers had been separated and sold, a deep keening broke out from the area where the rest of their family was being held. A mother's wounded cry for her children. Children torn from her never to be seen again. It was truly the most heart wrenching sound Emil had ever heard.

Emil returned to the salt works the next day. The back of the wagon now empty of salt was occupied by a young man with dark skin. Emil had spent the entire ride talking to the silent young man. He carefully explained the details of the expectations for the salt works and working for his friend the preacher. He told him that he would be provided with food and clothing. He would sleep each night at the preacher's home. The young man never responded, answered a question, or changed his expression during the whole ride. Emil later told Daniel he worried the young man might be deaf and unable to speak.

Daniel heard the pronounced sound of wagon wheels rolling over the rocky road that led to his cabin. Not many people came to visit, especially in a wagon. Daniel, as was his obligation, did the visiting.

Daniel looked up from the church journal where he was listing the names of the sick and elderly he had called on earlier in the week. He peered out the small window. As the rumble of the wagon got closer and closer, Daniel knew that it must be Emil returning from the delivery of the salt bags. His stomach turned in worry. He half hoped that Emil would be alone. Daniel walked to the porch.

Emil drew the horses to a stop in front of the cabin and looked down at his childhood friend with a bittersweet smile, spoke a greeting to his friend,

"Good afternoon to you, Daniel."

He then turned looking over his shoulder to the back of the wagon continuing loudly as though the young man in back was hard of hearing.

"This is Preacher Hughes who you will be staying with... Daniel, this young man is called Samson."

Daniel warily looked toward the young man. He felt the blood rushing to his feet and his ears began to roar. There, before him in the wagon, was his dream come to life. A young man's face that looked oh so familiar. The face that held brown eyes, wary like a deer in flight but with the strength of a bear. A face darker than Daniel's and no longer a dream. Daniel knew deep within his heart that something bigger was working before him. He knew at that moment his friend Emil had been right to take this next step.

Emil didn't seem to notice that Daniel had been on the verge of passing out before his very eyes. He was busy pulling bundles out from under the seat of the wagon. Two of the bundles were in brown paper and tied with twine. These held the clothes and a week's rations as promised by the salt company. The rest had been packed by Nelly and put on the wagon when Emil stopped by their home before making his way to Daniel's cabin. They included some bedding and some extra food that Nelly had prepared. Nelly knew that Daniel lived a simple life with no extras of anything for a worker that Daniel had never anticipated being in his care.

Daniel asked the young man to help carry the supplies into the cabin and wait there. There was a moment's hesitation. Daniel had prepared himself to witness the young man lumber from the wagon as best he could with shackles around his ankles. To his surprise the young man hopped limberly from the bed of the wagon and did as he was bid. Daniel looked over at Emil. Emil answered the question in Daniel's eyes.

"I removed them after we cleared the town of Abingdon. I figured if he was going to run, he would run. I am not sure why he didn't. Maybe because he didn't know the area well enough to know where to go. Maybe because he has all too often seen others suffer consequences for running."

Daniel could see the newcomer standing just inside the open door of the cabin as he and Emil shared information from the trip. Tomorrow would be Saturday, so Samson would have two days to settle into the cabin and his duties there before he was to report to the pumps at the salt works on Monday morning.

Daniel heaved a huge sigh as the wagon rolled away leaving him alone with young Samson. Daniel was unsure about what to do next but as Nelly had told both men "one step at a time".

Just as on the wagon ride back, Samson chose not to speak with Daniel yet didn't hesitate to carry out any instruction. Daniel asked him to help put away the food and supplies showing him where things belonged. He then guided the young man to the small loft above the kitchen area. It had been used for what little extra storage Daniel needed. Now, Daniel began shoving things to one side and making a makeshift bed for Samson. He told the young man that they would begin to build a bed frame tomorrow so that he wouldn't have to sleep directly on the floor.

Daniel had an extra chair given to him by a family from the church who felt that he probably lived so minimally he didn't have a seat to perch upon. The truth was that Daniel didn't have any extra pieces because his quiet life did not require them. Hardly anyone came by to visit. He took the gifted chair and placed it by the tiny window in the loft. Daniel told Samson they could also build a table to put up there as well. Daniel actually loved working with wood and building furniture. Although it had been a while since he had called on those skills , he knew that he could build anything they would need.

Sometime later, Daniel began pulling some of Nelly's good smelling treats out for dinner. She had sent a mess of chicken and dumplings, a loaf of homemade bread, and a small pot of honey. Daniel talked the whole time he heated up the dumplings before setting them on the table. Samson just stood stoically, not allowing his eyes to fix upon the food. The cabin was extraordinarily quiet except for the growling of the young man's empty stomach.

Daniel asked Samson to put the plates and utensils from the sideboard on the table. Samson brought one plate and a set of utensils, placed them in front of one of the chairs at the table and then stepped back with a sense of gallantry. Daniel wondered if Samson had been a houseworker and not a field worker at his old plantation.

Daniel looked down at the table and felt humbled. This young man thought that he was to look on as Daniel devoured the evening meal. Now it was Daniel's turn to become quiet as he stepped over to the sideboard for the extra table setting and placed it in front of the chair opposite of his own. Daniel pulled out the chair and asked Samson to sit. Samson hesitated and held back. Daniel came closer and looked Samson directly in the eye.

"No person stands and is hungry with me. If I eat, you will eat. Sit. Eat. This is the last time you will hear a command from me. From this day forward you will be asked, and I hope you will receive."

Chapter 14

A week later, Meg sat cross-legged on her bed sipping a steaming cup of coffee before getting ready for work. She leaned back against her pillows recalling the evening she had spent with Ben and Jessica and contemplating her next steps. She had spent a good part of the week bringing together a variety of corroborating data from the church journals provided by Ben. The rest of the time was spent searching through what was turning out to be terminus data from other colleges, universities, and historical organizations. A study steeped in numbers as the prime support of the hypothesis didn't have much further to go.

Meg smiled perceptively and glanced over to the small table she used as a nightstand. The two additional journals belonging to Daniel were resting side by side on the lace covered table. Ben had presented them to her telling her to keep them for as long as she needed. Meg reached over to touch the leather covers. She gently trailed her fingers across the worn leather-bound books. She swore she could feel a faint pulsing when she allowed her hand to come to a rest. The pulsing became stronger as if there was a heart held somewhere deep inside.

After the evening spent with Ben and his wife, Meg felt a new stirring deep within her own heart. She couldn't decide if it were the simple words read from the first journal or Ben's way of retelling the stories held inside that appeared to trigger a change in the way she began to feel about her place in this moment of time. Meg recognized Daniel's carefully penned words held the key to opening an important and long-locked door. A door that had been firmly shut hiding the stories and voices of people who had suffered horrifically while supplanting the lifestyle of a privileged few.

Meg worried the world of the academy would simply treat the narrative of Daniel and Samson's story as just a small point in time. Could she make them see the importance of that story and the way it could support the data points of the study? Meg's forehead wrinkled in worry when she thought of the people who lived around her. How would the people in her little town handle the information she was discovering? Would they be able to accept it as truth?

Meg pushed herself off the bed. She was moving toward her dresser with coffee cup in hand when she recognized a familiar smell. She curled her dainty nose and took a deeper sniff of the air around her. Vanilla extract. Her grandmother always dabbed a bit of vanilla behind her ears and on her wrists before going out of the house. Meg felt a heightened sense of excitement. Her inner senses were beginning to recognize the little things she had felt she would never experience again. Meg smiled in relief. She had always been able to "hear" her grandmother but now she could smell her sweet scent. A giddiness rose inside her. She knew this was real and not imagined.

"But how much do you have to include," a familiar voice echoed through the room.

Meg wasn't startled at all. She had been hoping her Granny would pop in and give her some insight.

"Good morning, Granny. How much of what? I'm not sure what you mean."

She heard her grandmother utter a grunting sound.

"Are you not paying attention? How much of the stories that you are wondering about do you have to tell at work? And don't you be concerned about the people in this town. They'll either believe you or not. Nothing much you can do about that. You know some people. If it doesn't affect them, what do they care."

Meg wasn't so sure she agreed with her grandmother. Granny was over on the other side now and didn't have to deal with the people of the town. None the less, she could at least explain about work.

"I would suppose I need to share all of it for my work."

Meg thought a moment. "At least all of it that could be supportive of data we are uncovering from other sources. The methods Daniel used for the church journals and his personal journals were different. He was very businesslike in what he included in the church documents. His feelings, thoughts, and opinions came out more in his personal journals. But the current study is based more on statistical data than narrative stories."

"Then you have quite a task before you.", her grandmother said succinctly.

"Just do your job and give them the facts. Then show them the connections to the stories in the journals. You know as well as I do, it's time to stop being just a girl with the numbers. Time to start remembering you're the girl with a heart. Give them all the facts they need but make sure you are getting what *you* need to do right by yourself and others."

The room went quiet for a minute. Then her grandmother's voice came through again. This time a bit more quiet and forlorn.

"Isn't it time you tell the stories that shouldn't be forgotten? If you don't tell them, aren't you just doing the same thing you think some of the people of this valley have done for hundreds of years? Surely you don't want that. You don't want the lives of so many to continue to be hidden and forgotten, do you? If you don't speak the truth, who will?"

The scent of vanilla faded away as quickly as it had come. The familiar voice did, too. That was her grandmother's way. Say her peace, make her point, and walk away to let you think about it. Same in death as it was in life.

Meg found herself ambling through the halls of Tobias later that morning on the way to John Peabody's office. Very few *living* people were in the hallways. Meg knew a few of the others lingered about. She gave a nod or two when she sensed a different scent or temperature as she passed certain doorways. She had no doubt they saw her even if she didn't see them.

Meg, however, was most unaware of the tall shadow following behind as she knocked and was bidden entrance into Dr. Peabody's office. She pushed open the door and made her way to the green leather armchair perched in front of the beloved professor's desk. She watched as John Peabody glanced up and nodded to the corner behind her as she sat down. It was as if he was acknowledging someone. She looked over but saw no one.

"What's up, Miss Meg?"

152

"I wanted to discuss a few things concerning the study. I want to run something by you related to what I am discovering. Quick and to the point, all the church journals that Ben provided correlate with the data we have found so far. The original hypothesis of the study is proving accurate in its scope. The end results are becoming apparent. Unfortunately, I am finding that any ties with a possible underground railroad may not be as easily documented. I believe that specific aspect would be better researched in a separate study in the future."

John Peabody glanced to the corner again and back to Meg with a furrowed brow.

"Are you saying you see the end of the study wrapping up? Basically, you want to drop the idea of the extension you asked for from the committee?"

John Peabody was concerned. If Meg stopped the research project now, she would never find what she was supposed to find, professionally or personally.

Meg smiled, trying to relieve the anxiety she was sensing in Dr. Peabody. Surely, he knew she was a professional and would not bring a study to a halt for no apparent reason.

"Yes. And no. The expansion of the current study has actually brought on further questions. So, I want to begin to draw that study to a conclusion in terms of the methodology and the heavy emphasis on data and statistics. I believe the expansion and further questions would be better researched and answered using a different methodology.

Meg took a grounding breath and continued,

"Basically, I want to begin a new project design of my own and I want the college to fund it. I will be using narrative and qualitative research. I will collect and analyze various accounts of the enslaved. Especially as it pertains to what has already been documented in reference to the Slave Trail of Tears, the utilization of the enslaved at the salt works, and any correlations as enslaved people were moved from Virginia farther south."

Again, Meg watched as the professor looked toward the corner with a sense of relief passing over his face.

"And if you can find a lead to possible underground railroad connections, you will include it?"

"Yes, of course. I know it may be difficult to get the full approval and I am prepared for that as well."

Meg went on,

"If the college is unable to fund the study, then I will undertake it myself. I will, of course, be utilizing my vacation days to travel for research purposes but that also means that anything I produce will be for my sole benefit."

John Peabody wasn't entirely sure where Meg had been hiding this self-assured persona, but he was immensely proud that it was finally shining through. If only she knew what he was keeping secret.

John put his hands together, fingertips to fingertips, giving Meg his most direct and studious expression.

"Let me get back to you on this. Have a good rest of your day," John said abruptly but with a smile spreading across his face. He rose from his chair and opened the door ushering Meg out quickly. He closed the door and looked back at the corner where the shadow figure stood. Could one high five a ghost?

Two weeks later, Meg found herself packing her car with the last of the things she would need for an extended road trip. Trust or blind faith. She wasn't sure exactly what to attribute the reasoning behind this trip. Her gut told her not to question and just accept that John Peabody had worked his professional magic. The original study results were accepted by the committee. Surprisingly, the committee had also voted to hold off doing anything with those results until Meg finished her current proposed project.

Meg was unsure of the details surrounding the approval and funding of her project, but John Peabody had given her assurance she had carte blanche with methodology and to some extent the time she needed to conduct her research. The most surprising aspect of the whole situation was that she did not have to report to or run anything by a select committee. The only person she would be working with or under the direction of was John Peabody.

Meg had used the past two weeks to continue looking back over Daniel Hughes's personal writings in the last two journals. Daniel had written of taking Samson southward in search of the family he had been separated from in Abingdon. Meg had decided to follow the trail and not just the paper trail.

Reading the journals, Meg learned the remainder of Samson's family, minus his brother Moses, were to be taken to Natchez. Once they arrived in Natchez, they were to be picked up by the New Orleans cousins of their original owners. Meg made the decision to drive to Natchez and then on into New Orleans in search of any evidence addressing the remainder of Samson's family. Meg could have easily flown to both locations. She could have driven using the major highways. She chose however to follow the exact same trail that the family had been forced to travel. She would be following the modern-day representation of what was historically referred to as The Slave Trail of Tears.

Meg intended to pick up where Samson left his family in Abingdon and drive down Route 11 into Tennessee. From there she would change over to Interstate 40 going westward toward Nashville and then finally down the Natchez Trace into the city of Natchez. Meg hoped that she would find the remainder of the family had been kept together and had made it to New Orleans as a whole unit. That would make her research a bit simpler. Later she would turn her attention to finding Moses, which should be an easier task. As soon as the thought of simplicity and ease ran through her mind, she found herself feeling pangs of shame. Samson's family and thousands of others had suffered atrocities that were mindboggling and nowhere near simple. They had been forced to suffer both mentally and physically because they had been deemed less than human.

Meg went back to the house and locked the door. Her childhood friend Lynn had agreed to care for her mother's cats and keep an eye on the place for another few weeks. Her parents were set to return home from their wild west adventure in about two weeks. When Meg had called them to share about her new project, they were supportive and appreciated that she had made the arrangements with Lynn. With everything in place, Meg had only one more stop to make before leaving town.

Meg pulled her car up to the old rusty gate that separated the parking area behind the old community center and the Hurley family cemetery. More than Hurley's were buried here but the primary residents were Hurleys and other folks who had settled this gap in the mountains. The grass was starting to get some height on it now that winter was coming to an end. It would soon need to be cut. Her dad always did this with her mom since both had family interred here.

Meg walked up to the round of the hill and looked down at the gravestone of a man she had never known. Her grandfather, 3 times great, was buried here with a headstone commemorating his service as a corporal in the Confederate States of America army. As a small child, she remembered going around to all the local graveyards with her grandmother, mother, and aunts to clean off graves and place flowers before Memorial Day. When their little group came here, they always packed a picnic lunch and sat at the top of hill overlooking the gravestones.

Meg had often looked at this specific stone and thought to herself that she should probably feel some type of pride. Yet she felt nothing. Thinking back now, she remembered the women of her family talking about the people buried here. The stories were really mundane and relayed everyday life for them. Meg reached back in her memory bank and tried to search for a brief recitation about the corporal. She came up with nothing.

Meg bent over and brushed stray leaves and tiny blown branches away from the headstone. She had seen an old black and white picture of him in his gray uniform. He sported a long beard as was typical fashion of the day. She held that image in her mind's eye now and spoke to him as if he were standing before her today.

"I wish I could believe that you didn't *want* to fight in that horrible war. I wish you had been one of the older men taken from this place against your will. Forced to fight even though it went against what you believed. We both know that is almost impossible. Your military records show you fought with a group from your native North Carolina."

Meg lowered her head and whispered,

"I won't say that I am ashamed of you. I don't even know how that could change anything. I can find nothing— no journals, no letter— nothing that will tell me what called you to take the side of the Confederacy. I do know what calls me. I am being led to uncover the truth of what we were as a people back then and how we conducted our lives. How did we allow such horrific things to happen to a group of people just because they looked different? I wish I could hear your voice. I wish you could give me some answers."

"One day I hope I can find your story. Everyone deserves for their stories to be heard. It doesn't matter if it's perfect, it just needs to be truthful. Hopefully, the truth will go a long way to heal us all."

Meg walked off the hill and climbed slowly into her car wondering if she would ever be able to move through the absence of feeling when she visited the Corporal's grave.

Meg drove a quick twenty minutes toward the college and arrived at John Peabody's office. John had just arrived as well. He hopped out of his old dusty green Ford pick-up and walked over to Meg's car. Meg rolled her window down.

"I was just coming by to see you before I head out. I wanted to see if you had a checklist or special instructions for me to start the project."

John grinned broadly.

"The hardest part of this project for you is going to be the freedom you have been given to take it in any direction you want to go. I told you last week the only thing you need to do is keep an account and copy of expenses. As far as the parameters of the study itself are concerned, let the trail lead you and go with your gut. I don't know… maybe try and stay away from too many checklists. "

Meg shrugged sheepishly.

"You are right, loose parameters are going to be foreign to me. I may have to hold on to a few lists to begin with and back away slowly. Can you at least give me some insight as a friend and mentor?"

John leaned back and looked over to the bench at the cobbled walkway meandering past the library. His elongated gaze enticed Meg to look over as well. She saw nothing but the empty wooden seat and looked back up at Dr. Peabody. After another moment, John Peabody nodded his head slightly and turned to look into Meg's eyes.

"Take your time. You are on no deadline with the college. Don't rush straight to Natchez. Stop along the way, just as the coffle that was being dragged down the trail hundreds of years ago had to make stops. You may find that a day or two along the way can make a difference in finding what you have been looking for all along."

Meg held back a moment and thought through what John Peabody had just said. Oddly, she felt it was the tone he used rather than the words that made her feel he knew something she didn't.

"Okay. I promise to take my time. Honestly, I won't be surprised if things in Natchez don't pan out the simple way. I'll check in with you each Friday before you head out of the office for the weekend. I'll also make sure to fax you all the week's expenditure paperwork each Friday as well."

John's fatherly instincts kicked in and he blurted out,

"No, I need you to let me know each day where you are even if it's in a text. I don't need to know details of your project, but the wife and I want to know you are safe."

Meg smiled at the sweetness.

"Will do. And I will do the same for my parents as well."

A final quick good-bye and Meg was motoring out of the parking lot and through the stone archways of the college. She rolled the passenger side window down and felt the warm spring breeze fill the car. A feeling of bliss and freedom coursed through her body. She was quite unaware of the shadow figure that had settled into the back seat of her car.

Chapter 15

Meg turned off the road from the college onto Route 11 heading southward. This familiar portion of the highway would lead her through the center of Abingdon and then into Bristol, where the states of Virginia and Tennessee converged. In Tennessee, she would move westward on what was now Highway 40 toward Nashville. Finally, just below Nashville, she would turn southward once again on the Natchez Trace. The swiftest traveling tourist could travel the Trace in at least four days. Meg had to remind herself that speed wasn't the goal. It was about slowing down, literally and figuratively, in order to try and understand what Samson's family and thousands of others like them were forced to experience.

Meg looked ahead at the sunny skies. It truly was a beautiful day to begin an adventure. A gentle breeze was blowing around big white cotton candy clouds against an azure blue sky. Meg had lowered the windows so she could feel the natural air wash over her. The sun was still at her back moving from east to west over the road as she entered the town of Abingdon and made a decision that would slow her down and probably cause her to arrive in the Nashville area well after dark.

Meg wanted to experiment and see if she could feel the "spirit of place" here in familiar territory. Meg parked on the tree lined Main Street, locked her car, and proceeded to walk up the hill past buildings that had been standing since the 1700s. As Meg passed by the worn stone wall of the oldest tavern in town, her hand brushed against the cold surface. She felt a jolt of electricity flow from the wall through her arm. She clearly understood this was a sign, but she wasn't sure what it meant.

Meg peered through the window of the building watching the modern-day diners. No one seemed to pay her any attention. She turned her head away from the thick paned glass just in time to catch a shadowy reflection from behind her. Meg turned slightly to see who might be standing there. She saw no one. She continued up the hilly street taking furtive glances behind her as she made her way toward the courthouse.

Meg's confidence in her abilities to detect certain sensations became stronger the closer she got to the areas where slave auctions had been well documented. She really wanted to cross the street and stand on the very grounds where those auctions had taken place. She wanted to whisper to the spirits there and ask them to share their stories. Meg looked around at the people and cars passing by the building. She was pretty sure someone would report her if they saw her talking to the empty air. She laughed under her breath at the picture in her mind of sheriff's deputies carting her off for some mental evaluations.

Meg thought she heard someone approach from her right. She turned but no one was there. All was quiet on her side of the street except for the voice whispering,

"You know it started here, but it is time to go somewhere new."

Meg silently agreed and turned to retrace her steps. Once she was back at the car, she hopped inside ready to continue her drive. Meg made sure to look over her shoulder to ensure no cars were coming from behind as she pulled out of the parking space. She did a double take when she saw a peculiar shadow in the back seat. *Odd*, she thought, *how the shadows of trees play with your mind.*

Meg continued her drive down Route 11, also known as Lee Highway in Virginia. As a child, she loved taking rides with her family up and down this road. The valleys that cradled the roadway were still breathtaking to her. But now, Meg realized as beautiful as they were, they held painful secrets as well. It was hard to reconcile everything that had taken place between the hills and mountains.

Only a few short minutes after leaving the town proper of Abingdon, Meg became entangled in a long line of traffic built up caused by an accident ahead. The flashing sign by the side of the road told drivers that the traffic would be stopped for a while. Meg had the opportunity to detour onto Interstate 81 where she could have driven at a much faster rate of speed. But Meg chose to stay with her original route. She found herself turning onto Resting Tree Drive just off Route 11. Resting Tree Drive ran behind a local recreation park. The park offered a cool spot for Meg to park her car while waiting for the accident to clear. Meg pulled her car into a spot overlooking a small field, picked up her notebook and camera, and began a short walk up to the Resting Tree.

Near the top of the hill, Meg stood in front of the wooden fence surrounding the grounds that held the huge old oak tree. A commemorative plaque had finally been installed which shared the story of the tree. This small plot of land had once been included in the plantation that had been situated here between Abingdon and Bristol. Ironically, it had been owned by cousins of the family who owned the salt works in Meg's hometown. Many of the

163

enslaved workers of this plantation had been allowed to take a brief rest from their work under this very tree. The same tree also shaded the graves of those who had finally found their ultimate rest and freedom… in death.

Meg walked through the open gateway of the fence. She made her way to a bench that offered a quiet spot to reflect on the lives that had been shared beneath the tree and now beneath the earth. Meg quietly jotted down a few notes and used her camera to hold on to the images before her. Smaller trees surrounding the fenced area were shedding small white flowers. The spring breeze carried the petals through the air to land on the bench beside Meg.

The drifting petals also covered the deep rich earth beneath the long arms of the tall elder oak. Tears from heaven trying to wash away the sadness? Or celestial confetti celebrating the ultimate freedom? Meg shook her head at the poetic turn her mind had taken. Time to get back to the secondary reason she had stopped by the park for. She wanted to take a few photos of the area around the old oak.

Meg pushed herself up off the bench to gently step closer to the tree. A few old stones protruded from the ground. Meg had read prior research and knew that each of the stones marked a grave. There was no etching of letters or numbers on the stone. There never had been. The stones were smooth and plain. Unlike modern day markers, they had never shared any information about the soul who lay beneath. Many had questioned this. Perhaps it was because those held in bondage had been refused the schooling it took to put together the words. More than likely however, it was because those who held the keys to their chains would have never seen the worth in acknowledging the lives they had lived. Lives that had ended long before they died.

Meg made her way around the width of the oak as she passed by flowers, real and silk, that had been dispersed throughout the hallowed ground. Such a sight made her eyes water, but it wasn't until she rounded the tree on the other side that her breath caught painfully in her lungs.

A pair of brown leather boots lay at the base of the huge old oak tree. They were quite small with rounded toes and laced up all the way up to the ankle. Seeing them nestled so reverently between the jutting roots suggested that the tree itself was embracing the spirit of a child. Meg knew logically they had been placed there recently. The color of the leather was still strong, not nearly as faded as the silk poinsettias stuck in the ground behind them. Meg sensed what the small work boots represented. Her stomach tightened with determination as she whispered,

"The footsteps you took upon this earth will not be forgotten or erased. Your story, your truth, will be shared."

She felt something akin to a warm breath on her right,

"Good, because there is more to the story than you now know."

Meg returned to her car and took a moment to steady herself before continuing her drive. By the time she arrived at the Strawberry Plains exit just outside of Knoxville, she had resigned herself to stopping for the night. Both her chosen stops and slow traffic had eaten away at the time she had allotted for the day's drive. She would spend the night in Knoxville, wait for the morning rush of traffic to dwindle, and then make her way across Interstate 40 toward Nashville. She laughed at the irony of already being a day behind her own schedule.

Once she had checked into her room, she kicked her shoes off and sat on the bed contemplating what she could do for the rest of the evening. Looking over, she saw that her copies from Daniel's journals were spilling from her bag she had placed in the armchair. She walked over and brought them back with her to the bed and began going through them once more.

Meg realized that by the second journal, Daniel had begun referring to Samson as Sam. She wondered if that had been a request from the young man himself or just a way for Daniel to shorten his writing in the journal. Her gut was that it was an agreed-on change between them both. Whatever the reason, Meg now found herself referring to the young man as Sam.

The pages before her shared how life continued with Sam as well as the stories of the treatment of black workers at the salt works. None of the treatment was fair in any way that Meg could decipher, but some of the stories were completely horrific.

It had taken a long time for Sam to fully trust Daniel enough to tell him about the days he spent at the salt works. True to his word, Emil never laid a hand on the workers and Sam verified that fact. However, Emil was not there every day. There were times that Emil was pulled away to the office or other responsibilities. On those days, Sam and the other workers experienced a different kind of treatment. Sam also shared the stories about what happened to the men working overnight. When the sun went down, the darkness became a tool to hide the evil acts of evil men.

Sam detailed how the night workers were constantly hounded and hit with a whip to keep them awake. Even more cruel were the tales of the foreman who gleefully waited for a worker to collapse in exhaustion. When the foreman was sure the man was soundly asleep, he would take cords with bones attached and tie those cords to the man's limbs. As the worker was awakened, the cords would shake and clatter the bones together like a macabre wind chime. The foreman would erupt into evil laughter as the worker would run trying to flee from the sound. Then the fleeing man would be taken and whipped for both sleeping on the job and trying to "escape."

Meg had spent some time trying to find an explanation as to why after the first incident the workers didn't catch on to the horrible trick. She began to wonder if the bones had a connection to some superstition or spiritual belief of the workers. No matter, it was a horrible thing to do to anyone.

Daniel also wrote that the description of the bones indicated they were human. Daniel himself knew that human bones had been found scattered on the ground in different parts of the valley. He had tried not to think about what that could mean. When Meg read this, she could only assume many more horrors were being inflicted and hidden. But she couldn't allow herself to dwell on that information. For now, Meg needed to concentrate on the journey that Sam's family had been forced to take and how that played out for both Sam and Daniel.

"And maybe just as importantly, I need to be present for my own journey."

The unseen figure in the corner of the room smiled at the words.

Chapter 16

Once Meg reached the Nashville area, she hopped on the Natchez Trace just outside of Franklin, Tennessee. She was surprised at how closely the roadway resembled the Blue Ridge Parkway back home. It took Meg almost two weeks to travel down the Natchez Trace. During that time, she found herself leaving the Trace for short unplanned stops along the way.

Meg also made two previously planned stops in the areas of Florence and Muscle Shoals, Alabama. Her decision was based on their connection to the salt works. The salt from her hometown had been loaded onto barges and floated down several rivers before reaching these two destinations.

However, the most intriguing stops for Meg seemed to occur at the oddest locations. She found herself stopping at the pullovers along the Trace to stretch her legs and take short hikes on the original trail itself. In these lush spots, she could almost hear the whispering of the past in her ear.

After two weeks of purposely slow travel, Meg finally exited the Natchez Trace just before the terminus of the parkway. She entered the small city of Natchez in the early afternoon and found her way to the Grand Hotel. The lovely old building sat high on the bluffs overlooking the Mississippi River.

After checking in, she made her way from the front desk toward the elevators. Just as she reached the elevator area, she turned and saw a huge portrait of an old plantation hanging above a restored credenza. Meg felt perplexed as to why the painting seemed so odd to her. She pulled her rolling case behind her and stepped back off the lift. She walked over to the credenza and took a closer look at the artwork.

The painting held a magnificent rendering of a fine old antebellum home. Pictured in front of a sprawling veranda was a finely dressed man and woman. The two were seated high upon two handsome thoroughbred horses. A couple of hounds angled themselves just in front of the horses. Meg felt something prickle and burn on her skin. Before she could study the painting further, the elevator doors opened with a swoosh. Meg quickly stepped back over to them and headed to her room.

Once in her room, she took a few moments to unpack what she would need for the evening and the next morning. Then she decided to take a walk before trying to find a place for her evening meal. She headed back to the elevator to make her way downstairs. As she exited the elevator on the first floor, she once again glanced at the artwork over the credenza. This time she kept walking by to leave the hotel for her walk.

Outside the doors of the hotel, she turned to her right and began to move down the street that led over to the walkway running by the river.

At the riverside walkway, she had the choice to turn right again and follow the hill down to a small casino. If she turned left, she could follow the sidewalk toward the park and gazebo. Meg decided to meander towards the park and the gazebo.

At the top of the slight incline, she climbed the steps of the gazebo to get a better look at the large river flowing south. She began to imagine all the boats and

170

barges that had left this town on their way to New Orleans. Had Sam's family possibly walked on these same bluffs to make their way to their intended destination? Did Sam and Daniel find themselves here on the bluffs when they were in search of Sam's family?

Meg walked through the park amid historic markers detailing the history of the Natchez. The Natchez that sat far atop the bluffs had been designated as "Natchez Proper." The portion of the town sitting below the bluffs was known as Under-the-Hill. There was a distinct difference between the two.

The Under-the-Hill section of town held the gambling establishments, the saloons, and the houses where prostitution was on-going. Meg noticed that only one small paragraph on the historic marker acknowledged information about the slave trade that occurred in Natchez. The marker ended with a sentence stating the river traffic also provided a route to freedom for those who had access to counterfeit freedom papers or who had been able to find a way to hide on the northbound steamboats.

Meg thought to herself, "One small sentence that provided a large promise of unearned absolution."

Meg walked back up to the hotel and went to the front desk to ask for dinner recommendations. Her plans were to make a quick run for dinner and then head back to her room. Once she was back, she could shower and curl up on the bed with her computer.

Meg usually spent her evenings transcribing notes about her daily stops and any information she had gathered during the day. Tonight however, Meg couldn't muster up the energy for the task. Instead, she decided to give her brain a break and watch something mindless on the television. She turned the volume to the lowest setting. She drifted off to sleep listening to the soothing tones played by the hotel's community happenings channel.

Meg closed her eyes and felt herself slipping into the warm fuzzy edge of sleep. It was a wonderful place to be. Not quite asleep but not really awake. Outside the hotel, she thought she could hear a passing rain shower pitter patter against the window. Something began to flicker against the darkness behind her eyelids. Meg opened her eyes expecting to see flashes of lightning. She looked through the slightly open window curtains. Everything outside of her hotel appeared to be bathed in bright daylight.

Meg recognized that she was dreaming. These types of dreams had happened before, especially when she was much younger. She had learned to simply accept what was happening. She didn't fight it. She didn't try to wake herself up. It was always more interesting when she went with the flow.

Meg looked around and found herself standing on the same sidewalk area she had traversed earlier in the day. When she looked down at her feet the sidewalk had disappeared. She was standing on dry rough ground. She looked up again. She could see the sun shining down from only a mild slant in the sky. There was a warm afternoon breeze tickling her bangs. Meg turned her head and looked at the road leading down to the bluffs overlooking the Mississippi River.

A line of women dressed in bright cotton dresses were ambling slowly down the road. The human parade was being led by a grubby looking man perched on horseback. Four other men were walking to each side of the line with two more bringing up the flank. Something wasn't right. Meg could feel it. She waved to the man on the horseback, but he just ignored her. Did he even see her?

Meg attempted to step off into the road to get closer to the line before they reached the river's edge. Meg looked down at her feet yet again. She tried as hard as she could to move one foot in front of the other. She realized no amount of effort was allowing her to move forward.

Next, Meg tried to call out to the men and women. She wanted to ask where they were going, but she couldn't find her voice. Meg looked more closely at the women as they were passing right in front of her. Did they not see her? Could they not hear her?

Meg quietly gasped in surprise. She now understood why the line was moving so slowly. The women were shackled together at their ankles. She also saw that while the men were armed, they held no whips. A deep understanding settled in Meg's core. Intuitively, Meg knew the outcome for any of the women if they somehow escaped their chains. They would have been shot before having their faces or bodies spoiled by the cutting leather strap. Better hobbled by a bullet than disfigure the goods. These women were on their way to the brothel by the river.

The women were of differing ages and differing skin tones ranging from deepest mahogany to a lighter café au lait. Their facial expressions were varied as well. The younger ones had a look of terror in their eyes while the

173

older women seemed to have a more resigned hopeless expression. When their heads turned her way, it was if they were looking straight through her as if she were an imageless ghost. She could see them in detail but none of them could see her, or so Meg thought.

As the last of the line made its way to the cut off leading down to the river's edge, Meg saw the last woman in line. To Meg's eyes she appeared ageless. She belonged to neither the group of young and fearful nor the older group who seemed so very despondent. She was not secured to the continuous chain with all the other women in line. Instead, she wore her own set of shackles around her ankles. Her hands were bound in front of her as well. She lagged a few feet behind the other women. The man directly behind her kept taunting her, poking her with a stick. She was wearing a lavender cotton dress and her hair was bound by a white tignon.

The woman in lavender turned her head and looked directly at Meg. Meg could see a different look on her face than all the other women. She looked neither terrorized nor resigned. Instead, she had a fierce look of determination in her eyes. Her chin was tilted upward in a defiant manner.

The line had been halted at the front by the man on horseback as a wagon came rolling past them. The woman in lavender turned slightly in Meg's direction. She did not speak to the women in front of her nor the men around her. She did not speak to Meg. At least not with her voice.

The woman looked directly into Meg's eyes. Meg did not need to hear the woman's physical voice to understand exactly what she was trying to communicate. She simply knew. Without speaking, the woman assured

Meg that this walk down to the river wasn't the way things would end. Clear as a bell, Meg "heard" the woman's last bit

of wisdom,

"Truth rings clear when someone actually listens."

Meg wanted desperately to ask the woman why she was saying these things to her. But just as quickly as the message came through to Meg, the line began to move once more. This time the pace was picking up and the women appeared to be melting into a phantom mist rising from the river.

Meg awoke to a new morning in Natchez.

It took several cups of strong black coffee to shake Meg out of the daze her long night of dreams had rendered. She looked over to the bed as she drank from the heavy paper cup. Her eyes took in the heavily tousled linens. Meg clearly remembered trying to move her feet in the dream. The covers around the foot of the bed were in such a tangle that Meg knew she must have been thrashing her legs in her sleep. Meg grabbed her journal and quickly jotted down the events of her dream. She felt it was important to capture the details before they slipped away.

Once Meg was showered and dressed, she left her room, locking the door behind her. She hopped on the elevator to head down to the first floor where she paused before the plantation painting. She got the oddest feeling in the pit of her stomach every time she looked at the painting. She would have taken more time to study the artwork, but she had a 9 a.m. appointment at the local historical archives. If she found the information she was searching for this morning, then she could be on her way to New Orleans by the afternoon.

Meg stopped by the front desk to inquire about a late check-out. The staff at the hotel were exceptionally accommodating. The desk clerk told her if she could be out of the room by 2:30 there would be no charge. As it turned out, however, Meg did not check out until the next morning.

The last day in Natchez turned out to be quite an unexpected experience for Meg. She drove her car slowly as she made her way through the older parts of the city. Aesthetically, the old part of the city certainly held true to the tourist brochures. The architecture, the antique stores, and the small coffee shops and bistros called out to a variety of visitors. Meg could see just how vested modern-day Natchez was in holding on to the antebellum heartbeat that once provided life for the privileged few.

Meg thought to herself, "Natchez wears the proverbial southern costume well, but what would happen if what lay beneath that costume was revealed?"

Meg's visit to the archives proved to be quite fruitful. Within an hour she was able to locate a manifest indicating the safe arrival of a southbound coffle. The document listed the date of arrival and provided a detailed list of names minus several men and boys who had died or been sold along the way. The manifest listed Sam's father, mother, teenage twin siblings and the baby sister. To any other person reading over the documents, the names might have meant very little. But for Meg, it felt as if she were forming a relationship with the people who were also the focus of Daniel and Sam's search.

In her mind's eye, she could visualize Nelson and Sarah. The youngish parents must have felt an initial relief that the owners of Graystone Plantation had allowed their little family to stay together rather than being sold separately back in Virginia. Of course, that reprieve was quickly altered when the oldest sons were sold just before entering the next state. That left Louisa and Henry, the twins, both 14 or so and Deborah, the youngest at six years of age, to travel along with their parents. The manifest clearly indicated that the parents and remaining children had arrived in Natchez alive.

Meg thought back to Daniel's journal entry when he wrote of Sam talking about his siblings. Daniel had written of Sam's recollections of how both girls were deeply ingrained in the hearts of all three brothers. Sam was especially protective of his baby sister. He had given the youngest girl a sweet variation of the name given to her by the master of the plantation. To the family, little Deborah became "Dibby."

Meg looked over the documents once more. Clearly listed were Nelson, Sarah, Henry, Louisa, and Deborah. Meg's heart sank every time she was reminded of the nullified promise made to Nelson and Sarah back in Virginia. Her heart completely twisted when she came upon additional paperwork indicating the promise continued to be broken once the coffle arrived here in Natchez.

Meg could barely breathe when she read that no one of the prominent New Orleans family had been there to pick up the family sent to them from Virginia. Shockingly, two days after the Natchez arrival, the twins were sold to a sugar plantation about an hour northwest of New Orleans.

Meg wondered why they both had been sold to the same location. She was sure that no one had taken into account the special bond between twin siblings. That would have indicated someone actually cared about them. There was no heart in the business of buying and selling human beings. Meg simply surmised that the two met the needs of the plantation where they were heading.

Meg continued to read through other documents, wondering if she would find the rest of the family sold apart as well. After a bit more digging, Meg found evidence that indicated the father, mother, and baby sister were finally turned over to an agent sent from the New Orleans family. A week or so after arriving in Natchez, the eldest and the youngest of Sam's family were heading down the Mississippi River to an entirely different life.

Meg inwardly seethed at the fact that the family continued to be ripped apart. Wasn't it horrific enough that these people were moved from the only home they had ever known down a dangerous trail, walking while chained all the way? They had nothing to call their own except for the clothes and rations provided. The only thing they had was each other and it seemed as if that one boon was heartlessly taken as well.

Meg now recognized her own naïveté in thinking the family from Graystone Plantation had actually cared about Sam's family. Of course, the LeGris family knew that a safe arrival couldn't be guaranteed just by the nature of the journey itself. Factually, Meg knew that Virginia plantations like Graystone were falling on hard times during that time period. It was in their best interest to trade and sell what would bring the most money to them. Meanwhile in Louisiana the plantations and business owners were experiencing a rise in sales of sugar and rice. They most definitely had the money to take on more workers. Clearly, it all boiled down to money and greed in both locations. There was nothing else more important.

Before leaving the building, the staff at the archival center shared a few points of interest that Meg might want to consider before moving on from Natchez. Meg stopped for a quick bite at a coffee shop sandwiched between antique stores and boutiques on Franklin Street. She took a moment to call her hotel and extend her stay for another night.

After lunch, Meg drove to a point in town nearest to one of the Trace exits. She pulled her car out of traffic beside a triangular grassy area. Directly across the street was an automotive repair shop. She gazed across the green triangle hugged by a line of tall pine trees. The trees were many feet taller than the building across the street, but not tall enough to have been growing here almost 200 years ago.

Meg stepped out of her car and found herself at the Forks of the Road. This was the point where the Virginia coffle had stopped to unload what was left of their shipment. This had been the point at which Sam, his brother Moses and the rest of their family were supposed to have been transferred to the LeGris' rich cousins of New Orleans. That had not happened.

Meg looked around the triangle of green. There were more than a handful of metal historical markers explaining the relevance of the Forks. At least here, there was public documentation of the slave trade that was so much a part of what established Natchez as prime location on the Mississippi River. Meg took her time reading and photographing each of the markers.

The knowledge that she was standing freely on a plot of ground where so many who weren't free and had been held in bondage humbled her beyond words. But she was never more humbled than when she walked around a set of historical markers to find a circular slab of concrete. Embedded into the concrete were the remnants of original shackles taken from legs of the enslaved.

Meg felt the world around her slip away. Everything around her was fading out of focus. It was as if all the modern-day buildings had just melted into thin air. The paved roadway that was filled with the hum of daily traffic disappeared as well. She could feel herself turning slowly in a circle to see what was left in her sight. The less traveled road behind her was now rutted dirt instead of rough pothole filled pavement but the old white boarded antebellum house that sat across the road was still there.

Meg felt faint. She wanted to sink down into the soft green grass under her feet. Meg heard a soft rustle beside her and turned. She was looking into the eyes of the woman in lavender that she had dreamed about the night before. Meg's voice came out in a rough but weak whisper belying her shock,

"Am I losing my mind?"

This time she could see the woman's mouth move as she replied to Meg.

"You are not. You know what is happening if you really think about it. Stop playing by everyone else's rules. Unlike the ones who were brought here in chains and had no choice, you can choose. Choose to tell the story. The whole story. It's time. Find the way. Believe in what you are being asked to do. Remember what I am telling you. The way must be your own. Not the way you *think* you are expected to do it."

And just like that, the woman faded away before Meg's eyes. The dirt roads became pavement again. Meg could see a few cars passing by and hear the clangs from the automotive shop across the way. She looked over and was relieved to see that no one was paying any attention to her. Her legs felt shaky as she walked the short distance to her car. Meg was in shock, not because she heard a voice but because, this time, she had a visual of who was speaking with her. Meg opened the door of her car and slid inside.

Meg's senses felt a bit more normal once she was in the car driving. Her shakiness had stopped, and she was clearly seeing the modern-day sights of Natchez as she traveled the short distance back to her hotel. About midway in her brief drive, she decided to grab something for dinner that she could reheat in the hotel microwave. She was sure she would not be doing much work on her project during the evening. She felt like she needed the quiet atmosphere of her room to integrate everything that had happened.

Something was changing for her. Something was on the cusp, and she instinctively knew it.

Meg parked her car in front of the hotel before grabbing the bag of enticing smelling food she had picked up and locking up her car for the night. She scurried into the front lobby smiling to the kind woman working at the desk and walked toward the elevator. Meg barely glanced at the huge painting over the credenza this time. She just wanted to get to her room where she could begin to relax her mind and body from the oddities of the day. After eating her meal, she took a long hot bath and contemplated calling John Peabody. She wanted to discuss her findings so far. She quickly decided against it. She was fine with relaying the information from the archives, but she feared if she shared her dream and the odd occurrence at the Forks of the Road, he might tell her to come back immediately.

"Who in the world can I trust with all this? I need someone to tell that won't think I am a raving lunatic."

Meg spoke her thoughts out loud to the steam covered tiles of the bathroom. Just as the last word reverberated through the room, Meg heard her grandmother's voice as plain as day,

"Call your mother."

Meg noticed that she still couldn't see her grandmother even though her voice was as plain as day.

"I will, but granny, why could I see that woman and not see you when you speak to me?"

"Girl, you always get what you need when you need it. Now call your mother."

Meg's mother answered on the first ring. Meg laughed and said,

"What were you doing, sitting on top of the phone?"

Her mother sighed, "Of course not. I knew you were going to be calling. So, I was ready."

How could Meg forget that her mother could "anticipate" a phone call or visit and exactly when it would happen. Meg's mother had her own gifts. She didn't advertise them, but she certainly had never denied them. She had always wanted Meg to live her own life in the way she chose. But deep down, she wished Meg could recognize what she was capable of and accept the bounties even if they held a certain responsibility.

The chat with her mother had been just what she needed. Her mother listened without judgement and simply asked pointed questions that allowed Meg to gain a better sense of clarity of all that had happened since she had left Virginia. The only deliberate advice her mother had offered was for Meg to continue to write all the inexplicable occurrences she encountered in her journal. They both agreed this felt important to Meg's journey. Meg looked over at the journal thinking if things kept going as is, she may need to purchase a second one for this trip.

Chapter 17

Meg made a spontaneous decision to make one more stop before heading into New Orleans. She drove with the windows down to take in the sweet spring scents along the Great River Road. Her car was pointed in the direction of the sugar plantation listed as the point of sale for Sam's twin siblings. She felt a strong push to try and discover anything she could about their lives there. She wondered if Sam and Daniel had been able to do the same.

When Meg pulled into the parking area for the plantation tours, she saw several large buses already parked. Thankfully, those folks had prepaid for their entry into the luxurious grounds, so the ticket line was relatively short.

Meg purposely lagged behind the group in front of her so that she could be alone as she moved through the property. Meg walked through the front entry of the estate and stopped dead in her tracks. There before her was the same grand home in the painting over the credenza at the hotel in Natchez. The only thing missing were the people on horseback and their loyal dogs trotting alongside. Meg wondered if this was a sign that today's investigation would be a success.

It was not to be. Meg was sadly disappointed with her visit but oddly enough not at all surprised. Except for the listing of the names of the twins, their arrival date, and the jobs they were assigned, she found nothing about their life on the plantation. This plantation shared very little of the details of those who had been enslaved here. The tours in this location were more about the grandiose way of life of those who owned the land. Even in the present day, the plantation tours centered on the beautifully manicured grounds as a site for lavish parties, dinners, and weddings.

Ironically however, Meg found another surprising connection to her hometown. She discovered the plantation had once belonged to the son of the very man who ran the salt works during the time Sam had lived with Daniel Hughes. Ownership for him had come through a marriage into a prominent southern family. The plantation as well as the slaves utilized in the sugar production had been gifted to the couple as a wedding present.

The thread of irony was woven tightly in this connection. From salt to sugar. This lavish plantation and her tiny hometown had one thing in common. Neither openly told the story of the enslaved.

Even though Meg had paid for a tour of the entire grounds including the interior of the great house, she could not muster up the feeling for exploring inside. She knew well enough that she could not listen to one more "ooh and ahh" over the beautiful estate. If she heard yet another person speak about how hard the Reston's must have worked to make such an enduring legacy, she would, well and truly, throw up her breakfast on the nearest damask sofa. It had never been the elite owners who had done any of the work.

Instead, Meg decided to take a solitary walk on the grounds before getting back on the road toward New Orleans. She meandered through Spanish moss-covered oaks and past sweet-smelling jasmine. She saw the most beautiful roses with their faces turned toward the sun. Their roots clearly could have been planted by the workers who were enslaved on these grounds at the same time as Louisa and Henry, twin siblings of Sam, who had lived here. She wondered if either of them had walked the same path she was taking now.

Meg felt an overwhelming need to walk back toward the grand house and back to her car. She wanted to leave this place well and truly behind her. As she turned and made her way through the Spanish moss-covered trees, she could have sworn she saw a woman in a white tignon and a lavender dress dart toward the river. She blinked several times. She looked from left to right and back again. No one was there.

Meg began to retrace her steps to the front of the house and came to an abrupt halt. Earlier she had noticed a friendly "warning" sign announcing a photo shoot for brochures being prepared for the estate. Cameras and special lighting equipment had been set up on the huge green expanse in front of the main house. Meg's breath caught in her throat as she saw a historically outfitted couple astride two thoroughbreds. In front of the shining steeds sat two fine hunting hounds. The scene was exact in every detail to the scene depicted in the painting hanging by the elevators in her hotel in Natchez.

Meg knew it would take her just over an hour to reach New Orleans, but her gut told her to stay in the vicinity for at least another day. She spent the evening in her new hotel adding to her journal. She thumbed back through to the beginning noting some patterns that were beginning to form. These patterns were definitely helping her to gain clarity on a personal level, which in turn was serving her research effort. For Meg, both were equally important.

After a comfortable night in the inn by the river, Meg decided a good cup of coffee was needed before finishing the last leg of her journey down River Road. Meg pulled her car into the first empty parking space she could find in front of the old hardware store turned coffee shop. People were milling in and out of the small building. Meg mentally crossed her fingers hoping she would be able to find a seat inside.

Meg pulled open the door of the shop and heard the tinkling sound of the brass bell affixed to the top of the door. She drew in a deep breath drawing in the scents of caramel and cinnamon wafting through the air. After placing her order, she found a small table beside the front window.

Meg stirred the coffee and sweetened cream together in her cup. She happily anticipated the sticky warm roll being prepared for her fresh from the kitchen. Gazing mindlessly about, she watched as the crowd inside the shop trickled down to only a few folks left chatting quietly over their food. Finally, Meg noticed that she and one older woman were the only two left sitting inside the café. Meg felt the eyes of the elderly woman sweeping over her. Meg looked over and smiled. The lady returned the smile. Meg watched in surprise as the lady picked up her cup and saucer and walked over to Meg's table.

"Do you mind if I join you for a few minutes," asked the elderly woman. Meg stood up and pulled the extra chair around for the lady to settle into.

"Please do. I'm Meg. How are you today?"

The lady laughed and it sounded warm and gooey like the inside of a pecan pie.

"I am well, thank you. I hope you don't think this is strange, but I know everyone around here, so I was sure you were new to our area. I thought you might want some information about the sights."

Meg was slightly taken aback, not at the smiling woman's friendliness but more at the fact that she assumed Meg might be looking for information.

Meg thanked the lady and explained about her work as a researcher. She gave a brief background as to why she had stopped by the plantation. The lady looked over with some sadness in her eyes.

"You are trying to find information about the twins? Well, I can't give you exact details with formal documentation, but I can tell you the old story about those two. It has been passed down for years. The current owners of the estate house don't seem to want to recognize the facts much less the folklore associated with the Reston estate. Reston House was and is famous for the wealth amassed as a sugar plantation. That could only have happened one way and you and I know that."

The woman took a long drink from her cup and continued.

"The foundation that runs the place might be good with a general ghost story, but they surely don't advertise the one about the twins."

Meg's freshly baked pastry arrived, and the waitress brought more tea to the lady across from her. Meg settled back in her chair ready to be captivated as she listened intently to the woman's mesmerizing voice.

"The story passed down actually begins with the overseer. He was charged with going to Natchez to purchase and barter for strong men and women to work the sugar cane. The man was called Hiram, I believe. He had started out in life as a blacksmith and tended to the fine horses for many of the plantation owners up and down the river. He had married his childhood sweetheart but was devastated when he lost her to the yellow fever. Some say he lost his mind and soul as well that day. The Reston family took him on as a full-time hire to work with their finest racehorses. In fact, they say that Mr. Reston trusted him more than anyone else working for him. So much so, he allowed Hiram to travel on his own with a great deal of funds when going to Natchez.

The tale goes that Hiram had just finished procuring a strong pack of men to put on the boat in Natchez to sail back down the river when he saw her. Louisa was her name. They say she had creamy skin much like the coffee in your cup and eyes the color of whiskey. They also say that her mystical eyes put a spell on Hiram without even realizing what she was doing.

Hiram had traded so well that day that he had a great deal of the funds left in his pocket. He knew Reston House was preparing for several huge gatherings and there was a need for an additional kitchen girl. Hiram decided to make an offer to the coffle agent who was holding the girl. When Hiram approached the man, he found that she couldn't be sold unless he took her twin brother as well.

The leaders of the coffle were trying to unload as many of their chattel as possible to fund their passage on a boat back up the river and still return with a hefty profit. The twin brother was slight in build but healthy. He had experience with horses in Virginia. For that reason, Hiram knew he could use him in the stables. If Mr. Reston had an issue with this last purchase, he would use his own savings to give the money back making Hiram the outright owner of the brother and sister."

The woman took a sip of her tea and looked out the window thoughtfully,

"Now what you have told me is that there was more than just the brother and the sister of this family being taken down river. The stories around here only talk of these two."

Meg sighed and wondered if the lady knew how hypnotic her voice sounded. Meg yearned for her to continue the story and leaned into the words as they flowed.

"The tale goes on that Mr. Reston cared not one whit about the fact that Hiram made the purchase of the brother and sister. He saw how useful the addition would be to his plantation. It would have been a sweet story in some ways if Hiram had fallen in love with the girl, but he had vowed never to love again. No, his interest was apprised of pure lust.

Both women sat with a disgusted grimace on their faces before the older of the two continued.

"And so, this young girl who worked in the kitchen from sun-up to sundown was "visited" shall we say in her quarters behind the house on a regular basis. She worked with a yarb woman to protect herself so that she would be less likely to bring a baby into the sad world she was forced to live in during her lifetime. However, she could not protect herself from the jealousy that festered inside of Hiram. Hiram watched as she was growing from a young girl into a lush woman. He saw that the workers in the fields and plantation buildings noticed her as well. It's been told that often on the nights he came to visit, he questioned her as to how many of the men she spoke to or looked at during the day. One night, her fiery spirit got the best of her, and she said, 'All of them.' Hiram gave into his temper and slapped her across the face leaving a bruise that lasted for days."

Both women were quiet for a moment before the older woman continued the story.

"Her brother, Henry, wanted very much to turn on Hiram in the stables and kill him, not just for the slapping but for ever putting his hands on his sister. Yet, Henry was smarter than that. Instead, he began working with a few trusted older men who worked in the stables and the household. They had a plan to escape. Henry knew he had to take his sister and run. Henry also knew if the two of them stayed on the plantation, he would certainly be killed for taking retribution on her behalf. Henry also knew that her spirited ways could lead to more than her receiving a beating by Hiram.

He waited until the plans were in place and the time to leave was near before even telling his sister. Several of the older men were making ready to go as well. They all were watching the moon as it dwindled down each night from full to crescent— just waiting for the night when it

191

would be hidden from all eyes. That would be the night when they would make their way into the swamp to load on to a pirogue to move as silently as they could away from plantation life. The brother was not told who would be whisking them away or to where they would be heading but he trusted the old men who had become like fathers to him. They knew and they would tell him when it was time.

At first, the sister never knew which night Hiram would show up in her quarters but soon it was if his jealousy would not allow him to skip a night. So, she again worked with the yarb woman to find a mix of plants that would cause Hiram to fall asleep quickly and remain soundly asleep through the night. She was careful to use them sparingly so that he would not catch on to her deception. He didn't question why he didn't even have the energy to begin much less finish what he had intended to do with Louisa in the first place. He simply thought that he was just that tired from a hard day's work.

After Henry shared the plan with Louisa, she began to watch the moon as closely as Henry in preparation for the night they would be able to leave. All she wanted was to leave Hiram and the godforsaken plantation far behind. She never even asked Henry where they were going. She didn't care if she could be with the last family member she had by her side.

Her thoughts often went to Sam and Moses back in Virginia. She pictured them back in those green mountains and hoped they had found a way to each other. She often wondered if her mother, father, and little sister had finally made it together and were safe in New Orleans. She had heard the talk among the house staff how folks were coming up to the plantation from New Orleans for parties and dances, so she supposed that the city wasn't that far away. Would it be too much to hope that Henry had plans to get them to New Orleans? Would it not be a joy for them to all be reunited again?

Louisa only held that dream momentarily. She knew it would not be possible. She and Henry would be runners. Even if they didn't get torn apart by the hounds or killed by the overseer, they couldn't just suddenly turn up in New Orleans to be with their parents. A brother and sister who had escaped from the river plantation could be easily traceable if not easily recognizable. Unless…

Louisa began to form a plan of her own. She had a pair of pants and a shirt that belonged to Henry that she was patching for him. She had scissors. That night she cut off the legs of the pants to match her height. She found an old piece of rope from the horse barn to fashion a belt. She folded the garments together and hid the scissors deep inside the roll. On the night that the moon went dark, she would put Hiram to sleep for the last time, throw away her Louisa clothes, and dress in her brother's throwaways. She would take the scissors and chop away her hair as close to the scalp as she could get it. Louisa would become Louis until they reached wherever they were going.

Louisa took the tightly rolled clothes and placed them behind a loose board under the floor of her bed. She looked over at the bed with a sense of shame. Almost everyone else from field worker to house worker slept on a floor mat or makeshift bunk, but not Louisa. She had an iron bed with a feather mattress because Hiram refused to be uncomfortable when he made his "visits."

Meg jumped ever so slightly when she felt the light bump of the server's arm as she refilled Meg's coffee cup. The lady across from her didn't seem to notice, just as she didn't seem aware of the fact that her own softly elegant drawl and the story that she was sharing had taken Meg to a place that wasn't inside the warm room of the coffee shop. It had only taken the woman the time it spent in Meg drinking a half a cup of coffee to tell the lead up to Henry and Louisa's escape. Meg had been transported so deeply into that realm that she felt she had been gone centuries. None the less, she was on the edge of her seat waiting for the woman to continue. The lady brushed away a refill for more hot tea but did ask for a glass of water. After the server brought the water and she had taken a sip, she leaned toward Meg drawing her back into the magic of the telling of the story.

"Finally, the day came they had all been waiting for: the day that would bring the darkest of nights."

With those last words, Meg noticed the woman's voice took on an ominous tone and yet she found herself leaning into the story more than ever.

"The older men sang in the fields and the outbuildings— an old spiritual song. A song that the overseers would seemingly pay no attention to because they did not realize that the words were a code announcing what was to happen later in the night. Henry briefly made passing conversation with the oldest of the men, again not wanting to draw unwanted attention."

The woman took a sip from the icy glass of water and continued.

"Henry and Louisa had come up with a plan for Henry to signal her that all was going to plan. Henry oversaw exercising all the horses, but on this day, he would specifically walk *only* the prize gelding around the stable three times just before the evening feeding."

"Louisa deliberately placed herself at the back kitchen window as she prepared the baking for the evening and the next day's breakfast. She could clearly see the horse stable from this vantage point. As she kneaded the bread, she watched her twin bring the strong fine horse around the stable. One round and no more meant their journey would not occur on this night and maybe not for a while. Two rounds and no more meant that the journey would be postponed one more night while there might be only a sliver of moon. Three rounds signaled that all was going to plan, and they would embark at midnight.

"Louisa finally saw Henry go into the barn and return with the beautiful horse he loved so much. One round and her brother went back around the stable out of sight. Louisa felt her hands sink into the dough and had to remind herself to keep working as if nothing that would change her life forever was happening. Suddenly, she saw her brother come around the stable on a second circuit. She held her breath tightly in what seemed an eternity until she saw her brother bring the fine horse for the third and final round in the late afternoon sun. She squinted a bit as she watched her brother out of the paned window. He seemed to be smiling and talking to the horse, but she knew that the smile was for her. Tonight, she and Henry would be turning their backs on this godforsaken plantation.

"After a fine dinner was served in the main house, Louisa made her way down the footworn path to her quarters. She had half a pie wrapped in a blue cloth. The lady of the house often gave her hardest workers leftover treats thinking this would make them satisfied and eager to continue to run a fine kitchen. Louisa was feeling generous herself. Rather than hide the pie away, she would serve it to Hiram with a fine cup of her "special" herbal tea. Louisa imagined watching him drift off to a deep sweet slumber and not awaken until the rooster's crows brought him around.

"Louisa had no fear surrounding the thought of Hiram waking up in the morning without her by his side. He knew she was required to be in the kitchen of the big house well before sunrise. It would be much later in the day before she might be missed. The women in the kitchen generously covered for each other if one was late occasionally. They especially took heart with Louisa because they knew Hiram took many advantages of being one of the overseers who had the ear of the owner. He had been given the special privilege of visiting Louisa in her cabin whenever he chose.

"Louisa shook her head slightly and glanced at the wind-up clock Hiram had brought to her cabin as a convenience for himself and not her. While he cared not one whit if he kept her to himself and made her late on the odd occasion, he refused to be late in his own duties. He knew well which side of his bread was buttered with Mr. Reston.

"Louisa swept the floor of her small cabin in nervous preparation for Hiram's arrival. She pulled out the special blend of herbs for his tea. She knew the dose she put in the tea would take at least an hour to do its job. Hiram would have to finish at least half a cup by 10:30 or 11 o'clock for her to fulfill her plan. He must be deep in his sleep so that he wouldn't see her slip into her "Louis" clothes. She would take the scissors with her and cut her long braids once she was safely away."

"Meg found her body leaning deeply into the small table that separated her from the older lady who sat across from her. Meg realized that her hands were gripping the sides of the seat of the café chair. She felt every inch of her skin tingle in anticipation as if she were there in the room with Louisa impatiently awaiting the very moment that the dash toward freedom would arrive. The woman took another sip of her water and continued.

"Meanwhile, Henry had gone back to the stable where he had hidden a pack of supplies for the journey. No one ever paid attention to his comings and goings at the stable. His love for the horses was well recognized and welcomed. Nothing seemed amiss if Henry was there late into the evening. He glanced out the barn door at the darkened sky. The moon could not serve as a time piece on this night. He would have to rely on the relaying whistles and calls of those who he would be traveling with to know when to make his way to the swampy alcove by the river.

"Henry knew that as soon as his sister had served Hiram her special tea, she would start to look for the light of his lantern leaving the barn. She knew that once Henry made his way from the barn to the edge of the riding yard, he would extinguish the flame and continue through the darkness to the small boat that would carry them all away from the sugar plantation. When she saw the light disappear, she was to follow. Henry had all the faith in the world that his sister could silently follow him without detection. She had somehow magically taught herself how to steal through the darkest of nights to gather the herbs she so often used in her teas and poultices.

"Louisa found herself pacing back and forth over the planked floor of her cabin. She thought Hiram would have already been through her door by now. The ticking of his small clock was anything but soothing. With every small movement of the clock's hands, she felt her stomach roll. What if he chose this night of all nights to stay away? It had happened before but not often. Usually, it was only when he was called away on a job for Mr. Reston and that didn't often occur on the spur of the moment.

"The self-importance that Hiram had developed often had him bragging to her about the special trips he would be taking. Louisa knew her place and knew he wasn't trying to impress her. He simply wanted to let her know that it was because of his importance that she was given the special cabin and time with him. Louisa pulled her tense shoulders up straight. Likely, if Hiram had not arrived by eleven, he would not be coming at all. That would more easily allow her to dart away into the night unencumbered by even his sleeping presence.

"However, if he did come to the cabin and it was much later than 10:30, she would have no choice but to add more of the herbs to the tea to ensure that sleep would be almost instantaneous. Louisa felt her stomach tighten once again. Her experience with the plants specific to the area close to the plantation was new. She was wary about the fact that too much or the wrong combination might result in a forever sleep for Hiram. No matter what he had done to her and how he treated her, she was not sure she could live with herself for taking another human's life. She hoped it would not come to that. All she wanted was to see that her brother and she could safely make their way to freedom.

"Henry had decided that giving the horses an extra brushing for the evening would help him pass the time. The rhythmic passing of the comb over the warm bodies helped to quieten his nerves. The horses who returned Henry's love relished his extra attention on this dark night. He reached the third stall, the stall that held Mr. Reston's favorite horse. Mr. Reston had brought a famous artist to paint him astride this beauty. The painting included the beautiful Mrs. Reston seated upon her own horse with one of their best hunting dogs ambling in front of the fine steeds."

Meg swallowed hard. Did this lady know that she had seen this very painting or at least a copy in the hotel back in Natchez? Before she asked if this was indeed the same painting, the woman continued with her story.

"Just as Henry opened the stall door, he heard it. The first whistle from nearby. His ears perked to listen intently, making sure that he had not imagined that the time had arrived. Unsure if it were anywhere close to midnight, he strained to hear what he hoped was coming next. The whistle was then followed by the remaining night calls that served as the signals toward freedom. Henry closed the stall, picked up his pack and the lantern, and made his way to the riding yard. Once there, he dared not turn around. He extinguished the lantern and fought the urge to run to the river.

"Louisa watched intently from her open door and saw her brother's lantern sway in the night as he moved deftly from the stable barn toward the riding yard and then his light was gone. She looked across the cabin, empty but for herself. The lamp on the table illuminated the face of the clock. Only fifteen after the hour of ten. Something was wrong. This wasn't the plan. Why had Henry moved from the barn well before the agreed upon time? Did she dare follow? What would happen if Hiram came and found her missing from her cabin at this time of night? Her absence could well and truly alert him that something was amiss on the grounds.

"Deep in her heart, she wanted to run as fast and far away as she could this very minute, but she could not put her brother and the others in danger. When Henry first shared the plan with her, she insisted that she would not be the one to hold him back if things did not go as they hoped. Her whereabouts on the plantation was well monitored by Hiram. She felt like a pet bird in the cage he had built for her. Henry was insistent that nothing would go wrong. Henry was the dreamer, and she was the realist. Characteristics that set the twins apart as much as it drew them together in name of balance.

"It suddenly became simple to Louisa. She would follow the plan and wait until just before midnight before heading to the river. If the boat had to leave before that and she remained behind, she was sure Henry would find a way to get her out by the next dark moon. If Hiram did indeed show up, then she would just have to risk increasing the dosage of herbs. She walked to the table, where she had the tea ready to go and added the mysterious herbs to the berry pie. One way or the other, there would be a long sleep for someone tonight."

Chapter 18

The lady across from Meg leaned back in her chair. Meg looked closely at her face. She seemed suddenly tired. Meg did not want to press her for more, but she hoped the story wouldn't stop there— without finding out what happened to Louisa and her brother. Meg watched as the lovely lady lifted her shoulders a few times, shared a melancholy smile, and continued.

"Hiram was nowhere in sight when the clock showed half past eleven. Louisa determined she had waited long enough. She quickly switched her clothing. It didn't take her long until she was wearing her "Louis" clothes. She was unsure why, but she quickly put her dress into her pack with the scissors, not taking the time to cut her hair. She would wait until they were on the water moving away from Reston House. She blew out the lamp and headed toward the swampy corner of the river.

"It's uncanny how a person's senses change in the darkest hours of night. Louisa smelled it before she heard or saw anything. Blood. Her eyes were adjusting to the darkness, and she had enough of a sense of self-preservation to hide herself behind some dense growing bushes. The first thing she saw was young Edward who worked in the sugar cane fields. He was strapped to an oak tree, naked, bleeding, and near death.

"At first, Louisa thought the intense bleeding came from lashes from the whip. Upon closer look, she realized that he had been cut. Long, painful cuts all over his body. She could see the long knife that had been used on him glinting in a very white hand. Her horrified gaze followed the length of the knife, up the hand, up the arm, until it landed on the scraggly face of one of the field overseers. Briefly, she wondered if he would mercifully put the young man out of his misery. But she knew the reputation of this overseer well enough to recognize that he would not. The pain he was allowed to inflict daily was evidence enough of what he would prefer in this moment. His raspy voice carried through the still night,

'You stupid animal. You thought I would stop cutting once you gave out the signals to the others. I know there must be more than you and that uppity stable boy. Where are the rest?'

"With that he slashed the knife across the naked stomach of the profusely bleeding man; just deep enough to bring more blood but not kill him out right.

"Watching the knife rip the skin from left to right, Louisa went slightly numb. She seemed to be rising from her own body as if she were a night bird flying above it all. Seeing everything without being seen. She had never been told how many or who would be leaving with her brother and herself on this night. She had no idea who else had been fooled into thinking all was a go for leaving, but she knew exactly who this piece of evil was referring to when he said uppity stable boy. Henry. He knew Henry was involved and he had to be here somewhere. The field worker was moaning now, and his cries covered the slight rustle when Louisa left the cover of the bush and headed onward to the river.

"She could feel one foot place itself in front of the other. She wanted to run screaming for Henry to come to her but if she had any hope of helping him at all, she had to move stealthily. Her ears quickly picked up the sounds of voices she would soon wish she had never heard. Just in the distance, she could hear a couple of men talking between themselves. The sounds of their voices were neither loud nor soft, but they screamed at her inner being.

'You know, Mr. Reston isn't going to like this.'

'Hmph, ain't nobody gonna miss Young Edward. He has been nothing but trouble since the boss traded Old Edward and the rest of his family to the Dupuy plantation for the caning equipment we needed. Hell, even the overseer for the Dupuy's could see what a mess he was. Dupuy's man refused to take him with the rest. Young Edward is a coward above all else. A useless coward. He didn't even have the guts to try and cover up for the runners. He told us everything after the first cuts. Well, almost everything, just not all of the names of who was heading down to the river.'

'I wasn't talking about young Edward, and you know it. Mr. Reston was counting on that fancy horse of his to win the River Race between the other sugar cane planters. He may not need the money, but you know as much as I do, he is a prideful man. He wants to best them all. He is, *was*, convinced that Henry could make it happen. I have even heard him tell you and anyone who would listen that Henry was filled with a special magic when it came to that horse. Hell, you saw what Henry could do with any of the horses but especially with that one. Henry could get that horse to run like the wind and never even look like it was sweating.'

"Louisa felt her heart drop to her stomach. Could do? Was convinced?

"She heard Hiram's rackety cough and heard him spit on the ground.

'I'll find him another. Henry should have known better. He should have recognized how good he had it being allowed to work in the stables rather than out in the sugar cane fields. He should have known better than to try and take what's mine away from me. No one on this earth takes what's mine. God has already done that and no man, much less a black man, is going to do that.'

"Hiram's voice slithered over Louisa's senses like an evil snake. The other man began to question Hiram.

'How do you know that he was going to take her? He never mentioned her even when…'

'No, but young Edward said he watched Henry closely and that in the last week he had visited with her a lot. Their heads bent together whispering and looking around to make sure no one could hear them.'

'Hiram, I don't know. We never saw any of the others or her around here tonight. Maybe young Edward was lying about it all. You said it yourself; he was never one to be trusted. We both know he was jealous of Henry. He wanted Henry's position even though he could barely clean out a stall much less work with stable of horses.'

'You are right about young Edward. Nothing will be lost there.'

'I know one other thing. I don't want to be anywhere around when you tell the boss the rest. That race is in another month and I doubt you will be able to find a way to get his horse to win.'

"If Louisa could have seen Hiram's face more closely, she would have seen his cheek starting to twitch in a moment of recognized fear of what was to come when he went to the boss later that night.

'Hiram, I guess you could just blame it on the gators. I mean, in the end it was the gator that got him. I won't be telling Mr. Reston or anybody that you actually fed Henry bit by bit to the gator. It was crazy how you roped him like a calf and began dunking him back and forth into the water, bringing the gator close to do the job for you. Was it like hooking and losing a fish? Did you feel the gator take the bait and move off?

"Hiram didn't answer. But Louisa had her answer. Henry was gone and so was what was left of her heart and soul. She turned and made her way back to her cabin.

"Louisa worked in reverse back at the cabin. She removed her Louis clothes and hid them away again. She put the scissors back in the mending basket. She emptied the tea behind the cabin and buried the pie in with the remains of the chamber pot. She hung her dress ready to be worn to do the kitchen work in the morning. She climbed into her bed, and she waited."

Meg felt tears burn her eyes. She had no brothers or sisters so she could only imagine the loss that Louisa felt for her whole family. At least Louisa had the hope that the rest of the family was alive somewhere. But knowing that her twin, her other half, was gone and never coming back must have been beyond devastating. Meg felt her voice roughly whisper,

"What happened to Louisa when that awful Hiram came back?"

The older woman smiled enigmatically.

"Well, that is where this tale gets even more interesting. The story goes that Louisa waited all night for Hiram, but he never came to the cabin. In the kitchens the next morning, she heard the other workers whispering about the rumblings of what had happened the night before. She saw the looks of pity and curiosity aimed her way. Supposedly one of the youngest kitchen girls walked straight over to Louisa and asked her if Hiram had told her what had been carried out near the river last night.

"Louisa stopped cutting away the fat from the ham that was to be served with breakfast. She gripped the knife tightly, holding back from cutting the smirk off the face of the young girl called Hazzie.

"No, Hiram did not visit last night."

The smart mouthed young girl did not have sense enough to know when to stop.

"Well, then what are you looking so tired for? You should have gotten to sleep the sleep of the dead."

"Just then Hazzie's grandmother entered the kitchen from gathering eggs and walked straight over to her. She promptly smacked the top of the senseless girl's head before shewing her away. The older woman gently took the knife from Louisa's hand and gave a warning look to the rest of the kitchen help. Miss Tassy pressed gently on Louisa' shoulders as they walked to the back porch.

'You pay no attention to that nosey grand youngin of mine. I'm sorry she was so disrespectful. I know Mr. Hiram did not come to you last night. I will tell you what I have heard from the cabins and the big house. There were some old men who wanted to move on last night. It would have been a perfect night for it under the cover of the dark moon. Except this morning, they are still here. They are going about their work as if nothing was different than any other morning. But there are some who are not to be found this morning. Young Edward and… my sweet girl… I'm sorry, but Henry is nowhere to be found.'

"The older woman watched for Louisa's expression to change but all she saw was a pair of ice-cold eyes looking back at her."

'Young Edward was found dead, tied to a tree, vultures picking at the blood pools and his body. But no Henry. Not a trace. Old John who serves the boss, well he told me Mr. Hiram came in the middle of night and told the boss that he had stopped a bunch of men from leaving here last night. He told the boss that they had to "make" young Edward tell them what was happening. He then had to tell the boss that Henry had been snatched by a gator before they could save him. Mr. Reston went crazy mad. Old John thought he was going to burst into flames, he was so angry. He said the veins looked ready to pop out of his temples.'

'Course, Mr. Reston didn't care what happened to young Edward. He accused Hiram of lying about the plan for running since Hiram couldn't tell him the name of anyone else that was supposed to make their way out of here, except for Henry. He then accused Hiram of being jealous of Henry and all his talents. Old John said he heard him say, 'If Henry had only been white, then he would have had Hiram's job.' Master Reston went all crazy and began ranting that Hiram would be the cause of our plantation not winning the race. That he should have saved Henry and now he had no use for Hiram.'

"Miss Tassy smiled for the first time since taking Louisa out to the porch.

'The reason you didn't get a visit from Hiram last night… well, Mr. Reston had him escorted from the grounds. Told him not to bother to try and find a job along the river. He would make sure no one would take him in— ever. The riders came back and said the last they saw of Hiram, he was heading toward New Orleans.'

"Miss Tassy then sent Louisa back to her quarters to have some time to herself so that she could deal with the news that had just been delivered. She told the rest of the kitchen girls that Louisa was in shock. Miss Tassy figured shock was why the girl's demeanor never changed the whole time the older woman was delivering the sad news about Henry. Miss Tassy was a wise old woman, and she had her own ideas about what had gone on the night before. None of the rest of the kitchen help needed to be privy to those thoughts.

"Miss Tassy also warned her granddaughter Hazzie that she was never to be anything other than kind to Louisa or she would wrap her in white and feed her to the gators herself. Tassy began to watch over Louisa as much as Louisa would let her. Tassy watched as Louisa began to double down in her work, often taking the work from the other women and giving them a rest. She watched as Louisa began to waste away and tried her best to get her to eat. Even Hazzie, who was a fine baker, made her special little pies with the leftover ingredients from the main table.

"A week or so after Hiram had been run off the grounds, Louisa was finally able to sleep a whole night through. Partly because there was no one waking her up for their pleasure and partly because she purposely worked as hard as she could so that her sleep was deep and dreamless.

"About a week before the next dark moon, one of the oldest men from the cabins came to Louisa. That same week, Miss Tassy noticed that Louisa remained her quiet self, but she was eating so much better. Tassy wondered if she had found she was with child from that awful Hiram. The day after the dark moon, Louisa did not show up in the kitchen. This worried Tassy so she hurried over to Louisa's cabin. There she found a floorboard jimmied open. Nothing inside. Louisa's mending basket was on the bed, nothing missing except a pair of scissors. Looking over at the small table, Tassy saw the wind-up clock that Hiram had provided. She shrugged her shoulders. Wasn't neither one of them coming back for that. Tassy put the clock in the pocket of her apron and closed the door quietly behind her."

Meg blinked as if coming out of a dream. She looked across the table waiting for the story to continue and was surprised to see the lady gathering her purse and rising from her chair.

"Ma'am, are you leaving? What happened to Louisa?"

The lady smiled and tucked her purse under her arm.

"You are about to find out very soon." And with that the lady left the café. Meg sat there with her mouth open in wonder.

Meg went to the counter to pay her check before heading on down the road to New Orleans.

The waitress gave Meg the change and Meg promptly dropped it in the tip jar.

Meg began hesitantly,

"The lady who joined me at my table, where does she live?"

The woman, whose name tag said she was Peggy, answered her promptly, "You mean the older lady in the lavender dress? I have no idea; I have never seen her before."

"You mean she isn't from here?"

Peggy answered with an assured voice,

"Cher, I own this place and I am here every day. I was born in a house across the street from this shop. I know everyone from this little town. I have no idea who she is. She has never been here before. I thought you knew her."

Meg whispered to herself,

"Maybe I do…"

Part Four
All But the Blood

We share all but the blood,
yet our bond is eternal.

Chapter 19

New Orleans was showing off all of her spring beauty in comparison to places further north. Back home in Virginia, some plants would be starting to bloom, and a few trees would be attempting to push out their tiny leaves. But April in New Orleans presented a breath-taking display of color. The warm afternoon breezes carried scents that were new and exciting to Meg. She especially enjoyed taking them in as she rode down St. Charles looking out at the lovely old oaks dotting the many gardens of the grand old houses.

Meg had quickly learned how to maneuver the streetcar line which delivered her to her temporary office at Tulane University. Thanks to Dr. Peabody, she had been connected to his counterpart at the University who provided her with a small room to use for her research while she was in town. Meg swiftly settled into a rhythm of working on her research obligations from early morning to the midafternoon hours. After that she was free to savor the later hours of the day exploring the area in and around the French Quarter.

Professor Gallo, the department chair at Tulane, laughed gently when she explained how she was spending her afternoons.

"You may well want to switch that up a bit when summer arrives. You most definitely want to be in an air-conditioned office during the hottest part of the day."

Meg made no response but thought to herself that by the time the heat of the summer arrived, she would be back in the mountains of Virginia.

Somewhere around the third week of April, Meg realized that she was beginning to hit a wall with her research efforts. She could find nothing relating to Sam and Daniel and their search for Sam's family. It left her to surmise what may have happened to the two men. Had they even made it as far at Natchez or had something happened to them? Beyond what was shared in Daniel's journal about leaving for the trip, there was no physical evidence of them in Natchez nor here in New Orleans. It was as if both men had either totally disappeared or had at least turned back and went home to the mountains. The journals that her friend Ben had shared with her from his grand uncle's collection stopped with the final entry describing the last preparations for the trip south.

Given the current circumstances, Meg decided the ethical thing to do was head back home. She did not want to take advantage of the benefactor's funding by spending more money on hotel and parking expenses. Festival season was ramping up in New Orleans and hotel rates would be ramping up as well. Perhaps if she went back home, she would be able to find some inkling of when Daniel and Sam might have returned to Virginia.

Meg waited until early evening to make the call to Dr. Peabody announcing her decision.

"Hey Meggie, great to hear from you! Please tell me you are getting ready to head out for some fun this evening."

Meg was sure that John Peabody's definition of fun was quite different than her own. She still did not feel quite comfortable being out and about on her own after sunset. Often, she grabbed a meal at a restaurant close to her hotel or something from one of the small corner deli markets of the Quarter. She would then spend the evening in her room or by the pool either working on her computer or reading.

Meg wasn't about to tell a man thirty years her senior that he was probably having way more fun in the hills of Virginia than she was having in the French Quarter of New Orleans. Meg proceeded to tell Dr. Peabody the reason for her call.

"Dr. Peabody, umm John... I was actually calling to let you know that I am heading back that way in a few days. I am at a dead end here. I can't find anything official to document Daniel and Sam's whereabouts or any activity in New Orleans. I certainly don't want to waste funding that could go toward a more productive project."

A strange silence filled the line between her phone and the professor's.

"Umm, John... are you there?"

"Yes, of course Meg. Sorry. I was processing something you said... Am I right... you said nothing official— have you found something "unofficial?"

How in the world did she explain about the woman in Natchez and the story behind Henry and Louisa, the twin siblings of Sam? Meg drew in a breath and just let it all roll out of her.

Thirty minutes later, she drew in another breath and waited for John Peabody to tell her to pack her things and head back in the morning. Instead, he asked her to give him an hour and he would call her back. Meg really thought she must be losing it because she thought she heard a wisp of excitement in his voice. She agreed to his request, pushed the call end button on her phone, and began to pack her belongings.

It was almost two hours before her phone rang. She opened the call and waited for her instructions. Instead, John opened the conversation with a question.

"Meg, do you want to come home for any other reason than you believe you have lost the trail on your research?"

Meg thought quickly. She loved her home, but she was finding a part of herself loving New Orleans as well. Not being a partier, that might sound strange to some people. But she could see there was much more to the city and its people than the infamous Bourbon Street.

Meg was enjoying her time at the Tulane office. There she had not only been working on her own project, but she had been assisting Dr. Gallo in helping some of his youngest students develop their research skills. Oddly, not every student came out of high school with those necessary skills. Most of all, and this was the hardest for her to understand herself or articulate… Meg's gut told her there was something still here for her to discover. She just wasn't sure it had to do with Sam or Daniel.

"No, John, the only reason I feel the need to come back is to save the funding provided by the benefactor. It's not right to continue to spend the money on a project that's going nowhere."

John hesitated a moment before replying.

"Meg, I wish I was able to let you speak to the funder personally but that's not in my wheelhouse right now. I have relayed your concerns. I can tell you that the backer and I talked for quite a while. We then called Dr. Gallo in on a conference call. We have a proposal for you."

"All of us want you to stay longer. If you can stand the heat as Dr. Gallo pointed out and I think he meant weather-wise, we would like you to stay until September. Dr. Gallo spoke highly of your research skills and the way you are helping him with his students. The backer and he agreed that your salary from the funding would extend to your work with the students at Tulane. You could keep trying to find any solid factual evidence that you can regarding the original project while you are assisting Dr. Gallo."

Meg felt her heart race at the thought of more time in this special place trying to learn more about Sam's quest. Still the responsible side of her won out and she questioned the amount of money in paying for the hotel and parking until September. Did the benefactor truly realize the amount of money involved and how it could be going to other more assured projects?

"Meg, benefactors like the one supporting this project don't just "willy-nilly" dole out dollars. They have money and they know how to make money. They also know exactly how they want to spend their money."

"However, you are right in thinking the hotel and parking costs could be better spent. That is why you are getting an apartment. Dr. Gallo will store your car in his home garage. Gallo's sister is a real estate agent, and she has a few apartments that are furnished or partially furnished. All you have to do is pick the one that best suits your needs.

"All of them are located in the Quarter so you will still have to utilize the streetcar system to get up to Tulane. You will be responsible for paying for your own taxis or car services if you choose to go out on personal business; umm... something fun we can only hope."

Meg sat on the edge of her hotel bed with her mouth wide open. In the manner of a few hours, she was going from packing up all her belongings to head home to beginning to dream what a summer in New Orleans would bring for her.

Meg was a bit stunned and John Peabody could hear it in the tone of her voice when she began to speak. Wait until he told her about the last message from the benefactor.

"John, are you sure? I mean, it sounds wonderful. . . exciting even. I'm confident that I can be of help to Dr. Gallo, but I can't honestly promise that the research into Sam and his family will turn up anything more."

John laughed as he tried to reassure Meg.

"Will you stop? I am sure. Dr. Gallo is sure. The benefactor is more than sure. I have been told to tell you one last thing. The benefactor said to tell you and I quote,

'There is more than one way to share someone's story. Facts are easy and sometimes cold. Human stories are often messy and filled with emotion. Support the story with facts when you have them but remember, a person's real story comes from the heart. Remember to tell the whole story, not just the easy parts.'

217

The morning clanking of the street cleaner rattling through the Quarter usually brought Wavery out of her deep sleep. Not today. Today she awakened much earlier. The first rays of sun sprinkled across Wavery's face as the dream settled into her mind's eye.

Wavery jerked awake and sat straight up in bed. Her heart was thumping and she could feel a sheen of sweat across her forehead. She pushed her sandy blonde hair out of her face and looked around quickly. No one was in the room with her. Alive or dead. It had been just a dream. She pulled her knees up to her chest and rested her head on her crossed arms. She remembered the dream all too well. The sounds of steps coming up the stairs, the door pushing open, feeling her body turning and seeing…

Wavery jumped out of the bed and tried to wipe the picture from her mind's eye. Wavery had to work harder each time the dreams came through. The feelings of shame and disappointment were still fresh and hard to shake off. She had been wishing more and more that the ability to "see" would fade forever.

She had put all the strength she had into leaving behind her ability to vision during her waking hours. Metaphorically and literally, she always kept her head down as she traversed the streets of New Orleans. All manner of things, seen and unseen, meandered through the Quarter attempting to grab her attention.

They were everywhere. Here in the building where she resided, in the streets of the Vieux Carre, in the bar where she worked, and all points between. They were especially thick in the Square as she passed by going to the market on Royal or on her way to work. They were around her and they wanted her attention.

The readers in the Square, the authentic ones, saw them gathering around her. They would wave to Wavery offering to read the Tarot for her, but she would look at them stoically declining. As soon as she made eye contact with the reader, they recognized Wavery's ability to see what they saw around her and would simply nod in commiseration.

Many years ago, Wavery had been trained to read as well but with something beyond the typical Tarot cards. Eventually, Wavery rarely needed any divination tools because her abilities became well-honed, and her mind's eye did all the work.

Wavery could remember a time when she relished her innate abilities. However, it became uncomfortable when folks began to call on her to perform on call like a circus act. They also couldn't understand her reluctance to tell them exactly what she saw, especially when she knew it might be something they didn't want to hear, even if they needed to hear it.

By the time she had finished high school and the first few years of her undergraduate, Wavery was done with either being asked to perform on demand or with being treated as a freak show. She felt it would have been simpler to just stick with her divination tool if she did anything at all. That way she could box it up and put it away. Blame the tool for what showed up and what did not.

A chill ran over Wavery's body, and she felt the nausea rise to her throat when she remembered the last time she had used the glass pieces to delve into a situation. A situation that had best been left alone. The result had been more devastating to her than simply being labeled a freak. It had changed so many lives other than her own. The community loss and pain and her family's loss and pain were` just too much for her. So, she carefully packed the glass pieces in an old box and vowed to never use them again.

In the end, she decided to box herself up and step away from anyone who knew the gift she had been given. The easy part was moving thousands of miles away to a place no one knew her. The hard part was coming to an understanding that you can't hide yourself in a tightly bound box. The knots eventually begin to unravel, and you are left seeing yourself well before others see you.

As much as Wavery tried to push away the dreams and the memories of her gift, she knew something was afoot and soon would show itself. But for now, she would continue her self-prescribed method for dealing with her anxiety: physical activity and work. She would continue to push herself in every way possible to tire out her body in hopes her sleep would become dreamless. Her daily schedule included a run in the morning, plugging away at her graduate studies at Tulane, and working in the bar. Maybe she could find a way to add an extra run or two in somewhere.

Wavery dressed quickly and slipped on her running shoes. She grabbed her keys and her phone off the dresser and headed out the door. As the door clicked behind her, a figure slipped out of the shadowed corner of the apartment and moved in a gray mist to the dresser. The figure reached out a gossamer finger and touched the tiny bottle attached to a silver chain dangling from the mirror. She moved to the window watching the young woman run down the street she herself would never walk again.

Toulouse Street was still quiet on this Monday morning as Wavery began a slow jog toward the river. As badly as she wanted the physical activity to push away the thoughts in her mind, it seemed to work the opposite way this morning. The sweet thoughts of her childhood came flowing through her mind. It had been an idyllic time when she was surrounded by those who wanted nothing but good for her and wanted nothing but love from her. Wavery let the memories lift her feet as her body moved swiftly through the streets toward the water.

Wavery finished her run through the Quarter and returned to her building in somewhat record time. She had pushed herself to finish the run as quickly as she could. She wanted to avoid the oncoming heat of late morning plus she was working a double shift at the bar today. Wavery unlocked the entry gate and door to the building. She entered the cool stone breezeway of the building and met one of the other tenants from her floor. She hoped her sweating body was not off-putting.

Glen, her neighbor, was always neat as a pin and smelled heavenly. His partner, Conrad, was a lucky guy. The couple had moved to New Orleans several years ago, working in different restaurants. They had worked and saved until they were able to open their own small eatery serving soups, sandwiches, and gelato. Tourists could find a quick and affordable small plate that would stave off their hunger until it was time for a night out on the town. Locals were really turning out for them as well. The carriage drivers often had standing orders for lunch. So much so that Glen had hired a couple of Tulane students to bike around delivering to the drivers and others who worked the shops nearby.

Wavery, was quite the loner, but somehow a friendship of sorts had blossomed between her and the couple from the floor above. Glen spoke briefly before rushing out to the eatery. Wavery continued her own hasty dash to her apartment for a shower.

After showering, Wavery walked over to the dresser with the mirror to begin her quick make-up routine. No need to overdo it with the expected humidity. She reached for the tube of mascara that rolled out of her bag and glanced up to look at her reflection in the mirror. Her breath caught in her throat. In the mirror, she could see the outline of someone. The figure stood with an outstretched hand.

Wavery wasn't frightened. It happened so quickly and naturally that she simply followed the line of direction of the hand and pointing finger. The figure was pointing toward the chain hanging over the corner of the mirror. Wavery reached out to touch the gift that had come from her grandmother. She had not worn the necklace in years, but she always kept it in sight. Since moving to the apartment, she had been careful to hang it so that the bottle charm would not bounce against the mirror avoiding any accidental breaking of the bottle or the mirror.

Looking closely, Wavery saw that the bottle was resting boldly against the mirror. It caught the sunlight flowing through the gauzy curtains on the tall French door windows leading out to the balcony. A rainbow of light sparkles reflected throughout the room. Wavery had not moved the necklace since the last time she had dusted and that had been quite a while.

Wavery gently wrapped her fingers around the charm bottle that held a tiny piece of amber brown glass. She looked into the mirror and over her shoulder. The figure she had seen was gone, but the feeling that she was supposed to do something was firmly implanted. She touched the necklace again. Was she supposed to put it on? A feeling grew inside her. Words, not her own, danced through her mind.

"No, the other glass. You know where it is. It is almost time."

Wavery walked to the front window of the dressing room and looked up. A bed loft with a ladder had been built into the old apartment a few years before she had moved to the city. Wavery, had no family or friends who would need to make use of it, so she had never purchased a mattress for it. Instead, she used it as a place of storage.

Wavery found herself hypnotically drawn to the short ladder and was up in the loft with barely a thought. She found the cardboard banker's box toward the back wall. She gently removed the lid and pushed the tissue paper away from a bubble wrapped wooden box. She unlatched the box and pulled out a drawstring bag made of age-stained linen. She knew exactly what was inside. Eleven pieces of amber glass. Wavery could remember a time when she would "throw" the glass pieces across a quilted piece of cloth just as her grandmother had taught her. Her grandmother guided her to read them as easily as reading a child's picture book.

She didn't have to throw them today. She didn't want details. Not yet. She instinctively knew something was about to happen that would change things for so many people. Strangely, that knowing held no fear for her and for now that was enough.

Wavery climbed back down the ladder and walked back to the dresser. She took the necklace carefully from the corner of the mirrored dresser and placed the chain around her neck. Wavery tucked the small glass charm bottle inside her white cotton shirt. Only she would know it was there. The charm nestled well below her neckline and against the center of her chest. She felt as if a spark was trying to warm the cold wall that had been surrounding her heart. Was it the amber glass and its magic? Or was it the visitor who seemed to be floating around her apartment moving her things around and trying to get her attention?

Wavery grabbed her purse and headed out the door for work. As she closed her door, she popped her head around the corner and spoke quietly,

"I know you're there. It's okay, as long as you behave yourself. Don't move my necklace again."

Wavery walked down Toulouse and made her way to Chartres and toward the Square. She didn't feel the need to avoid the area nor the need to avert her eyes from anyone or anything. Perhaps she *was* ready to see what was to come.

Ann was livid. She wasn't sure which one of her know-it- all brothers were to blame, maybe all of them. She had specifically told Jack and Luke, her two youngest

brothers, not to put her special bag inside the small moving van. She wanted to carry it with her on the drive to New Orleans. She could only suppose her brothers thought there was plenty of room in the van since at this point, she had very little furniture to move. She was only taking the basics: a bed, a comfy chair, some lamps, a small dining table, and chairs. The van also held all her personal tools and special keepsakes passed on to her by the grandmothers. Everything else she would find once she was sure she was living in an area that appealed to her most.

Ann had watched the van roll out of sight barely an hour ago, trusting that her brothers had followed her directions. Hopefully, they had at least placed the special bag in the cab of the truck. When would she learn?

Luke and Jack would be getting a text from her in about an hour giving them the address of the location they were to unload her belongings when they arrived. It would be their turn to be livid.

Ann was tapping her foot impatiently when Gray, her oldest brother, came down the front steps carrying his travel bags. Gray was headed back to New Orleans and his two-bedroom house near the school where he was training. He had convinced Ann to tag along with him on the drive. He was hoping the long drive would give him enough time to convince her to move into his house with him on a permanent basis. He had already been chipping away at her over the last few days and Ann had placated him with the promise to think about his offer.

Little did Gray know that she had already signed a lease for a place in the Marigny. She had shared her plans for living arrangements with her parents and they completely understood her need for independence. None of her brothers would like the fact that she was not living with or near Gray, but they would have to deal with it. Ann looked over to her oldest brother. Gray had to learn that he was not the overall caretaker for any of the siblings. All three of her brothers needed to finally come to an understanding that she was a fully capable adult able to care for herself.

Ann thought back on the years growing up when she had worked so hard to try and convince the males in the family that she was always capable of keeping up with her brothers and that she could take care of herself. The boys had finally begun to wean themselves just a bit from their constant hovering once she had settled into the university.

As she grew older, she also tried to demonstrate her capability for working side by side with her brothers and father in the family business. Ann's plans had always been to work a few years under her father's tutelage and then be ready to strike out on her own in a location a distance away from her dad and brothers. She was more than surprised when Gray ended up beating her to the punch.

A couple of years ago, Gray had finally been forced to admit to himself that the family business was not for him. He was exceptional at every aspect of the restoration process, but it wasn't his true passion. Just as Ann had been Nana Grace's and Nona's shadow learning the ways of healing passed down from their respective lines, Gray had watched and learned all the delectable recipes from those respective lines as well.

Ann loved watching her oldest brother lose himself in the kitchen amongst stew pots and spices. Ann especially liked to watch him out of the corner of her eye when he served and waited for the family to taste his latest dish. While he wanted the entire family to enjoy his preparations, he was most attentive to the reaction the grandmothers shared with him. Their approval meant the world to him.

One evening after a particularly great dinner, their dad, Joe, asked Gray to follow him out to the workshop behind the house,

Gray stood nervously at the door while his father settled back in the creaky old desk chair smiling smugly.

"You know Gray, there was only one thing wrong with that meal."

"Sir?" Gray questioned apprehensively,

"Yep, Gray, the one wrong thing is that you weren't serving it to more than our family. I know that the grans have taught you everything they know about cooking regionally, but I think it's time that you take your next step."

Gray swallowed loudly, "Next step? I don't understand."

Joe pushed back the chair and put his hands on his oldest son's shoulders.

"Son, you need to open a restaurant. As smart and talented as you are, I think a bit more professional training is a step you should consider before getting your own restaurant open for business."

With that, Joe walked over to the filing cabinet, opened a drawer, and pulled out a handful of brochures for culinary training programs across the country. A year later,

Gray found himself living and working as a line cook in New Orleans while training in culinary studies at the local community college.

Gray had been in New Orleans for almost a year when he found out that Ann was coming to town to open a branch of Rossi Restorations all on her own. Surprisingly, he took the news of Ann's move in stride. His acceptance of the situation went a long way in calming the younger brothers' fear about their little sister's new endeavor. Gray clearly understood everything that the grandmothers and even their mother had taught Ann about the world. He understood, more than the younger brothers, that the skills and gifts Ann had cultivated under the guidance of the grandmothers would help her both professionally and personally. Their mother had stated it perfectly,

"Ann's small but she's mighty and she is forever protected by those even mightier."

Gray looked back one last time at the Rossi house before Ann and he turned the corner heading to the interstate. He saw that his sister's eyes were glassy with unshed tears. She had to make a tiny gulp before she could speak.

"Thanks for not teasing me. I thought it would be easy to leave because I am so excited about this new job. I really think it would have been less emotional if mama hadn't given me that gift."

Gray looked over at the small box Ann was clutching in her hands. He knew that his curious little sister was aching to tear away the silky blue ribbon to look inside. He also could tell that opening the box might start an avalanche of tears. Gray was a strong man and could take just about anything in stride. Except his sister's tears, even if they were happy ones.

"You know mama said not to open it until we were at least an hour on the road. Are you going to be able to do that or will the unknown push you to the edge," Gray asked laughing trying to lighten the mood.

"Usually I wouldn't be able to contain myself but something mama whispered to me tells me there is a good reason to wait."

"Really? What was that? Or can't you tell me this time?"

Gray had been privy over the years to some of the lessons the Grans had taught to Ann. Some of the magic of the wisdom they shared with Ann required a grand amount of patience and faith. The younger brothers had never been around to overhear the lessons. Even as much as the younger boys loved the Grans, their interests in girls, sports, and work kept them out of the house and out of the kitchen where the most wonderful things were conjured.

"Mama said that the item in the box had a connection to Nona and Grace. That it would offer me a place to keep my hidden treasure *and* protection for me while away from home. I think she didn't want to see me cry when I saw it. Maybe she didn't want to cry either."

Gray found himself almost as eager as Ann just thinking about what was inside the box. The Grans never did do anything halfway. Everything they ever did or said always had an underlying meaning.

It was a bit over an hour before the siblings stopped for a break and a cold drink. Gray offered to stay inside the rest area while Ann opened the box, but she wanted him with her for support. The two took their drinks and went to sit on a bench under an old pine tree to open the box.

Ann tenderly removed the silky blue ribbon and pulled the top of the gift box off and laid it to the side. Inside she found a small square of stationery with her mother's graceful cursive script. She slid the note to the side as well and pulled back the translucent tissue paper. Nestled inside the delicate wrapping she found a beautiful silver chain with one charm attached. The charm had been etched on the front and the back with a strange set of marks. They looked like the symbols of a language of sorts. The charm looked like a small puff or silver bubble. Upon closer inspection, Ann could see that the top part of the circle could be twisted off and that the inside was a hollow that could hold a small object.

Ann took the note and quietly read the words out loud to her brother:

Dear Ann,

Your grans asked me to pass this gift to you when you were finally ready to strike out on your own. Your grans and I know you have the knowledge needed to protect yourself and others if need be. Even though they seemed overprotective at times, your father and brothers have shown you how to stand up for yourself physically. The Gran taught you well in calling upon those mightier than us for care and protection. I hope that I was able to help you learn how to maneuver the physical world just as your Grans have given you the knowledge to make your way through the spiritual world.

More importantly, the Grans felt you needed to have something of them to remind you that you are never alone. The chain was a gift from Grandpa Tony to Nona. Nona said it was to show you that you will always have a connection to family and home. The charm is from Grace. It was a charm that you might have noticed her wearing throughout the years. Sam had given it to her. She wanted me to tell you that she had the etchings engraved just for you.

I have no idea exactly what they say, but she said they would always connect you to your spirit and the spirits that protect you wherever you go. Grace also said to tell you that the amber glass now has a home. She said you should know what she meant, but just in case to remind you of the piece that you hid in your pink shorts once upon a time.

Nona and Grace were adamant that you weren't to have this gift until I was sure that you were ready to make your way in the world on your own. I am sure. Just know that home will always be here for you, but also know that the women of this family, past and present, stand behind you no matter where you settle.

Love,

Mama

Ann's breath caught in her throat. She knew exactly which piece of glass Grace meant. It and the broken amber bottle was somewhere in her treasure box, hidden down in the depths of the bag she had asked her brothers not to put in the trunk.

Only she and Grace had ever witnessed the fiery sparks that seemed to emit from that tiny shard of glass broken from the bottle. Grace had helped her to understand that some spirit had placed energy into the bottle that Ann found in the wall all those years ago. Even the small piece of glass that had broken from the bottle's neck held a great deal of energy.

Grace had assured Ann that the energy was neither good nor bad. But it could be manipulated by Ann if she wished. It was her choice how she would interact with it. Ann had never been wary of anything that Grace had taught her within the conjure world. She knew how to respect the energies, but the bottle had not come from Grace, so Ann was especially careful with it. She had kept the bottle and tiny piece of glass secure for all these years without much thought. Out of sight, out of mind as the adage conveyed.

Grace had told her that one day she would recognize when the time had arrived to take the shard of glass out of hiding. Ann knew that the time had come.

Gray looked over with tears in his eyes and wondered how in the word Ann could look so stoic. He gave her a second look and decided that look on her face wasn't stoic at all. She looked mad and he wanted to know why.

"Ann, you look angry. Are you mad at mama or the Grans for waiting so long to give you the necklace?"

Ann looked at Gray, shocked that he could think such a thing. They began walking back to the car.

"No, I am mad at those doofus brothers of ours. They took my special bag and put it in the moving truck when I clearly told them not to do it. "

Gray popped the electronic locks open, and Ann slid into the passenger side. She began texting her brothers to see how far ahead they were, hoping she and Gray could catch up with them. She wanted to retrieve her bag.

Gray opened the driver's side door and held out a woven bag towards Ann.

"You mean this bag?" Gray asked smiling ear to ear.

Ann sat gaping at the brilliance of her brother. He explained he had grabbed the bag just as Luke began to toss it into the cab of the truck. Ann dug through the bag to find her treasure box. Once she had the box in her hands, she retrieved the amber shard that was wrapped in a linen handkerchief.

Gray glanced over as she pulled back the embroidered cloth and watched in awe as tiny sparks of firelight shot from the amber. Ann seemed unfazed by the magical light. He watched as Ann uncapped the hollow charm and placed the amber fragment inside. She tightly recapped the charm and held out the necklace to Gray. His hands were almost shaking as Ann lifted her dark hair. He helped to secure the clasp of the chain at the back of her neck. Small but mighty. His mother had spoken the truth. His sister was indeed protected by those even mightier.

All But The Blood

Chapter 20

June was proving to be an exciting month for Meg. She had settled into a studio apartment on lower Bourbon Street close to Esplanade. It was a perfect size for her needs with a well-appointed kitchenette that she could hide by pulling pocket doors. The small bathroom did not have a window, but it was clean and brightly colored in yellow and white ceramic tile reminding her of a chic 1940s style. The open living area came furnished with a table that could be used for dining or work. Meg had placed the table in front of a wall of brick original to the building. The owner of the building, who was an alum of Tulane, had provided the apartment for visiting instructors. He generously allowed her to pick out new seating and a bed.

Meg decided to go with an antique twin bedframe from a local shop. Choosing a twin frame allowed her enough room to include a love seat and a wing back chair with a foot stool. The apartment owner picked up the items and made the delivery along with two of his sons. By the end of the delivery, Meg somehow found herself trading cell numbers with the two at the insistence of their father. The older man had slyly suggested she might need their contacts in case she ever found herself needing some type of assistance. Meg had wondered if the man was trying to play matchmaker. She decided to think of it as southern hospitality and waved them off with her thanks.

Meg had always been a creature of habit and that didn't change now that she was in New Orleans. Every morning she was up early enough to have her coffee on her balcony as she watched the street cleaners plowing away the previous night's party leftovers. She then quickly

234

dressed, locked up, and scurried down the two flights of steps to walk through the stone hallway leading out to the street. After locking the gated entrance that she shared with the other residents of the building, Meg made a quick right on Bourbon and turned up Saint Ann towards Rampart. There she would catch the first streetcar that would carry her to work.

Her work routine varied only slightly. Her Monday, Tuesday, Thursday, and Friday mornings were dedicated to assisting Dr. Gallo. Wednesday mornings, she worked on her own research, sometimes at the University and sometimes at other locations. Each afternoon and the weekends were her own time.

Meg had decided that one of favorite things about the city was riding on the St. Charles streetcar. The morning and afternoon rides provided her with the opportunity to see something new every day. She loved looking at the old houses as the ivy green car rattled ahead and then stopped for folks to climb on and off. Meg had begun to recognize familiar faces who were regulars in both the morning and afternoons. It hadn't taken long for shared smiles and brief nods to be exchanged. The people in New Orleans were truly the heartbeat of the city.

Meg recalled the morning she was looking out the half-open window of the streetcar and noticed an old house that captured her eye. It was not the largest on the route but there was something about it that nudged her curiosity. Maybe it was because it seemed to have been a bit forgotten. The front steps looked a bit rickety, and the paint was peeling all around. The landscaping certainly needed attention. Actually, she would bet both the inside and outside could use a little extra love. She wondered who had lived there before and why no one seemed to be living there now.

Mid-June arrived and with it the overheard chatter about the horrid heat coming in July and August. Her fellow passengers on the streetcar wondered aloud as to what the tropics might bring their way in terms of storms and hurricanes. Meg herself wondered what would happen to "her" seemingly abandoned house on Saint Charles if the storms did come.

Meg stopped listening to the conversations going on around her and looked out toward the house in question. She was surprised to see a landscaping company hard at work in the early morning hours. The foreman of the group was speaking with a lady and pointing around the large yard. The petite woman was dressed in a chic summer frock with matching sandals. She had long dark hair held back off her face with a headband that matched the fabric of her dress. Meg supposed that this must be an owner of the house there to give directions to the crew. Meg found herself feeling jealous that someone besides herself had the privilege of owning this beautifully mysterious house. At the same time though, she was thankful that the home finally had someone to take care of it.

Meg monitored the home's rehabilitation progress every day on her way to work. She was more than excited to see loads of materials being delivered signaling the beginning of work on the inside of the house. Not long after her first sighting of the well-dressed owner, Meg saw someone on the porch holding what appeared to be blueprints giving instructions to a crew of big burly men. The smaller person was dressed in jeans, a white shirt, work boots, and a baseball cap. Meg could see a long dark ponytail of hair pulled through the back opening of the cap. Meg blinked and recognized that this was the same petite woman from before. Just then the woman looked up and saw Meg peering out of the window of the streetcar with her mouth slightly ajar. The young woman looked at Meg, waved, smiled, and then went right back to work.

Every day, Meg ensured she was positioned on the streetcar so that could clearly watch the progress being made on the old house. Some days she saw the woman and some days she did not. Every time she did see her, the woman was obviously working as hard as any men on the crew. She seemed as capable as any of them at using any of the power tools strewn about, but she also seemed to be the one in charge. Even not knowing this woman, Meg was intensely proud of her accomplishments. She was also still a bit jealous of whoever had the right to call ownership of the house. For whatever reason, Meg felt a strong connection to the lovely old home. Over the weeks leading into July, Meg saw the female supervisor less and less and wondered if she had moved on to another job.

June had also found Meg changing some of her own personal routine. As the afternoons grew warmer, she found herself walking around a lot less. More of her time was spent browsing the used bookstores and reading in the various coffee shops around the Quarter.

One Monday afternoon on the way back to her apartment, she decided to stop by the Rouses on Royal for a few groceries. She was going down the sundry aisle making her way towards the front counter when she looked down and saw a stack of spiral notebooks. Without hesitation, she picked up a couple with black covers along with a pack of fine line pens and headed to the check-out.

The next morning, her office time seemed to drag along. She loved her work with Dr. Gallo's students, and she loved being immersed in her own research but today she felt something different calling her. An idea had been building in her head since she first learned of Daniel and Sam's quest. There was a flurry of excitement building inside and she found herself hoping for a quick streetcar ride home. She simply couldn't wait to pick up her bag with the newly purchased notebooks and head out to a coffee shop.

By the time Meg arrived at her apartment, changed clothes, and grabbed her bag of notebooks along with her laptop, she could hear the unexpected sound of thunder rolling about in the sky back toward the lake. The weatherman had broken his promise of a clear but breezy afternoon. Meg grabbed an umbrella before scurrying out to the street.

The change in weather did not stop Meg. It only solidified her decision to spend the afternoon at her favorite coffee shop on Royal. The shop was close to her apartment and Meg loved the view from the windows and the seating. It also afforded her the ability to either use her notebook or transcribe and write using her laptop. It was perfect for rainy afternoons.

Meg's daily routine extended into an afternoon of writing and then returning to her apartment to prepare whatever she needed for work the next day and pulling together an early evening meal. Unless the weather was abhorrent, Meg would also take an after-dinner stroll as the sun was setting. As a lone woman, her walks would keep her within the confines of the Quarter's busiest and well-lit areas.

Meg especially loved this time of the evening when day workers were making their way home and visitors were popping out for a bite before going dancing or to music venues. Meg loved people watching but more than that, she loved what she felt and experienced at the twilight hour.

Her favorite place to be at that time was just in front of the cathedral. Meg would stand there quietly facing the Central Business District as the day faded into night. She watched as the lights of the high rises in the distance blinked against the darkening sky. The Quarter came alive in a totally different dimension. At that pivotal point in time, Meg questioned which world was real. Was it the world out there beyond Canal? Or was it here with just old spirits, broken sidewalks, and the languid flow of the Mississippi River? If Meg had a choice to live in just one world or the other, she knew which one she would choose.

July started with a strong blast of heat on the very first day. Travelers coming into the city for fireworks and festivals were certainly going to feel the effects. So far, there had been no mention of impending hurricanes. Meg was glad, not just for herself, but for the native New Orleanians who had endured the devastation of Katrina. Meg had decided to take the first week of July off from work. She had thought about a quick visit to Virginia, but her parents were off on a camping vacation with their best friends. So, Meg remained in New Orleans and decided to play tourist.

Meg was not used to the Louisiana summer heat so she gave herself grace and made all the visits she could to inside attractions. She went to all the museums across the city during the hottest parts of the afternoon, taking advantage of the gloriously air-conditioned buildings. She took a taxi over to the New Orleans Museum of Art at City Park and she toured the Audubon Aquarium amid the laughter of visiting children.

When Meg wasn't playing tourist, she found herself back at the coffee shop writing. This short vacation schedule enabled her to visit the coffee shop on Royal in the early morning each day. Once she arrived, she would quickly grab a coffee and seat herself by a window. There she would sit for hours furiously tapping away at the keyboard of her laptop, barely looking up.

If Meg had taken a moment to glance up, she would have noticed the tall blonde woman who jogged by each morning and passed again later dressed for work. She would have also noticed a more familiar person. The young woman with long dark hair from her favorite house on St. Charles. She walked by frequently. Had Meg been looking up, she would have seen the dark-haired woman peering into the coffee shop, noticing Meg with her head bent over her computer. She would have seen the questioning look on the small woman's face seemingly asking, "Where have I seen her before?"

As the week moved on, Meg realized that the number of visitors crowding into town was increasing as the holiday approached. People were driving and flying in for the Fourth Of July celebration as well as the upcoming music festival. Meg, neither a native nor a tourist at this point, wanted to be respectful of those who wanted to find a nice place to sit and have some iced coffee or tea. So, she started her morning writing sessions at the café early and ended them by noon, heading back to her apartment or out to one of the museums.

On Wednesday afternoon, Meg could feel her nerves tingling and she uncharacteristically wanted to be out among the people in the Quarter. Temperatures were still climbing, and she was craving something cold to drink. She decided to head out to find a place to sit for just a bit and enjoy a cold beverage. Just as she was locking the door to her apartment, she decided to step back inside for her canvas bag, her "writing bag" as she now dubbed it. She pulled out her laptop and locked it in her closet, making sure she had her notebooks and pens. Coming out of her apartment building, she turned toward the Marigny neighborhood, hoping the crowds there would be slightly less.

Meg could hear the clip clop of mules' hooves as they ferried tourists all around the Quarter. As Meg made her way down Bourbon toward Esplanade, she saw some of the carriages decorated in plastic flowers and ribbons. Sometimes the mule would be as well.

Meg knew that many of the carriages made a stop at Lafitte's, along with some of the groups on the evening ghost tours. Both the carriages and the tours brought a nice spot of business to one of the oldest operating bars in the United States. Meg often passed by the bar on her evening walks. The nights brought larger crowds and she had never felt the desire to go in on her own. Today as she passed by, she could see several open tables by the windows. There were very few smokers in the chairs along the front wall and side patio. It was probably too hot for them to give into their vice under the blazing hot sun.

Meg could feel her own perspiration starting to drip between her should blades. It really didn't make sense to walk the rest of the distance to the Marigny in this heat and humidity. Meg turned and headed into Lafitte's.

Meg walked through the open front door into the stone building and felt the sudden change in temperature. The small windows and the thick stone provided an age-old coolant method, but there was also some modern air conditioning and fans working away to provide comfort for the employees and patrons.

Meg walked up to the bar wondering what she should order that would be refreshing and not overly strong. She looked up to see a cylindrical barrel churning away behind the bar. The sign above the container labeled the concoction as a Voodoo Daiquiri. Inside the container was a swirling blend of dark purple. It reminded Meg of the icy slush machines at the local gas stations back home. Looking at the rhythmic spinning of the concoction was almost hypnotic. Meg knew instantly she was having a taste of that magical purple drink.

Wavery watched from the other end of the bar where she was mixing a to-go drink as Jimmy pulled a cup full of Voodoo Daiquiri for the woman with a canvas bag and a blue and gold baseball cap plopped on her head. The woman had pulled her sunglasses off as she entered the door looking around. Wavery guessed she had never been here before or was looking for someone. Wavery squinted her eyes a bit trying to get a better look. She was sure she had seen her before, but where? She squinted a bit harder and then she knew.

This was the woman in the coffee shop on Royal that she had seen bent over a laptop. She looked just slightly behind her and saw him. She was right. It was the same woman. He had been bent over her shoulder in the coffee shop too. She wondered if the woman had any idea that she was being "followed." Wavery shrugged her shoulders to no one and decided it was best she minded her own business.

Meg could see the female bartender out of the corner of her eye. The woman working behind the bar seemed to briefly concentrate on her, and then look over to her fellow bartender grabbing the purple delight. Then the staring woman quickly dismissed them both. Meg paid for her drink and tipped the pleasant man serving her. She walked over to a small table at a far window where the heat of sunlight was dappled by a Myrtle plant growing outside.

Meg took a couple of long sips through her straw. The drink was sweet and refreshingly cold. It seemed to be a quiet afternoon for the bar, so she didn't feel guilty pulling out her notebook and writing until at least her drink was finished. She took a few sips in between putting her thoughts down on paper. The delicious drink truly tasted like the gas station slushy of her youth. Maybe she would have one more and stay for a bit longer to write.

Meg was bent over her notebook when she felt the words coming through her pen in a furious manner. She wanted to slow her brain down to let her hand with the pen catch up with the words that were flowing from…

somewhere. Meg felt like she was taking dictation from someone whispering in her ear. She just couldn't seem to write the words fast enough.

Over at the bar, Wavery watched the woman at the table. She didn't mean to watch but she just couldn't seem to help herself. She watched him, too. The same man had been with the "writer girl" at the coffee house. She watched as the man bent close and just to the right side of the woman's head. Occasionally, he would stand straight and nod with a smile. Then he would lean in close once more.

Wavery felt sure the woman in the baseball cap had no idea he was there. Wavery purposely blurred her vision and then refocused her eyes looking deep within the man's space. She saw that he meant no harm to the woman, but he needed something from her. Was he able to sense that Wavery could see him? Did he even care?

Wavery chastised herself for stepping into someone else's business. What in the world was she doing? Had she not learned her lesson about using her tools and gifts long ago? She walked over to Jimmy, the other bartender, and asked him to switch bar sides with her. She didn't want to tempt herself into continuing to watch the peculiar situation over at "writer girl's" table.

The bartenders at Lafitte's weren't exceptionally busy on this steamy Wednesday afternoon. So much so that Meg didn't even have to go back up to the bar for order number two. Jimmy came over to her table to ask if she would like another. Within moments, he had brought back the second drink and they introduced themselves and struck up a brief conversation.

Jimmy told Meg that Wednesday afternoons were almost always slower than other days regardless of the weather. It was an in-between time for visitors coming in and going back out of the city. He told her that a lot of locals chose Wednesday nights to come by so they could avoid the crowded tourist times. When it was this hot, Wednesday afternoons were especially slow. Meg immediately decided she would be writing here on Wednesday afternoons. She wasn't sure what was going on, but this space felt very conducive to her writing.

Halfway through the second purple drink, she could feel a difference in her body. She reached up to her nose and it felt slightly numb. Dang, there couldn't be that much alcohol in the purple stuff! Jimmy walked by and she asked about the ingredients. She was shocked to learn exactly how many kinds of alcohol were camouflaged by the sweet grape flavor. She took one last sip and pushed the Styrofoam cup away. If she finished the rest, she might not be able to walk home. She laughed to herself. Wonder if this was what Dr. Peabody was thinking when he suggested she should go out and have a little fun?

A concerning thought flittered through Meg's head. What if it had been the drink that prompted the furious writing spree? She certainly was no Hemmingway, and she definitely didn't want to mimic his choice to rely on alcohol as a muse. Little did Meg realize that it wasn't that type of spirit that had contributed to such a productive afternoon of writing.

Wavery watched as the woman carried her two cups to the trash bin by the bar. She tipped Jimmy and waved goodbye. Wavery hesitated only briefly before dashing to the door to see which direction the woman walked. She saw the woman walking up the sidewalk facing the Central Business District, the CBD. The figure of the man was walking behind and slightly to her left. Anyone, especially men, who walked too close to the woman suddenly looked around as if something or someone had touched them. Then they instinctively moved away from her. The figure of the man that Wavery could see was actually trying to protect her. Wavery told herself that it was still none of her business, but still she let go a sigh of relief.

The hazy figure of the man turned suddenly and looked straight at Wavery. Did he see her? She hesitantly lifted her hand in a wave. Wavery saw his hand lift in return. Dammit. Wavery chastised herself again. Why couldn't she just have let it go? Wavery turned around and headed back to work.

Once Meg got back to her apartment, she sprawled across her bed for a short nap. She blamed her sudden sleepiness on the heat and not the drinks at Lafitte's. Once awake, she took a shower and decided to venture out onto her balcony now that the hot evening sun was setting. Meg decided that spending the evening on her balcony that night would be entertaining so she pulled a folding camp chair out of her closet. Just a few steps from her building were two music clubs on either side of the street. Both loud and boisterous. Meg watched as folks went back and forth up the street and into these clubs. People were out living their lives and having fun.

By the end of the evening, Meg had made a few decisions for herself. First, it was time to start having some fun herself and only she could decide what that would look like. Second, the story she was writing needed to be told. She reveled in thoughts of hours spent in coffee shops, by the river, or even on this balcony taking in the spirit of place as the story unfurled. She especially looked forward to a return to Lafitte's on Wednesday afternoons to see what other breakthroughs might happen. She laughed to herself. Only one caveat. There had to be a one purple drink limit while writing.

Luckily, the remainder of July cooled down from boiling hot to seasonably hot. For a mountain girl that was still saying something. Meg was thankful for the mornings spent in the well-air-conditioned offices at Tulane. She was equally thankful for any breeze that flowed through the windows of the streetcar as she looked out to the sights on the ride home in the afternoons.

Meg decided that the work on the special house on St. Charles Avenue must be close to being wrapped up. She didn't see half as many construction trucks parked there anymore. She also hadn't seen the young female construction boss around either. Meg secretly wished her well and hoped she had moved on to making yet another house feel appreciated.

Meg had purchased a small outside table and chairs for her balcony. The addition to the balcony made morning coffee a real treat plus she was having lots of fun sitting there in the cool of the evening. She was surprised, when one night, she looked down to the street below and saw the dark-haired woman from the St. Charles construction site.

The woman was walking with a tall man by her side. Meg assumed this was her boyfriend or husband. Meg caught herself being especially nosey when she leaned over attempting to see if either one of them had a ring on their left hand. Just then, the woman looked up at Meg. There was a moment of recognition as the small woman smiled up at Meg before moving along with the man by her side.

Meg thought to herself that for such a large city this was really a small place. Several nights later while sitting out watching the comings and goings, she saw the woman once again. This time walking from the direction of the Marigny. The petite woman was looking up at the balcony as if she were searching for Meg. Meg peeped over the banister and gave a tentative wave. The young woman stopped under the balcony and tilted her head as if deep in thought.

Suddenly, with a bright smile she gently popped herself on the forehead and called up to Meg,

"I got it! You are the one from the streetcar!"

Meg felt slightly embarrassed but relaxed when the young woman continued,

"I am so glad I remembered where I saw you. You seemed to like the house we were working on! I hope you have gotten to see the work in completion!"

Meg smiled back,

"Yes, I pass by just about every day on my way to work. It looks so much better. It looks like it is loved again."

Ann loved that this stranger could feel the spirit of the house and its need to be cared for and maintained. She wondered if the woman on the balcony would like to see the inside and so she made an offer.

"The owners are coming into town later in the month. After I have their final approval, you could come by and take a tour of the inside. I've been doing a couple of other projects but will be going back to the St. Charles site on a regular basis— at least until the final meeting with the owners. Once you see the work complete statement on our advertising sign in the yard, stop by and ask for me, Ann Rossi. I'll take you on a tour."

Meg couldn't believe how exciting the offer sounded. She quickly introduced herself and shared that she worked at Tulane. The two women continued their conversation for a few minutes longer before Ann had to remind herself that she was headed to the restaurant where her brother worked. Meg waved good-bye as Ann sashayed up the street.

An hour or so later, Meg left her balcony and closed the tall French doors. She closed the drapes that helped to block out the lights and sounds from the revelers in the street below. The drapes didn't help with the base sound thumping through the walls from the club on her side of the street, so she turned on the turbo fan she had purchased for ambient noise. With the help of the fan, the thumping of the music became more like a heartbeat that lulled Meg to sleep each night. Meg settled down among her fluffy pillows giving a prayerful thanks for all the good things in her life including finding what just might turn out to be a new friend.

It was a sultry ride on the streetcar that Tuesday morning. Everyone seemed a bit grumpy about the humidity as they got on and off at their various stops. Meg had to learn to deal with the humidity on more than one level. It was bad enough that every outfit was more than a bit damp when arriving at work but what truthfully bothered Meg was her hair.

Curly, wavy, slightly coarse, and thick. Most women would beg for a head of hair like hers. Meg had been raised to be grateful for everything. But she had to admit that this climate made it hard in regard to her hair. To say the least, her hair was not her best friend right now. Meg could not find a hair product except for a massively strong hair spray that would help. If she used that, she ended up looking like a horrendous caricature of a 1960s beehive. So, she found she had only a few choices. Hair oil and ponytail or hair oil and a bun for the workplace. A hat for casual times.

This morning she had chosen to put her hair up in a tight bun but the humidity was so extreme that she felt like every strand was ready to escape and stick out as if she had been electrocuted. Once she made it inside the building, she would take a few minutes to herself and fortify the mess that was ready to explode.

Her department at Tulane was mostly filled with men this summer. The female staff were working remotely or off on sabbatical for the next couple of months, so she really didn't have anyone that she could ask about such things as hair and humidity. Maybe she could ask Ann or the blonde bartender at Lafitte's for their secrets dealing with the humidity. The thought made Meg smile and feel like she was making new friends. Meg's smile faded quickly. On second thought, maybe not the bartender. She really hadn't been all that friendly. In fact, Meg remembered looking up to see the blonde watching her with a strained look.

Meg had been working at her desk for barely an hour when her cell phone rang in with a familiar tone. Dr. John Peabody was on the other end. Meg blew her unruly humidity-swollen bangs out of her eyes and accepted the call.

"Good morning, Dr. Pe…. John." Meg wondered if she would ever feel truly comfortable calling her former professor and mentor by his first name. She supposed that was a right of adulthood but all the same.

"Good morning, Ms. Hur… Meg." John Peabody was nothing if not sharp and quick on the draw. He laughed out loud at his own attempt to make a joke about their greeting and continued, "How goes the sultry city today?"

Meg reached up to the curly frizz that was again escaping her once tightly wound bun.

"Oh, she is sultry all right as evidenced by my hair from the ride in to work. How goes it back in the mountains?"

"Not as humid here, I am sure. We've only had a few hot days so far. Just wanted to give you a heads up. The wife and I have decided to brave your humidity and venture on down to experience a bit of the sultry ourselves. Gabby and I will be road tripping, making a few stops to see some friends. We should be in New Orleans by the last week of July. We plan on getting there for the Satchmo Summer Fest. More importantly, we want to have a visit with you. Do you think you could possibly work us into your schedule?"

"Without a doubt! I have a few things I want to share with you when you get here, too!"

John Peabody could hear the excitement in Meg's voice.

"Want to give me a preview? Have you found some more information for the research?"

Meg hesitated briefly,

"In a way, but I would really like to wait until you get here to show you in person."

After a few more minutes of general conversation, John confirmed he would text Meg on their trip progress as he and Gabby made their way south. Meg disconnected and began to make serious plans to delve into her personal project surrounding the research. She would love to get it completed by the time John and Gabby Peabody arrived. *If* that were going to happen, she would need to stick to a disciplined schedule making sure she left the office on time each day.

The next day, Meg was back at her apartment by noon. She changed into comfy cool clothes to head out into the Quarter with her notebook and pen. It was mid-week, and the accompanying heat of July ensured tourist traffic was low and slow. She walked to the coffee shop on Royal and peered inside the front window. It wasn't overly crowded but for some reason her instinct was to walk on. She turned the corner going up St. Phillip back toward Bourbon. There was a soft rumbling in the distance marking another afternoon storm brewing over the

Pontchartrain. It wouldn't be long until it reached the Quarter so stopping at Lafitte's would be convenient until it passed. At least that was the reason Meg professed to herself.

Meg dipped into the front entrance seeking the coolness of the darkened bar. Jimmy was at the bar pulling beers for a few older gentlemen. He nodded and smiled in a familiar way toward her. It gave her a feeling of welcome, like a neighborhood regular. Meg supposed in a way that this was exactly what she was becoming.

Jimmy seemed to be on his own this afternoon. Meg was kind of glad that the tall blonde bartender wasn't around. Meg felt like she gave off such a strange vibe. It had made Meg uncomfortable to be around her. Jimmy finished up with the gentlemen and came over to where Meg was standing at the bar.

"Hey there! Want to start with your usual?" Jimmy was the one who took her order most of the time and he knew now that she always started with a soft drink before having one of the dangerous purple slushies.

"Yes, please Jimmy. Here's my card, let me start a tab."

Jimmy's eyebrows perked in surprise. Meg usually paid in cash and only purchased a few colas and one purple drink. Meg recognized his look of wonder and quickly explained.

"I may be here a while. I have some work I want to do over at "my" table, unless it gets overly crowded but with that storm heading this way, I think it will be okay."

Jimmy smiled. "It will be perfectly fine but if you think you might want more than one of the daiquiris, you might want a bite of something to eat. I just ordered a pizza to be delivered in about an hour. I am willing to share. Oops! Unless you are a vegan or vegetarian. I ordered pepperoni with extra pepperoni."

"Thanks, it sounds really good. But only if you will let me pay you."

"No sirree! This one is on me. You can get us one the next time you come in."

Now Meg really did feel at home.

An hour later, Meg looked up to see Jimmy standing by her table with a paper plate full of pizza and her first purple drink of the day. She had been so intent on her work that she hadn't noticed the pizza delivery guy biking hurriedly up to the bar trying to outrun the storm. Meg thanked Jimmy and offered to pay her part again. He waved her off as he made his way back to the bar.

The bar was empty except for Meg and a few tourists who had wandered in while her head was bent over her notebook. The soft rumble of faraway thunder had morphed into more of a base drum sound as the black clouds began rolling over the Quarter. Meg took a generous bite of the good smelling pizza and looked out toward the street. Folks were scurrying to try and avoid the rain that was sure to pelt down into the streets soon. Suddenly, a bolt of lightning moved across the sky diagonal to the bar, stretching across Bourbon toward the river. With that, the blonde bartender dashed into the front door ready to start her shift.

Jimmy greeted Wavery and waited for her up front while she put her things in the back office. It looked like a slow rest of the evening for them with the rain coming so Jimmy decided that he would go upstairs to work on the inventory. He would also open the boxes of the bar merchandise to be ready for the weekend. Weekends were when they sold most of their shirts and baseball hats printed with the bar's logo. Before heading up the stairs, Jimmy told Wavery that all the patrons had been paying by drink except for Meg who had opened a tab.

Wavery looked puzzled, "Meg?"

Jimmy nodded his head toward the table opposite the bar and in front of the wire screened window. Wavery looked over and saw the woman in question with her head bent over a notebook writing away.

"Oh, writer girl. She's back. She usually doesn't stay that long."

And for that, Wavery was glad because she really didn't want to communicate with the man standing to her side. Of course, Jimmy didn't see what she saw floating around this hundred's year old bar, much less the figure of the man that was always with Meg. Jimmy made his way up the old wooden stairs to the attic area. Wavery decided to bite the bullet and go over to see if this "Meg" wanted another drink.

Meg became hyperaware of the blonde bartender approaching her table. She braced herself for another strange look wondering what it was that seemed to bother the taller woman so much.

Wavery began. "Excuse me. I wanted to let you know that Jimmy is working on inventory so if you need anything else to drink, I'll be glad to help you."

It was Meg's turn to offer a strange look toward the bartender. Her voice sounded so familiar or rather the accent in her voice sounded familiar. She certainly didn't sound like any of the natives Meg had met from New Orleans or the surrounding area. Meg realized that the tall blonde woman's accent sounded more like her own.

Meg hesitated for a moment and then plowed right in.

"No, I'm good right now but I will probably be getting one last purple before I head back to my apartment. Hopefully, the rainstorm will pass quickly. I'm sorry but my curiosity is getting the better of me. You aren't from here, are you?"

Wavery instantly recognized the familiar accent in this Meg's voice as well.

"No, I am a graduate student at Tulane University. I'm originally from North Carolina. A place called Foothills. Where are you from?"

Meg hoped she didn't imagine it, but she felt a softer glance from the woman standing by her table.

"Small world, I am working on a research project at Tulane in partnership with the college I work at back in Virginia. The southwestern corner of Virginia. I'm Meg Hurley by the way, nice to meet a fellow mountain girl."

Wavery decided she was already in for a pound so she might as well make a proper introduction.

"Yes, it is nice to meet someone when we are both so far away from home. I'm Wavery Parker."

Meg thought the name was both pretty and different.

"I have never heard the name Wavery before. It's lovely."

Wavery wasn't used to sharing anything about herself, especially with a practical stranger but for some reason, Meg didn't feel like such a stranger.

"Thank you. I was named after my two grandfathers. Wade and Avery. My mom decided to be creative and pull letters from each name to come up with my name."

Just then a group of soaked tourists came dashing in out of the pelting rain and Wavery quickly headed back to the service area of the bar. Meg watched Wavery methodically fill the orders as the group sat at the big table close to the bar. Meg realized that the group seemed to have settled in for the long haul. It was time for her to close out her tab. The dripping wet streets were no fun to slog through as Meg made her way back to her place. It was still early so she decided to transcribe her written notes onto her laptop once she dried off.

Meg mused over the afternoon. How odd to have wandered upon a person who was practically from the same place that Meg had been raised. She had recognized the lilt of Wavery Parker's accent and it had pulled her in. Oddly, that small similarity could have made for instant comradery, but Meg could still sense a wall between them.

It had been so different with Ann. There were no walls, just an instant connection. Ann was obviously a more open person. Meg realized that Ann's voice didn't have the same enunciation as the locals either. It didn't sound like the folks from her home area, but it definitely contained a soft southern drawl. Meg looked forward to chatting with Ann again and finding out her story.

That night after dinner, Meg sat cross-legged on her bed with her calendar to map out a plan to complete her little project by the time John and Gabby arrived in New Orleans. It was going to require some effort, but she could ask off work for a day or two if she needed. She could always make it up after the Peabodys left to go back home. For whatever reason, Meg felt her best flow of writing occurred at Lafitte's using a pen and her notebook. That meant she had to transcribe to her computer at night. She softly bit her lip wondering if that would end up making her use up more time than she wanted.

The possible loss of time was a deciding factor. She would just have to concentrate on working in the cafés during the afternoons and even work in the evenings at home. She wasn't going to return to Lafitte's for a while. She needed to proceed more quickly than writing by hand than transcribing would allow. It would also ensure that she wouldn't be on the receiving end of Wavery's unnerving stares.

Meg's legs had begun to tingle from sitting in the same position for so long. She pushed herself off the bed to stretch her legs and walked over to the door leading out onto the balcony. Opening the door, she could see the rain had stopped. It was just before sundown and people were starting to mill about on the streets once again. Some carried umbrellas and those thin plastic ponchos sold in almost every shirt shop in the Quarter. Meg leaned her head against the doorframe speaking to no one there.

"All of those folks looked prepared if a storm comes their way. I wonder if I am. Dang, this little project of mine could change a lot... or nothing. Either way, it's definitely going to affect me. I wonder if I am ready?"

Meg closed the door once again, locking it against the night, and pulled the drapes tight. She shook her head at her worries. What were they compared to what others had endured for hundreds of years? Again, out loud she whispered to the emptiness of her apartment,

"Please let me find the words."

A shadow in the corner heard her plea and took them to heart.

Chapter 21

Wavery's grad school schedule was open for a while, so she was spending this week working her own shifts and a few extras. Every day, she found herself unconsciously looking for Meg to come through the doors and head over to her usual table. She never showed. Wavery realized she was surprisingly disappointed. Not that she wanted to interact with the shadow of the man that seemed to follow Meg almost constantly but because she was interested to find out more about Meg and where she came from. Wavery couldn't help but wonder what all they might have in common since they both came from the same region.

Meanwhile, Meg was purposely avoiding Lafitte's and any interaction with Wavery Parker while doing her best to dodge the afternoon storms that July brought to southern Louisiana. Those daily storms fed the humidity infusing the Quarter with a thick soupiness, but Meg barely noticed. Her passion for completing her secret project blocked everything around her.

Meg was sitting in the coffee shop on Royal when the ping of a text broke through her concentration. She reluctantly stopped typing to pull her phone out of her bag. John had left a message. He and Gabby would be in New Orleans by Sunday. They would love it if she could meet them on Monday afternoon around 2 o'clock at Lafitte's on Bourbon.

Meg really didn't want to meet there. Especially at that time. Hopefully, Jimmy would be working the afternoon shift with someone besides Wavery Parker. Meg felt only slightly guilty about the thought, but her nerves were being pulled tightly right now. She just didn't have the bandwidth to suffer through those odd stares from the blonde bartender. Meg nervously twisted a strand of hair as she went back to her writing. Her real worry should be the fact that she couldn't seem to find an ending for her story. Hopefully, Gabby would still agree to read over her work.

Monday afternoon came in what felt like a blur and Meg got her wish. When she arrived at the bar, the blonde bartender was nowhere in sight. Uncharacteristically, Meg greeted Jimmy, grabbed the magical daiquiri rather than a soda to start, and went over to "her" table waiting on John and Gabby to arrive.

Meg anxiously watched for them to approach from the window facing Bourbon Street. She was mildly surprised when they entered the doorway coming from St. Phillip instead. The heat and the humidity kept hugs short and quickly the three of them were seated at the table. Frosty drinks in front of the two women and a beer for John set the mood. Everyone seemed to be talking at once, sharing all the news from back home, and catching up with Meg on her work at Tulane. The conversation was light and comfortable. Both John and Gabby could see a change in Meg. Her shoulders were more relaxed, and she seemed happier than they had seen in a long time. Gabby looked over at John with a look that seemed to say, "I told you so."

Usually, it would have been John who would have delved into the subject, but Gabby took the lead.

"I think John will agree with me when I say that you look absolutely wonderful. So content. It seems that the time here has been good for you. Are we right?"

Meg thought for a moment and agreed wholeheartedly but then went on to add a second thought.

"You both are right, at least to a degree. I love living here. The people, the music, and the food. Who wouldn't love all that? I really enjoy my work with Dr. Gallo and assisting with teaching others the ins and outs of research. Of course, you both know that I really felt the need to end my time here when the research turned up so many dead ends. But I thought long and hard about something you shared with me from the project benefactor. They were right. There is more than one way to share a story. I took the advice to use my intuition and that's what I have been doing since we had that conversation."

Meg reached into her canvas bag and pulled out a binder. Inside the binder was the culmination of all the work she had been doing for the last few weeks. She held it tentatively against her heart and then passed it over to Gabby Peabody. Gabby was taken aback that Meg had not handed the bound work over to John. John didn't seem to notice, as his eyes seemed focused on something just over Meg's shoulder. Gabby raised her eyebrows in question and Meg answered the unspoken query.

"Gabby, I think I have written a book. I pulled together published facts, passed on stories, and my intuition to tell what I know so far about Sam's journey. My only conundrum is that I don't have an ending… yet. If I don't find any more facts to corroborate, I very well may just have to write the ending solely based on my intuition. I want you both to read it and give me your input. I'd like you to share your input from an author's perspective and I'd like John to review it from a historical perspective."

John Peabody had finally refocused on what was happening at the table. Meg really had changed. She would have never turned over an unfinished project before. It would have had to have been complete and proofread a dozen times before she would have allowed any eyes but her own to look over a product of hers.

Meg was truly and confidently beginning to trust her own intuition. It looked good on her. John looked over to see a glaze of proud and happy tears in his wife's eyes. He could also read her body language. She couldn't wait to tear into the binder. She liked nothing better than to support a budding author. It would have to wait for a bit though for they had a few more stops to make while they were out and about in the city today.

Gabby handed the binder over to her husband and then reached across the table to take Meg's hands in her own.

"Meg, I am absolutely honored that you shared this with me… with us. We do need to take off because we have a few stops we have to make before we head in for the evening. As soon as I get in and get my comfy clothes on, I am going to sit down with your book. That's right, John. I get it first so you will just have to be patient."

They both rose from their seats to hug Meg good-bye. John looked over Meg's shoulder once more before saying,

"We're going to be here for at least two weeks, so getting your book read will not be a problem. We'll call you soon to set up some dinner and some fun outings as well. You tell Dr. Gallo that your time is ours for the next two weeks. Never mind, I already did that when we had dinner with him last night."

Meg watched two of her favorite people walk out of the bar hand in hand like two young sweethearts. They turned the corner heading up St. Phillip toward Rampart. Meg bought a drink to take with her and headed to sit by the river just to think. Her canvas bag felt strangely empty and bereft, but her heart felt full.

Wavery's meeting with her advisor to plan her fall schedule ran a little late and then there was stoppage on the streetcar line. Thankfully, Jimmy was covering for her until she could get to the bar. She was practically in a jog when she came through the doorway. Jimmy laughed at her for worrying about being only a tiny bit late.

"Slow down 'Carolina Blue'! You aren't that late, and besides, business has been slow. Well, slow except for Meg, the *writer girl* as you call her. She finally came back, and I think she met up with her parents here today."

Wavery felt oddly disappointed that she hadn't been around to watch that. She glanced over toward Meg's usual table.

"Did she introduce you to them?"

Wavery couldn't figure out why she even cared but still she waited for Jimmy's answer.

"No, I just figured they were a couple about the right age. There was a lot of hugging 'hello' and 'good-bye' when they left. I even saw Meg give them something, I figured it was a gift of some sort."

Wavery thought to herself, *Hmm, and I thought I was being nosey.*

If she hadn't met Jimmy's husband, she would have mistaken Jimmy's interest for a crush.

Wavery quickly put her things away in the back room and began prepping the garnishes for the evening. She would occasionally glance out to the street as she was cutting the lemons and limes. Her interest was piqued when she saw two men unlocking the heavy wooden door of the building directly across the street. One of the men looked vaguely familiar. She watched them chat before going inside. Then she saw a shadow in the corner of her eye.

Dammit, the shadow was the man she usually saw standing over Meg's shoulder here in the bar. He typically stayed right with her when she left the bar. Did that mean she was somewhere over that way as well? Wavery looked up and down the street. She even walked from behind the bar to get a closer look. Meg was nowhere to be seen. The shadow man appeared to be watching the men.

Wavery watched as the men made their way through the door and shut it tightly behind them. The shadow of the male figure turned to looked her straight in the eye and waved. He then turned and disappeared before her eyes. To anyone else, that would have felt unusual, but to Wavery, it was just an everyday event. She shrugged her shoulders and turned to go back into work trying to remember where she had seen the tall, dark-haired man before.

The next day, Wavery had her answer, or at least a partial answer. She came in early to her afternoon shift to "pay" Jimmy back for his coverage the day before. Her morning had started early with a run before the sun started moving the temperature and humidity into an almost unbearable range. Wavery always felt better both physically and mentally when she was able to get her body moving. She had learned a long time ago that if she stayed busy, she had less of an opportunity to think and brood. Wavery busied herself with the daily task of prepping drink condiments and checking the levels of the rotating freezer barrels that doled out the magical frozen concoctions for the bar's patrons. It looked to be a hot one so Wavery needed to make sure there was plenty of yummy slushiness ready for the afternoon.

Wavery stole a glance across the street to the old building that had been standing there since around 1830. She looked at the parts of the windows not covered by shutters and up toward the balcony. The shadow of the male figure from the day before was nowhere to be seen.

Just as her mind went back to the nosey wonderings of the previous afternoon, she saw the same tall, dark-haired man approach from the Canal Street direction. He paused in front of the building and looked toward the street heading toward Esplanade. She saw a bright smile light up his face and he lifted his hand to wave. Wavery leaned over the bar just enough to watch who was approaching. She saw a petite woman with equally as dark hair. It then dawned on her that this was the couple she had noticed walking down the street together not so long ago.

Just then, two of her regulars popped in and ordered a couple of Hurricanes to go. Wavery could mix that drink in her sleep. She was able to quickly serve her customers while keeping up with the goings on across the street. She made herself look busy by wiping an already clean counter as she watched the couple move around the side of the building inspecting every nook and cranny. The man pulled a ring of keys from his jeans pocket and unlocked the front door to allow the woman to enter. He turned to close the door, glanced across to the bar, and shot a brief smile to the bartender who seemed to be rubbing the finish off the wooden bar top.

An hour later, Jimmy joined Wavery for the remainder of the day. A pre-wedding party had informed management that they would be bringing a large group in for the late afternoon and early evening gathering. It seems this was the anniversary day of the couple meeting at this very bar. Both bartenders began moving some tables together at the end of the room nearest the patio in preparation. Jimmy noticed that Wavery kept looking through the window and across the street.

"Hey there, woman, what's up out there that you are so interested in?"

Jimmy looked to the street and saw nothing of excitement. There were only a few folks walking about the Quarter and a couple of carriages of mules clopping past.

Wavery shrugged her shoulders,

"Nothing really, saw a couple go into the old building across the street about an hour before you came into work. I haven't seen them leave yet," Wavery laughed, "I guess I was just being nosey."

"You sure your spidey senses aren't up?" inquired Jimmy.

Jimmy and Wavery both had an uncanny knack for recognizing when someone came into the bar and wasn't feeling safe. There had been several nights that Wavery had tipped Jimmy off concerning a female who was being followed and harassed. Wavery usually took care of getting the woman to a safe spot while Jimmy showed the man (or men) the door.

"No, it wasn't anything like that, honestly. I really am just being nosey. Something about that building is… interesting."

Jimmy nodded and continued, "I heard it was for sale— privately. Maybe someone is interested in purchasing."

Wavery had never seen anyone enter the building for as long as she had worked at the bar. That didn't mean that someone had not done so on the hours she wasn't around. If buildings could have feelings, Wavery felt this building was feeling lonely and abandoned. Hopefully, if someone could buy the property, they could give it what it needed to feel alive again. Wavery shrugged at her own fanciful thoughts.

Wavery looked across the street once more. She tugged Jimmy's arm nodding in the direction of the building. The two men who had entered the building earlier were exiting through the door and locking back up. Both were covered head to toe in dust.

"Well," said Jimmy, "Do we have us a little mystery going on here?"

Meg was on pins and needles. The weather was beginning to morph to hot as Hades as August quickly approached. Everyone she worked with had told her that August and September in New Orleans would be downright stifling. She was beginning to believe them. Meg knew it was more than the growing heat keeping her up at night. She was anxiously waiting to hear what Gabby and John Peabody had to say about the contents of the binder she had handed over to them. Both had her number and had texted her off and on during the week. They mentioned doing some "touristy" things with old friends and a few meetings but had made no remarks about her project. Then late last night just before going to bed, Meg saw a text from Gabby.

It read:

"Let me know if you can swing by Lafitte's tomorrow at noon. Look forward to chatting with you."

Meg quickly responded in the affirmative and hopped into bed. She tried to sleep. The attempt to quiet her nerves and her mind was weak at best. She spent most of the night tossing and turning, overthinking all the possibilities of the upcoming "chat" with John and Gabby Peabody.

On Friday morning, she gave Dr. Gallo a call to request a work from home day. Meg quickly completed the data spread he needed and attached it to an email wishing him a good weekend. Once her obligations were fulfilled, Meg decided to head out early to the bar on lower Bourbon, stopping by Clover Grill on the way. A good burger might be just what the doctor ordered. The carbs could go a long way in soaking up the drinks she might be consuming with the Peabody's. Drinks that could be a celebration or a drowning of sorrows.

Meg sat at the counter of the iconic dive and watched the animated cooks at the grill. A fine dining restaurant in New Orleans was quite the experience but so were the antics of the smiling staff at Clover Grill. Meg watched as the tall, thin man in the grease-stained apron placed her burger under the famous hubcap cover that would seal in all the yummy juices. Meg loved a good burger. She was hoping she could get this one down without an embarrassing incident. It wasn't that the food here was subpar, it was just her nervous tummy. Knowing that the butterflies in her stomach might not allow the whole burger to be consumed, she asked for a knife to cut it in half. She would take the uneaten portion in a box.

Meg often did that when she ate out in the Quarter. She would then give her untouched portions to someone who looked down on their luck. Sometimes she would leave it atop one of the trash receptacles where she often saw older folks digging for something to eat. At least with her box, Meg knew it was clean and untouched. Many residents would probably chastise her for her actions, thinking it was encouraging the homeless to hang around. She didn't care about that. Meg came from a place where even folks with a roof over their head often went hungry. She would always do whatever it took to help people.

Meg arrived at Laffite's about 10 minutes early. Weekend visitors had already started arriving, many of them flying in on Thursday night. The flow into the bar was already beginning to build, leading into the party that would be called Friday night on Bourbon Street. Meg saw Jimmy and two other guys working behind the bar. Wavery, thankfully, was nowhere in sight.

Jimmy smiled at her and nodded with a questioning tilt of his head toward the rotating barrel of frozen purple slush. Meg returned the smile and gave him a thumbs up. Meg handed him her card to start a tab. She turned and made her way over to the table where she usually sat but it was already taken by a large party. The only place left to go was back by the piano. No one would be playing there until the evening hours, so Meg pulled three stools up close together around a high top. She texted John to tell him where to find her.

Within minutes, John and Gabby appeared with drinks in hand but no binder. What could that mean? Meg could feel beads of sweat pop on her forehead and not from the heat. After a few hugs, they settled down in the cool dark quiet behind the piano area. John and Gabby gave each other a quick knowing look. Gabby gazed directly into Meg's eyes as John spoke first.

"Let's get to it. Meg Hurley, your research skills are spot on. You have certainly utilized all the information you found to support your writing. As a historian and researcher myself, I applaud you. But I'm not the writer in the family. That's Gabby's area of expertise. So I am just going to sit here quietly now," and with that he looked back at his wife,

"Okay. I am going to TRY and sit here quietly while Gabby gives you her input."

Gabby reached out and patted John's hand and laughed quietly before turning back to Meg.

"Meg, I am not sure really quite what to say…"

Meg's heart felt as if it had plummeted to her feet. This sounded like an attempt at a gentle letdown.

Gabby continued,

"Well, actually, I have a lot to say but I am not sure how to say it. And that is quite something coming from a poet and fellow writer. I am usually very good with words."

Again, another quiet laugh erupted from the woman sitting across from Meg. Wait a minute? Fellow writer? Could that mean that Gabby considered that Meg was now a writer, too?

"You did exactly what you were asked to do. It's clear that you have done it with your whole heart. Once you trusted yourself and your intuition, you were able to let the story flow from Daniel's journals and everything you have learned about Sam's family. Their forced journey took on a life of its own."

"As I read through each chapter, I felt like you were channeling the story from beyond your own being. I felt myself sinking into the surroundings of the settings and the emotions of the people who you were writing about. Sweetheart, you do indeed have a book on your hands."

Meg's heart began pounding in her chest. It felt like it was going to leap out into the room. The two people sitting by her were two of the most important people in her world besides her parents. Their approval and praise meant the world to Meg.

As much as she cared for John and Gabby Peabody as surrogate family members, she knew without a doubt they would not risk their professional reputations on blind adoration of her efforts. Gabby Peabody was a published poet and essayist. She taught creative writing and helped her students to get their work out in the world if and only if their work merited such action. Meg caught Gabby's eye again and thought there was a "but" coming. Her intuition was spot on even now.

"Well, I hope that is the good news you wanted to hear. I do have something to add. There is something I want to say but knowing your personality and work style, I recognize it might not make you very happy."

Meg braced herself even though she knew that every first draft had to be worked on and reworked before it was ready to go out to the public. She would just have to get ready to deal with all the parts of being a writer. Both the pleasant and the not so pleasant. However, what Gabby shared next didn't have anything to do with the logistics of publishing a finished product.

"Meg, as hard as it is going to be for you to accept, you may never be able to support the ending of Sam's part of the story with hard facts. I think you should just go ahead and finish up the book even if you must make it up. I know that goes against every fiber of your little research being, but the story needs to get out there and the sooner the better."

It was Meg's turn to chuckle, "Oh, Gabby, no worries. I had already decided to do that. In fact, I had already begun to do a scrappy little outline of what that may look like. Even if I can't prove everything, my gut is giving me all kinds of suggestions of how to wind this down."

Both Gabby and John were surprised. Meg had always operated in a by the book manner since they met her as an undergrad student. Thinking back, they both remembered how her parents had told them she had not always been that adamant about operating on pure logic and fact. The young child they had described had once been quite a dreamer. It was only after losing her grandmother that she had become so strict with her own feelings and actions.

Gabby's face showed her every emotion. There she sat with a satisfied smile and a proud gleam in her eyes. Sitting beside her was a writer who could both utilize research and produce a story that would have many mesmerized. Gabby was as excited for herself as she was for Meg. This was going to be quite an adventure.

John excused himself from their little gathering to run back out to the bar for refills for the three of them. As he returned, John saw that their favorite table was now available. He sat their drinks down and waved Gabby and Meg over to sit. Once they were settled again, John began to speak.

"So now that it's settled that you intend to write the remainder of the story as you see fit, it's time to think about next steps."

Meg had only briefly thought about what would happen after the story was complete. She was glad to have Gabby guide her through the process and said as much to the couple.

"Well, of course we can guide you, but Gabby is prepared to go a bit further than that. There are a few things we have never shared with you. Now we think the time has come to enlighten you on some background," continued John.

"Background," queried Meg.

John continued, "Would it be true to say that you think the benefactor that is funding your working sabbatical is an alumnus of the college or perhaps a donor to the college?"

Meg had secretly thought it was an alumnus the whole time and told John as much.

"Well, you would be incorrect. The benefactor never attended the college but does donate to certain functions of the college dependent on Gabby's requests and guidance. For many years, he would never have listened to my advice because he was not happy that I had brought Gabby to the college in the first place. Although later, he softened up on me a bit."

Gabby's laughter floated throughout the room and several people turned to listen to the pleasant sound. Gabby patted her husband on the hand,

"Well, it helped that you assisted in providing him with a couple of grandsons. You see Meg, the benefactor is my father. After graduating with my master's from Tulane, he really wanted me to stick around New Orleans. Of course, after I met John Peabody at a poetry reading down at the Maple Leaf during my senior year, that was that."

"John was completing his doctorate, but we were still able to spend the spring courting, and, in the summer, we got married out at City Park. My mother was not happy that her only daughter had taken away her chance at a fancy wedding and one of those darling second line parades through the Quarter. John had secured a position in the history department of Byars Creed, and we needed to be in Virginia by the end of August. Quite by chance, an opening came in the English Department beginning the following January and the rest is poetical history."

It took a few minutes for all this information to settle into Meg's brain. The amount of money that the benefactor had spent over the years, beyond Meg's own project, was mind blowing to a girl who had been raised in the frugal Appalachian Mountains. Basically, Gabby Peabody was from a very monied family. Gabby had never exhibited what Meg believed would have been the demeanor of rich girl… woman. John had shared a little of his background growing up on a farm in Virginia but had never mentioned his wife's background or how they met.

Still stunned, Meg was unsure if she should ask more questions or just let Gabby continue. Gabby took a long drink through her straw and kept her explanation going.

"My father didn't always have money as a child. Around the time he turned ten years of age, his father made a smart investment with a trusted group of friends. It paid off quite well. My grandfather was a prudent and careful man. He never took a risk that he couldn't recover from quickly. It took a few years but by the time my father graduated from high school, my grandfather had amassed a fortune he could pass down to my father. Father was equally smart and careful. You know I really believe that it wasn't just smart investments in a variety of companies and businesses that brought either of the two men their rewards. I firmly believe it was that they continually paid it forward. Sometimes it was for local folks in need and sometimes it was for organizations. Anyway, we can talk more about that some other time."

Meg did have a question and she felt like it was a good time to bring it up.

"So, Gabby, does your father still want to support my time here in New Orleans?"

Gabby nodded her head excitedly, "Absolutely, if you want to stay. We did share your concerns about being away from your regular duties in Virginia. He wants to use his contributions to fund your position as a dual partnership there and with Tulane. That way if Byars Creed wants to utilize their budgeted monies to fund another more typical position in the research department, they will have the availability to do so."

"My father also has recognized a dream of mine. He is going into partnership with me, and we are opening a small company, LeBlanc Publishing. We should be ready to take on clients by November. I hope you will decide to work with us and let us publish your book. Of course, I understand if you want to submit to larger companies. I will respect whatever decision you make."

For a split second, a look of doubt crossed Meg's expression. Gabby knew at once what was going through her mind.

"Meg, the idea for this publishing company has been in the works for over a year. I did not ask my father for a new toy to play with just to entertain myself or to help you specifically. I have wanted to go beyond guiding new authors with their writing and publishing for many years. Now that our sons are grown and out on their own, I can put my efforts into this dream. I will be stepping back from my duties with the college and more fully into this new endeavor. I only just found out that you are a budding author, so as much as we love and care for you, I honestly did not start this project with you in mind. That has just become a happy synchronicity."

Meg felt a pang of guilt for making this revelation all about herself, but she realized everything Gabby had just shared with her simply highlighted the fact that Gabby believed in her. Gabby believed that Meg could write and be a published author. Another concerning thought flitted through Meg's mind. She turned and looked at John Peabody.

"Are you stepping down as well? Does this mean you guys are moving here to New Orleans?"

John pushed back in his chair, "No, I am still staying on full time. We are just going to be traveling back and forth more. Gabby wants offices in both places. The main business office will be here in New Orleans manned by her father. He is as energetic and sharp as ever and Gabby has sparked a fire within him for this project. Gabby will have her satellite office in Virginia."

Gabby pushed back her chair and came around the table to give Meg a big hug.

"First things first, let's get the final portion of your story written. Then you can decide if you want to become one of LeBlanc Publishing's first authors."

John went back over to the bar to close out his tab, taking care of Meg's as well. John left a generous tip and Jimmy watched to make sure Meg's card was returned to her. Unless Meg was or had been married, the different surnames on the two cards alerted Jimmy that the older couple may not be Meg's parents.

John returned to the table and made a suggestion to the women,

"Now that we have that all settled, well, almost settled, I vote that we celebrate this day. Let's grab some food, more drinks, and find a place to listen to some good music. I believe the evening will be funded by LeBlanc Publishing. Am I correct, Gabby?"

Meg finished putting her card away and quickly mentioned the binder with her manuscript. Gabby winced a bit and said,

"I know I should have asked your permission first, but my father came in when John and I were discussing your work. My father loves reading as much as I love writing. His curiosity peaked, and he asked if he could take a quick thumb through. When we left, he had made a pitcher of sweet tea and was settling down with it for a thorough read. I am so sorry."

Meg grinned from ear to ear,

"Well, if your partner is going to join with you in taking me on as a client, I think it's only fair that he has a chance to see what he will be getting in this deal. *Especially* if he is paying for our celebration tonight."

Chapter 22

Meg rolled over on Saturday morning to hear the very early roar of the street cleaners rolling past her building. Cleaning up after the Friday night revelers was a huge task. Meg was tired from her own celebration that had taken Gabby, John, and herself all over the Quarter and beyond. The little group had spent hours eating really good food, listening to music and dancing. They ended their evening down on Frenchman Street well past midnight.

Meg had never had so much fun in her life. But boy, did that fun come at a price. She could barely hold her eyes open, and her calf muscles were screaming from all the walking and dancing. She was happy though. She had learned yet another beautiful thing about New Orleans. Everyone danced. They danced with each other and sometimes all at the same time. It was fabulous. Meg turned and decided to sleep just a bit more, dreaming about the things she loved.

It was close to noon when Meg finally came out of her slumber. She stretched and popped her legs over the edge of her bed. She tentatively tried to stand and was a little anxious when she found that her calves weren't happy with her. They were extremely tender as she made way to the tall French doors. She pulled back the drapes and let the light fill her studio apartment.

Meg spoke out loud to no one in particular,

"I should probably try to walk this soreness away. Maybe just a slow walk over to the coffee shop for a bite to eat and to work on the ending of the book."

Meg recognized then that she had been talking to the air more and more when she was safely tucked away in her apartment alone. Thinking back, she could see that it had increased exponentially once she started writing her book. Her book. It was no longer an addendum to research or a project. It was a *book*.

Again, out loud to no one particular,

"I wonder if this is what happens to writers. They begin talking to themselves. Maybe I should adopt a pet and blame these crazy one-sided conversations on them."

Meg had half been expecting someone to answer her questions and confirm her plans. Deep down she had hoped it would have been her grandmother's voice ringing through. It had been quite a while since she had a conversation with Granny Del. Meg bit down on her lip worrying why Granny wasn't talking to her.

Meg walked over to the kitchenette to make a cup of coffee. She reached up to brush away a strand of hair tickling her right ear. She tucked the strand back up but could still feel the tickling sensation like a soft breath of a whisper. She heard no voice but immediately had a totally different thought about her time. She needed to slow down. Meg decided to take the rest of the weekend and have some more fun. She would start back in on the final chapters of her book on Monday.

Meg dressed while the coffee perked and then took her cup to sit on the balcony. She watched as the street was beginning to fill with people sashaying up and down Bourbon. Her building was just down from the St. Ann and Bourbon crossing so she was often privy to many interesting sights. Ever the logical one, Meg had brought a small notepad out with her as she sat at her table overlooking the street below.

She began making a list of all the touristy things she hadn't done yet in New Orleans and there were quite a few. Today she would concentrate on the ones she could do in the Quarter. The list was short but could take what was left of the day. She would visit a few of the metaphysical shops, take a carriage ride, and eat beignets at Café Du Monde. Her tummy growled in agreement with the last idea so that made food first and then the shops. She would complete her meandering with a ride to rest her sore legs.

The line for beignets was quite long but Meg was not in a hurry. She wanted the quintessential experience of sitting at one of the wrought iron tables sipping café au lait and being baptized in a torrent of powdered sugar. Meg was anticipating the enjoyment in watching people from all over the world coming together to delight in the three puffs of fluffy heaven.

Just as she was nibbling her second beignet, a notification on her phone grabbed her attention. She wiped her sticky fingers on a napkin before pulling her phone from her purse. It was a text from Gabby. Gabby's father wanted to meet her. Mr. and Mrs. Leblanc wanted to have them all over for lunch next Sunday. Mr. Leblanc would be out of town for the week but would return next weekend. Meg texted her acceptance for the lunch date and wondered to herself about what she should wear. She would ask Gabby for her opinion. Maybe they could go shopping together.

Meg finished her decadent goodies, and carefully brushed away the remnants of powdered sugar from her clothes. She made her way down Decatur and up to Dumaine to the first of the shops she had on her list. The city was full of various types of metaphysical shops, but the one Meg had decided to investigate was closest to her present location. She peeked inside the plate glass window and saw only a few folks inside. She opened the door, and an old-fashioned bell tinkled a welcome above her head. A gorgeous woman with auburn hair was at the back checkout counter. She looked up from the item she was wrapping up for a customer and called out a welcome.

Meg wasn't exactly sure what she was expecting but she was surprised at the brightness of the shop. There were a variety of shades of pink sprinkled throughout the long room. Meg glanced over and saw an antique mantle that had been painted in a rich creamy champagne color. In the center was a doll adorned in shades of pink and rose. The face was fashioned of cork, and she was appointed in a head dress most recognized as the tignon. There were dozens of oddities placed on the shelf surrounding her: perfume bottles and wine glasses, pieces of jewelry, and a plate of goodies. There was also a hand lettered sign in calligraphy asking shop patrons not to disturb the altar. A placard to the side explained that this was an altar dedicated to a goddess/lwa of love and decadence.

Meg continued to browse the other shelves. She made a circuit back to the front of the store passing by the plate glass window display. Just as she was about to cross back to the luscious smelling soaps, a very strange thing occurred. One of the dolls in the window display literally flew up in the air and landed at her feet with a soft thump. The woman with the auburn hair smiled as she walked towards Meg.

Meg stammered, "Honestly, I didn't touch it."

The woman told her not to worry about a thing as she placed the doll back in its display stand.

"Please just keep browsing. I can help you find what you need as soon as I finish with the lady in the back."

The shopkeeper went back to her other customer and Meg ventured over to the soaps. Each soap had a magical intent listed on the wrapping, but Meg was more interested in the way they smelled. She picked up a bar that was wrapped in black with purple lettering and decided this was the scent for her. She idly circled the shop once more patiently waiting her turn at the checkout. She passed the front window again just as both the customer and the shopkeeper were looking her way. They were all witness to the doll escaping its holder once more. It flew through the air, landing at her feet yet again.

The shopkeeper laughed out loud,

"Looks like someone wants to go home with you."

The customer at the counter looked straight at Meg and said,

"Miss, if you don't buy that doll for yourself, I'm going to buy it for you. That was clearly a sign."

Meg was a bit taken aback but the shopkeeper assured the other customer she would take care of it. The customer soon left out the door with a black bag filled to the top, leaving only the shopkeeper and Meg standing alone in the store.

"Sorry about that. She's a regular and not shy at all. My name is Amelie and I own the store. I do have to agree with her though, it was quite the definitive sign for you. I take it you are not a practitioner?"

"No, I'm sorry but I'm not. I was just wandering about today. Is it okay if I purchase the soap without being a practitioner? I picked it because it smelled so good," said Meg.

Amelie smiled,

"Of course. The general intention of the soap you picked is often connected to the scent that drew you toward it. The one you have chosen is great at cleansing the energies you have picked up throughout your day. It would aid in allowing you to not take on the energies of others. It would assist you as you move into new pathways. Do you tend to meet up with a vast number of energies daily?"

Meg thought about her general workspace and living in the Quarter. Even though her personal interactions were sparse, she could definitively feel all the energy surrounding her. Then she thought about the work she had been doing with her research. Yes, there were indeed some energies, both positive and negative, associated with that.

Meg answered Amelie in the affirmative and went to pull her wallet out to pay for the soap, but Amelie's next question stopped her in her tracks.

"You do want the doll as well, correct?"

Meg answered in a puzzled voice, "I am not a practitioner. I don't think it would be respectful for me to purchase … a tool… that I wouldn't be using in a dedicated manner."

Amelie respected what the woman was telling her and felt more confident in selling her the doll than before. Amelie walked to the window area and brought the doll back to the counter.

"You know most people who do practice would at least silently agree that a non-practitioner should not make such a purchase. If you do not know what you are dealing with concerning the spirits, you could get into a lot of trouble. However, that doesn't mean that more than one of the shops like ours refuses to sell to any customer that comes through the door. All we can do is offer advice and some warning."

Meg was still a bit perplexed, "So are you telling me that I should buy the doll?"

Amelie nodded, "Yes, I do think you should. And not because I want to make a sale. Quite honestly, I have *never* seen anything like that happen in my store. I am positive it was a sign for you. Let me ask you a couple of questions. Are you contemplating something new in your life? A new venture or job?"

Meg nodded and thought about the new opportunities that Mr. Leblanc and Gabby were offering to her.

Amelie held the doll up, "This doll represents the spirit or lwa of road openings. He came to you for a reason. He came abruptly too, so I can't help but think he wants to guide the way for you. It seems he knew you needed a shocking introduction to convince you to take him home with you. I would suggest that you take him. Place him by a doorway or window. Make sure you keep him clean and in a clean space. Just show him the respect he deserves. If ever you decide to work with him in a more committed fashion, you should research both the positive and negative aspects of doing so. You can always email or call the shop and I can offer you further guidance."

With that, Meg found herself purchasing both the figure and the delicious smelling soap. Amelie offered to wrap the doll in bubble wrap to ensure safe travels on a plane and was somewhat surprised herself to find that Meg was a resident of the Quarter. Amelie tilted her head to the side as Meg exited the store and spoke to the lwa around her,

"I believe we shall see her again."

Carrying the small black shopping bag around allowed Meg to blend in with the other visitors to the Quarter. She especially blended in with all the visitors who filled the mule drawn carriage she had just boarded. The cover of the carriage was decorated with silk flowers and made for a festive ride through the Vieux Carre. She listened attentively as the driver shared interesting information about certain points and made a promise to herself that she would look more deeply into some of the information that piqued her interest.

All in all, it was a fun little trip until she realized they had turned onto Bourbon Street. The carriage was heading in the direction of Lafitte's. How in the world could she have forgotten that many carriages not only rode by the bar but made a short stop for anyone wanting a beverage?

Meg was thankful for two things. She was seated on the outside of the carriage away from the bar and she was wearing a baseball cap to cover her unruly hair. She pulled the cap lower over her forehead as they neared the bar and rolled to a stop. Meg did not look towards the bar as the two people beside her left to go in for a drink. She wasn't sure why she worried about Wavery possibly seeing her, but it was the first thing that popped into her brain when she realized the direction the carriage was taking.

Meg looked at the elegant black shopping bag in her hands. She remembered the doll inside and what it represented. Meg sat up straighter and pushed her hat back from her face. She was starting a whole new path in her life. She was a talented researcher and soon to be a published writer. What did she care about what some stranger thought about her? The next time she was in the bar and the opportunity presented itself, she was simply going to ask Wavery about her demeanor. It was childish for two grown women not to be up front with each other. If she had offended Wavery in some way she would apologize. But *only* if she had truly done something. Otherwise, Wavery would just have to deal with it.

Meg's attention was captured by a slow creaking sound to her right. She looked over to the building sitting directly across the street from the bar and saw the front door open. A tall, dark-haired man came out carrying a bag of tools and turned to head down the street toward the center of the Quarter. A moment later, a petite, dark-haired woman came out of the building and locked the door behind her. Meg instantly recognized her.

The woman looked up at Meg all smiles and waved,

"Hey Meg! It's me, Ann. How are you?"

Ann walked over to the carriage and leaned in to speak with Meg. Meg briefly explained the day off she had given herself. Ann suggested that maybe they could get together soon and do some more exploring as well. Ann pulled two business cards and an ink pen out of her bag. She hastily wrote her personal cell number on one of the cards and gave it to Meg. She then handed her pen and the other card to Meg so that she would have Meg's number as well. Everyone was reboarding the carriage as Ann watched the group pull away.

Meg heard her call out, "Let's make it happen real soon!"

Neither Meg nor Ann noticed the blonde woman at the entryway of the bar's patio entrance watching them. Wavery wrinkled her brow wondering just how those two knew each other.

The carriage returned to the area in front of Jackson Square and Meg hopped off to make her way up the Saint Peter side of the square. She had decided to let the deli at Rouses on the corner of Royal provide her evening meal. She was hoping against all odds they still had some of their yummy mac and cheese and some roasted chicken in the hot case. It always sold out so quickly and for a very good reason. Their prices were reasonable, and their food was quite good.

She was in luck and as she cashed out, she made plans to put her things away as soon as she got home. Then she would hop into the shower to wash away the day's heat. Afterwards, she would prepare a little picnic to enjoy on her balcony. Tonight's entertainment would be the comings and goings on the street below her apartment. The music from the nearby clubs would provide the backdrop for all the wonderful characters dancing their way up and down Bourbon Street.

Meg only felt the slightest twinge in her calves as she climbed the two flights of stairs to her apartment. She opened the door and walked inside flipping the switch to the overhead light. She placed the black bag and her purse gently on the love seat and took the food to the counter of the kitchenette.

Meg walked over to the small walk-in closet that held hooks, a rod for hanging clothes, as well as a chest of drawers. After hanging her hat on a hook, she pulled some light gray lounge pants and an oversized t-shirt from the chest. She decided a long shower and comfy clothes were exactly what she needed.

After the shower, she pulled her hair up and made her way to the kitchenette. Meg hesitated when she saw she had left her bags on the love seat. She took her purse and put it on the undershelf of her nightstand. This was something both her grandmother and mother had always done. Now she carried on that tradition without knowing why. The next time she talked with her mom, she would ask about it. Meg picked up the black shopping bag. Darn, she wished she had remembered to take the soap into the shower with her earlier. How could she have forgotten that delectable smelling bar of goodness? She pulled the elegantly wrapped bar out of the bag and walked back into the bathroom placing it in the top drawer of the sink vanity.

Meg went back to the bag and gently removed the doll that Amelie had wrapped in deep purple tissue paper.

Where could she place the doll? Amelie had suggested by a window or door. Meg looked between both areas of her studio apartment. She just wasn't feeling the area near the window. She looked over to the doorway.

Just inside the entrance to her apartment was a small table. It was large enough for the doll and the small old wooden bowl she already kept there. The bowl was a gift that her grandfather had made for her grandmother. She kept nothing on top of the table but the bowl to hold her keys. Meg ran over to the cabinet below her kitchen sink and grabbed a cloth and some dusting spray. After she had given the table and bowl a thorough clean, she took the doll over and began to figure out a way to safely place it on the table so that it wouldn't fall into the floor. She just wasn't sure it could stand on its own and the bowl really wasn't deep enough to place it in.

Meg started to put the doll back into the bag until she could ensure it was displayed in a respectful manner. The bag still had some weight to it. Meg put the doll gently down on the pillow of the love seat. She reached under the folded up purple tissue paper that had cushioned the doll on its journey to her home. Under the paper at the very bottom of the bag was the wire doll holder with the wooden base that had been in the display window. Amelie had gifted her with the very thing she needed.

Meg promised herself that she would drop by the shop to thank Amelie for the extra kindness. Once the doll was in its proper place in the stand, Meg positioned the old wooden bowl in front of it. She then grabbed her keys from the sofa and laid them in the bowl. It appeared that the doll cast a glow once the keys were in the bowl. Meg logically reasoned the enchanting glow came from the lamp posts flickering on as the sun began its descent over the Quarter.

Meg's evening picnic on the balcony was a huge success with her tummy. She was full and satisfied and she had a bit left over for tomorrow. She took her plate back to the kitchen and washed up quickly so she could return to the balcony to enjoy the rest of the evening. Meg looked down at her phone on the charger by the sofa and realized she had a missed call from John Peabody. She saw that he had also left a voice mail. She replayed the message.

John's voice came through to let her know that he and Gabby had a surprise for her, but the surprise wouldn't arrive until tomorrow. They wanted her to keep her schedule flexible and be ready to meet up sometime in the afternoon. Just as she was finishing up listening to the voice mail, she heard a notification ping and looked down to see an additional text from John that read:

"Hey, I know I just left you a voice mail and Gabby says I am being too overprotective but could you just text to let me know you are okay."

Meg smiled and gave a silent thanks for the blessing of the people in her life who cared so much about her. She quickly texted that she was fine and had a great day out and about. Meg let John know that she was back home safe and sound. She then went back to the show that was Bourbon from her balcony.

Meg stayed out on her balcony until way past midnight. She knew there was no way she would be able to sleep with the promise of a surprise coming her way. She felt like a kid getting ready for Christmas or her birthday. The folks in the street were starting to become more and more rowdy and the energy was a bit much for her. Just as she decided to head back inside, she noticed a familiar looking tall, dark-haired man. Meg realized that it was the same man who had been walking with Ann on the street in front of her apartment and who had emerged from the building across from Lafitte's today. Tonight, he was dressed in black pants and a crisp white shirt jacket. He was carrying a tool bag but not the kind from earlier in the day. Meg recognized the bag that all the chefs moving about the Quarter carried with them. The black bag held their most precious tools, their knives.

The man seemed to sense that he was being watched. He looked up to see Meg sitting quietly on her balcony. He smiled a tired smile and moved on down the street. Meg's curiosity was on fire. Another mystery besides the upcoming surprise for Sunday afternoon. Meg decided to take another quick shower. This time she used the special soap she had purchased from Amelie. Oddly enough, once Meg's head hit the pillow, she was sound asleep without any tossing and turning.

It wasn't the early morning rumble of the street cleaners that roused Meg from her peaceful slumber. Instead, a loud clap of thunder provided the nine a.m. alarm. The storm appeared to be stationed at full throttle over her building. Meg stretched and pushed herself out of bed to get dressed and ready for the day. She looked over at the handmade figurine by her door and spoke directly to him.

"Today is the day for my surprise. Would you happen to have anything to do with that?"

Meg laughed to herself and decided she wouldn't need a pet after all, she could just direct all her musings toward the doll she had purchased at Amelie's shop.

After getting dressed, Meg pulled out an umbrella in case she needed it later. The rain was still coming down, so she had to drink her coffee and nibble her toast while sitting inside on the love seat. She sat there wondering how she would have any patience at all waiting for John and Gabby to let her know when and where to go for her surprise.

Meg almost pulled out her laptop to continue writing the ending of her book, but she stopped in mid action. She had promised herself a weekend off from her special project, so she decided to tidy up her apartment and sort her laundry to do later in the week instead.

Thankfully, the noon hour brought a message from John and Gabby. She was to meet them at 2 o'clock at the bar of a small boutique hotel on Toulouse Street. Gabby was surprised they hadn't chosen their favorite bar on Bourbon. Thankfully, the storm and ensuing rain had moved away by the time she headed out her door, but she could feel the humidity building in the air once again.

Meg scurried down Bourbon and made a right onto Toulouse. She walked excitedly past the lobby doors of the hotel and directly into the small adjacent bar. Meg saw Gabby chatting away with the woman tending bar. Gabby looked over to see Meg in the doorway and said a quick thank you to the bartender before making her way over to Meg. Gabby's eyes were sparkling mischievously as she gently took Meg's arm and guided her through the back door of the bar into a short hallway. As they walked from the hallway to the dining room doorway, Gabby said,

"We are just going to grab a bite of lunch. I hope you are hungry."

Gabby led Meg over to where John was waiting at a table covered in crisp white linen. He stood up and pulled a chair out for each of them. It was then Meg noticed that the table had place settings for five. She briefly wondered why the waiter had not placed them at one of the smaller tables. She said as much to John and Gabby, and they just began beaming smiles that lit up the room. John was sitting directly across from Meg. She watched as he nodded toward the doorway behind her and said,

"Well, I suppose your surprise is the reason."

Meg half turned in her chair and looked toward the doorway. Her breath caught in her throat, and she began smiling as much as John and Gabby. Ben and Jessica were walking towards them. The three shot up out of their chairs to greet the couple. Lots of hugs later, they finally settled down long enough to give the waiter their drink orders. Quick explanations about the surprise visit were shared in between receiving their drinks and making their lunch choices.

John and Gabby had invited the younger couple to come down for the music festival held at the U.S. Mint during the first weekend of August. They wanted to keep it as a surprise for Meg. Gabby joked with Meg about John's inability to keep anything a secret, but she was so proud that he had succeeded for once.

The waiter brought around cups of chicory coffee after they had finished their meals. The dining room was clearing from the onslaught of the Sunday crowd, and they were practically the only party left. The little group began talking about Meg's project and its progress. Meg gave Gabby the go-ahead to share the news about turning the project into a book that would be published by the newly formed Leblanc Publishing.

Ben and Jessica listened intently as Meg explained how she was practically finished with the book, but that her research on Sam possibly being here in New Orleans just wasn't coming to fruition. During the conversation, Meg noticed Ben nod at Jessica. Jessica quickly excused herself for a moment.

"I'll be back in a jiffy. I forgot something up in our room."

Ben adroitly turned the conversation to the upcoming music festival and John was talking non-stop about all the bands that usually performed as well as the scrumptious goodies at the food tents. When Jessica returned to the table, she had a canvas bag over her shoulder.

Ben looked around the table and then turned to Meg,

"Jessica and I aren't the only surprise for you. We brought something with us that we think you will want to see."

Jessica reached into the bag and pulled out a very old journal and passed it over to Ben. Meg instantly recognized it as the same type as the others that had belonged to Daniel.

Meg asked, "Is that what I think it is?"

Ben nodded,

"It sure is. We just found it a couple of days ago. My uncle brought us an old pie safe he had gotten from Granny Roberts' house years ago. He thought it would fit perfectly in our house. It was in bad shape, so we were trying to do some minor repairs and refinish it. When we turned it on its side, we saw a loose board underneath and found it had a hidden bottom. Inside, we found this journal. I can understand the hidden bottoms of the boxes we found earlier, but the hiding space in this cabinet took some real effort. It was after I read the journal that I realized why Daniel had gone to all that trouble."

John and Gabby looked as astounded as Meg felt in this moment.

Jessica joined in,

"I haven't read it yet, but Ben has. Things seem to get more and more interesting. It seems like the universe just keeps providing you with what you need to finish your project. Am I right Ben? Will she find the answers she needs for her ending?"

Ben looked down at the journal and then at Meg.

"I think you will, well, at least somewhat. Depending on the twists and turns you have written in the first part of your book."

With that, Ben attempted to hand the journal to Meg. Instinctively, she momentarily reached out her hands but just as quickly drew them back and clasped them tightly in her lap.

Ben laughed and said, "Oops, I forgot you won't touch an artifact without your gloves. Jess, do you have some in the bag?"

Meg shook her head as Jess began to dig down into the bag to find the gloves they had packed.

"No, it's not that. I mean, yes, I would prefer to use gloves when I look at it, but right now, I don't want to read the journal."

This time Ben and Jessica joined in with John and Gabby in their looks of abject surprise.

All four people around her spoke simultaneously.

"You don't?" The voices of the four carried across the room and even the waiter looked up startled.

Meg was certain how she wanted to move forward.

"I have finally begun to trust my gut and listen to the voice of my intuition. I want a chance to finish the ending of my book based on what bits of historical research I have about that specific period of history and the messages my intuition is receiving. Can you give me a few days to complete the book on my own? Then I will read over the journal to see how closely they align."

The young couple nodded. Jessica took the journal from Ben and placed it back in the bag. John Peabody was itching to ask to read the journal himself now, but his respect for Meg outweighed his curiosity. Gabby looked around the table at the group of friends, beyond thrilled to be an observer of this very interesting literary experiment.

It took every ounce of willpower that Meg could muster to leave the journal behind with Ben and Jessica. However, she was adamant that she would go back to her apartment without it. The plan was simple. She would take the next week off from her duties at Tulane and dedicate herself to completing the book. She wanted to have the ending written before Ben and Jessica returned to Virginia.

These new circumstances changed her original plans for the remainder of the day. Now instead of playing tourist, she would go back to the apartment and firm up the outline she had begun. She felt sure if she wrote all day on Monday and Tuesday, she could complete the ending and hand it off to Gabby and John to read. They would hold on to it until she had a chance to discover the information found in the latest journal. The plan was for all five of them to gather on Thursday evening. Together they would compare the information garnered from the journal and what Meg had intuited as the ending of her book.

Ben and Jessica had several day outings planned for the week prior to the beginning of the music festival. John had shared that they were going to be working on a project for Gabby's family during the week and he offered to help Dr. Gallo with anything he needed while Meg was out of the office for the week. Everything was set for Meg to concentrate on her writing.

Meg walked the few blocks back to her apartment within a very short time. Once there, she hastily unlocked the door, placed her keys in the bowl on the table, and walked over to put her purse away. She showered and changed into comfortable clothes. Then Meg walked over to the tall French doors and pulled the drapes to shut out the activity of the street below. Meg reached over and turned on the box fan she had purchased for background noise. Nothing could be allowed to disturb her during this final writing spree. As she made her way over to her small sofa, she looked back towards the table by her door. She smiled mysteriously at the doll on its stand.

"Okay, Papa, we have some work to complete.

Chapter 23

Monday morning found Meg up bright and early. After brewing a whole pot of coffee instead of her usual single cup, she sat down to work at the table near the window. She had pulled the drapes open and cracked the door to hear the background noises of the street below. The morning and early afternoon street sounds were becoming familiar and comforting for Meg.

Meg realized she had been working for hours without stopping when she heard chimes on the tower over at the Saint Louis Cathedral ring out eleven times. Her tummy was rumbling but she didn't have the urge to cook for herself. Meg decided that a quick walk to grab a bite was just the break she needed. She hastily made herself presentable to the outside world and headed out to the street.

Meg remembered there was a sweet little soup and sandwich place over on Dumaine. She had only visited a couple of times, but a sandwich would be just the thing to tide her over until dinner. After Matthew, one of the owners of the food shop, had whipped up one of his mother's famous egg salad sandwiches, she sat at the table by the window to eat.

As she sipped her sweet tea, she noticed that Amelie was just opening her store across the street. Meg had a sudden thought. She finished her lunch, bussed her table, and complimented Matthew on the delicious food he served, before dashing across the street.

Amelie welcomed her back into the store as Meg made her way back to the shelf of wonderful smelling soaps. After completing her purchase, Meg walked up Dumaine and then to Bourbon. As she passed Lafitte's, she glanced in to see who was working. Neither Jimmy nor Wavery were about, so she asked the bartender on duty if they were coming in today. The bartender told Meg that Jimmy had the day off, but Wavery was due in at three o'clock.

Meg made her way back to her apartment. She wrote diligently until it was time for her to return to Lafitte's. Today was the day. Meg was going to find out what she had done to elicit Wavery's strange looks and chilly attitude.

It was a little after the hour of three when Meg paused her writing. For once she did not pack up her writing bag to take with her. Instead, she picked up the elegant black bag holding the soap that she had purchased at Amelie's shop earlier in the day. Meg was non-confrontational by nature, but she needed to know if she had caused something amiss with Wavery.

If Meg was going to be in New Orleans for any length of time, she was not going to avoid one of the places where her writing energy seemed to surge. Maybe it would seem odd to others, writing in a bar, but she wasn't going to question what worked for her. She had found a flow of ideas there more than she had in any other place.

There were only a few people inside the bar when Meg arrived. A couple of older gentlemen were sitting in the chairs that lined the sidewalk next to the front entrance. Wavery was standing behind the bar replacing the condiments needed for the Bloody Mary and Hurricane drinks. Meg walked straight up to stand in front of the bar.

"Hey Wavery, how are you?"

Wavery looked up in surprise. There was a new tone in Meg's voice. It was a stronger, more confident tone than she had heard from Meg in the few times they had spoken. Wavery wondered what had brought on the new attitude.

"Hey Meg. I'm okay. How are you," Wavery asked hesitantly.

Meg stood a little taller, continuing with her undertaking and said, "I'm doing well. Mostly. I have something I need to ask you and I want your total honesty. Forget that I am a customer. Don't worry about playing nice with me, just give it to me straight. Every time that I have been here... when you are working... I have caught your gaze aimed at me. Especially when I am over at my... I mean *the* table working. Sometimes it has felt like you were studying me. The way you wrinkle your nose and scrunch your eyes, almost in a scowl makes me feel uncomfortable. And it has happened more than once or twice. I just need to know, have I done anything, anything at all, to offend you?"

It was Wavery's turn to feel uncomfortable. Feeling uncomfortable was not a familiar emotion for Wavery. She had blocked anything that pushed her toward that reaction for a long time now. Wavery had purposely developed a somewhat brusque if not surly attitude since her late teens and early twenties when she had first felt the need to protect herself both emotionally and physically. The protective armor had served her well in her job. It had kept well-meaning patrons from becoming overly familiar. More importantly, it had kept rowdy drinkers from thinking they could get away with anything in her presence.

Wavery had worked hard to present herself as a tough cookie. She hadn't been about to let anyone hurt her ever again. *But* she certainly didn't want to be the cause of anyone else's discomfort.

Wavery could feel the burning heat crawl up her neck. She didn't need a mirror to know that her neck was transforming into a bloody crimson color. The color was inching higher and higher toward her face. She reached up to rub the itchiness on her neck and felt her cheeks beginning to burn as well.

Wavery couldn't believe that the mild-mannered writer girl had unknowingly found a way through her defenses. Wavery was embarrassed beyond words. How did she let Meg know that the looks and attitude she had suffered through had nothing to do with anything Meg had done. Meg was definitely in the clear with this situation. Nope. Once again Wavery's problems with her own past, with her gifts, had resulted in someone else being hurt.

It certainly wasn't Meg's fault that Wavery saw people and things that others could not. She hadn't been making sour faces at Meg. She had been disgruntled about the fact that her gifts wouldn't go away and neither did it seem did the shadow man that accompanied Meg. All of that had come through in her expressions that she thought she had been hiding so well. How was she going to explain all of this to Meg without making Meg think she was totally bonkers?

Meg watched in awe as the red stain rose on Wavery's neck and onto her cheeks. Meg associated the bloody color with anger and waited for the bartender to explode. It certainly wouldn't have surprised Meg given what little she had already observed in Wavery's attitude before.

Wavery looked around. There were very few bar patrons milling about, leaving the two women some space to talk. Meg was shocked with Wavery calmly, almost beseechingly, asked Meg to pull up a barstool. She offered her a drink on the house. Wavery walked over to the rotating barrels to pull a cold cup of the purple frost. She turned to take the drink back to Meg and saw him. There he was standing behind Meg once again. She had not noticed the figure when Meg entered the building. Yet, he was here now, standing just over her shoulder. Wavery looked straight at the man's misty face. He cocked his head and then nodded toward Meg. It was if he was telling Wavery to share her truth... and she did.

Wavery looked around to make sure that the few patrons in the bar weren't close enough to hear the conversations she was about to begin.

"First of all, you have done nothing to make me feel uncomfortable or for that matter to anyone else here at the bar. Jimmy is crazy about you. He makes sure you are looked after when he isn't around."

Meg interrupted, "Jimmy isn't the one I am worried about."

"I know. I get it. It isn't anything you have done, it's my own... for lack of a better description... strangeness.," Wavery said quietly, hanging her head just a bit lower.

"I know you're from the mountains, same as me. I'm sure we have a lot in common or at least might be familiar with some of the same things." Hesitantly, Wavery went on,

"Have you ever heard people say that someone had 'the sight'?"

Wavery held her shoulders tight waiting for Meg's answer. If the woman across from her had no idea what she was talking about, this could lead to an uneasy explanation on Wavery's part. If she did know, she still might think Wavery was totally nuts.

Meg's reaction was not what Wavery expected.

"Well, of course. The sight and other gifts are rampant among the people of the Appalachian Mountains and valleys. I only wish I had a more defined gift like many of the women in my family."

Wavery couldn't believe what she was hearing.

"You would actually *want* gifts like that? Wouldn't it bother you for people to know you were different in those ways? Especially when you aren't back home," asked Wavery.

Meg looked at Wavery intently. The woman from North Carolina was holding something deep inside. Meg really wanted to understand what was going on in her mind.

"Do you have the gift of sight? Does being able to predict what is to come frightening for you," asked Meg.

Wavery was deep in the conversation now and there was no turning back.

"I see people, people that aren't here... well, that have been here, they are just not here now— if you know what I mean. I have at times been able to... put things together to decipher what might happen.

Meg knew exactly what she meant. Her great aunt Retta had been known for having that special gift. But still Wavery had not spoken to her fear of her gifts and Meg was unsure whether to push that part of their conversation. Fear is a personal thing and not to be dealt with lightly.

"I know exactly what you mean. You see the spirits of people who were once alive. Dang, I think you are very lucky. That's a gift I have been asking for, but if I am to be honest just to see my grandmother."

Wavery had so many emotions and thoughts wash over her. The woman sitting in front of her casually sipping on a frosty drink thought nothing at all strange about what she had just shared. It was as if Meg were saying "tell me something I don't know". Wavery wondered if Meg understood that having that gift had its pitfalls as well.

Meg tilted her head to one side. It had finally dawned on her that Wavery might have been scowling at someone besides her.

"Wait a minute," Meg continued, "does that mean when you were looking my way you were seeing spirits or a spirit near me? Was it my grandmother? Is she here now?"

Meg whipped her head around looking for any sign that might suddenly show up but saw nothing as usual. Wavery could see the disappointment in Meg's eyes because she couldn't see anything, especially her grandmother.

"No, your grandmother isn't here and as far as I can tell, she never has been."

Meg was disappointed but she had half resigned herself to the fact that she was not going to be able to have the same gift that Wavery had been given. Meg knew she should be grateful to at least be able to tune in to her granny's voice. But that hadn't happened since she left the Natchez area and she now worried that she may have lost that gift. She turned to Wavery and said,

"Oh well, this old building is filled with history, so it only makes sense that it has spirits that go along with the memories that were made here. All this was really my mistake. I thought you were looking directly *at* me and not *around* me. I guess everything floating around catches your attention."

Wavery leaned over the bar closer to Meg and said,

"You didn't make a mistake. I was looking in your direction specifically, because I was looking at the misty figure of a man that stands behind you when you are at that table. Well actually, just about anywhere I see you, I see him. Not all the time but most of the time."

Meg wasn't sure what reaction Wavery was expecting but it probably wasn't the curiosity of the researcher that erupted.

"Ooooh! Have you seen the man before? Do you know how he is connected to the bar? When was the first time and the last time you saw him?"

Wavery shook her head in wonder. The woman before her certainly wasn't put off by any of the information she had shared so far, but she might be once the answers to her barrage of questions sank in.

"No, I have never seen him before. Not before I noticed you coming here to the bar. As far as I know, he has no connection to the bar unless you have a connection to the bar. The first time I saw him, he was at your table, leaning over your shoulder. It looked like he was whispering in your ear. You were writing furiously away in that black notebook of yours. The last time I saw him…well…is now. He is standing right behind you."

Meg felt a shiver of excitement go up her arms and whispered,

"What's he doing?"

It was Wavery's time to be nonchalant, "Nothing. Just watching. I don't think you need to whisper on his behalf. I'm pretty sure we aren't going to shock him. Do you have any idea who he is and what he wants?"

Meg thought back over the past weeks, remembering how easy the flow of her writing had been when sitting here in the bar. It hadn't been the location necessarily but the spirit who had been "whispering" in her ear. Meg could only think of one spirit it could be… Daniel. Daniel Hughes. The man who had tried to help Sam find his family. After all, it was his journals she was using as fodder for her story. This had to be the sign that she was on the right path.

Meg looked at Wavery and answered, "I do. It must be the man whose journals I am using for the research portion of my book. This is good, very good. In some ways I really wish it had been my grandmother, but it is what it is as the saying goes."

Meg was excited. She had not only come to an understanding of sorts with Wavery, but she also felt she had received validation that she was on the right path. Meg wanted to give Wavery a hug for all her help, but she knew they weren't quite ready for that level of friendship. At least Wavery wasn't. Instead, Meg thrust the little black bag from Amelie's shop toward the taller blonde woman.

"Oh, here, I almost forgot, I brought you something."

Wavery took the bag with a questioning look on her face. Meg giggled a bit awkwardly.

"I stopped in at a local shop and bought it for you as an apology gift just in case I really had done something to offend you. I hope you like the way it smells, that's kind of important."

Wavery opened the top of the bag tentatively and a waft of something incredible filled her senses.

"It smells incredible. What is it?" she questioned as she reached into the bag and pulled out a cardboard container with purple lettering. "Soap?"

Meg looked delighted that Wavery liked the scent. She went on to explain the story behind the scented soap and its properties. Wavery thanked Meg and decided to cut a bit off to keep in her purse to use at work just in case the spirits and the patrons became a little too much.

Meg thanked Wavery for her drink and explained that she was on a self-imposed deadline and needed to get back to her apartment. Both women felt much lighter as each went on about the remainder of their day.

Meg worked well into the late evening before taking a quick shower with her special soap and once again she drifted off into a sound sleep. After her evening shift ended, Wavery walked down Bourbon going home from the bar. She unknowingly passed under the balcony of Meg's apartment. She didn't notice the misty figure standing guard outside the darkened French doors.

Meg slept a little later than the day before but was still up and working away as the sunshine sprinkled through her window. For the first time, she was truly looking forward to resuming her afternoon writing sprees at Lafitte's. She was anticipating the intuitive whisperings of her special spirit friend.

Meg abruptly thought about Ben and Jessica. Could she tell them about the spirit of Daniel being her muse? Well, of course she *could*. They were both open-minded people and would not criticize or demean the idea of folks having certain gifts. More importantly, *should* she? After all, Daniel was Ben's long ago relative. How would he feel about the grand uncle coming through to her and not Ben? Meg decided to keep that information to herself for the time being. Actually, the information really belonged to Wavery. It was Wavery's vision and not hers. The only thing Meg had were the inspiring writing sessions.

Meg could see the final bit of her work coming together. She was confident that she would be ready to hand the ending section of her book over to Gabby and John by tomorrow night. She wandered over to the sofa to stretch out and take a little break. As she leaned back into the cushions, she thought about what an eventful summer it was turning out to be. Her career had morphed into something she truly enjoyed. She had become a writer with the promise of being published. She had made a new friend, no, make that two new friends. She was counting Wavery even though she still had to work on building the connection between the two of them. Meg wasn't sure the woman was still entirely comfortable with her but then again Meg could sense that Wavery had gone through something that didn't allow her to feel at ease with most people.

That was quite the opposite with Ann. The connection between Ann and Meg had been positive and immediate. Meg looked over to where her phone was lying on the table beside her laptop. She thought about giving Ann a call. Then she thought better of it. Meg really needed to get back to work and she knew that Ann's infectious demeanor could lure her away from the job at hand. So instead, she walked over to the fridge, grabbed a soft drink and a snack to fortify her next round of writing.

It wasn't long after Meg returned to the table with a snack and drink that she heard the ping of a notification on her phone. She looked down. Meg was only half surprised that she was looking at a text from Ann. They were definitely on the same wavelength. Meg picked up her phone. She read the invitation to meet up with Ann at the house on St. Charles Avenue for the promised tour of the grounds. Meg accepted the invitation to see Ann on Thursday at two o'clock. She offered to bring a late lunch.

With a few back-and-forth texts they decided to have a picnic under the giant oak on the back of the property. Ann was sure the owners would be fine with their luncheon under the tree.

By the time the chimes at the Cathedral rang out one p.m., Meg was back at "her" table in Lafitte's. Wavery wasn't due in until two, but Meg wanted to settle in and get deep into her writing. She had concocted a little experiment in her own mind. She wanted to see if the flow of her writing increased from her arrival and continued when Wavery arrived. Meg has thought about asking Wavery if she saw Daniel over her shoulder again, but she didn't want to treat Wavery's gift as a sideshow.

Meg's flow of writing was as grand as before. So much so that she didn't even notice Wavery arriving for her shift. Wavery waited until three and finally walked over to Meg.

"Hey, there. I don't want to interrupt. You seem to be having a good go at your work, but have you had lunch?"

It took Meg a moment to switch her focus from the words coming out of her pen to the words that Wavery was speaking.

"Oh, hey there. It has been really going well. I hadn't even noticed you or Jimmy coming into work. Umm, no I haven't eaten yet. I thought I would just wait until I go home."

Wavery made a friendly offer.

"Well, I brought an extra salad. I thought you might like something to tide you over. Can I get it for you?"

Meg's tummy gave a little growl of acceptance and Wavery went to the back to get the salad out of the employee fridge. Jimmy nudged her arm as she carried it and a plastic fork back out front.

"So, now who's the one taking care of writer girl?"

If Jimmy wasn't such a sweetheart, she would have been taken aback by his teasing. Instead, she played right along.

"Well, somebody needs to see that she is fortified. She shared she had a deadline she was trying to meet. I understand that all too well. It's just like when I am writing a paper for class, I forget the world around me, and I forget to eat."

Wavery turned her back to Jimmy as she walked across the bar room. Jimmy smiled, watching a bit of the ice melt from around Wavery's heart. *Finally*, he thought to himself.

Wavery approached Meg's table and set the salad down for her. Wavery pulled out the chair to sit without a second thought. Meg raised her eyebrows in question. It was going to take a while to get used to Wavery actually being friendly.

Wavery began, "I just wanted to let you know about one of the things you missed when I first came into work today. You were so entranced in your work I don't think you saw me talking to one of the owners. She has noticed you once or twice before. I told her you were a writer with a deadline and that you had found you could do some really good work when you were here during the quieter parts of the day."

"She and I had an idea we wanted to run by you. I need to come in around eight in the morning to work on inventory before we open. I have permission for you to come in with me if you want. You can sit here at your favorite table and work in peace. We won't have the windows or doors open but it will be nice and cool. If you need to bring your computer, you have permission to charge it up in the back office."

Meg smiled at the offer and wondered if this was Wavery's way of opening a door to building a friendship. She was fairly positive that was exactly what was happening when Wavery pushed back her chair to return to the bar and called back,

"By the way, he was behind you when I came in and he has never left. Seems like he wants you to get this project of yours written as much as you do."

Meg was far enough ahead with her writing that she decided to take a break after leaving the bar. She walked back to her apartment and left her writing bag on the table. Her plans were to transcribe her work from her notebook to the laptop once she came back to the apartment. For now, the water was calling to her and she headed back out to sit by the river until the sun started going down.

The next morning Wavery was standing at the patio entrance of the bar when Meg arrived sharply at eight. The two women hastily made their way inside and Wavery locked the door behind them. Meg didn't bother to ask Wavery if Daniel was anywhere around and Wavery didn't offer. Instead, both women went straight to work on their individual tasks.

By eleven that morning, the inventory was complete and Wavery was filing orders with their liquor supplier. The beer delivery trucks had already come and gone. Meg needed a break and headed out to the coffee shop on Royal to grab some coffee and a pastry for each of them. She bought an extra pastry to put back for Jimmy when he came in later in the afternoon.

Wavery was working her last few hours for the day when Meg announced to her that the project was complete and saved on a thumb drive. Wavery wondered if this was a cause for celebration but hesitated to suggest it to Meg. They still weren't quite there yet.

Meg thanked Wavery for all her help and headed out to leave her writing bag at the apartment. While at the apartment, she took a few minutes to freshen up, place the thumb drive in her purse, and call a cab to take her to Tulane. She didn't have the patience today to take the longer streetcar ride to her office. She wanted to get there as quickly as possible and get everything she needed printed out and put in a binder. On the way, she called John Peabody to let him know that the work would be ready in a few hours. He excitedly relayed the message to Gabby. She could hear Gabby in the background,

"Ask her if we can come by Tulane and pick it up? I can't wait!"

Meg was both thrilled and nervous at the same time. She hoped Gabby liked the ending she had written. Meg knew once she had the information from the last journal that Ben had found, there could be more rewrites and additions ahead.

After she had turned the binder over to John and Gabby, Meg decided to take the slower route back to her apartment via the streetcar. She wanted that extra time to soak in the spirit of the city, letting the rhythmic turning of the car's wheels help her wind down. She felt as if she had been running a marathon and she simply wanted to breathe. Slowly. Deeply.

When Meg finally reached her apartment, the sun was still shining. She decided to forego dinner and take a long hot bath instead of a shower. She used the last of her special soap, realizing she needed to purchase more. Tonight, she was simply going to pull her drapes shut tightly, sink into her bed to sleep, and let the lingering scent of the soap work its magic.

Chapter 24

The sun was beaming rays of heat through a cloudless sky. Thursday in the Quarter promised to be a scorcher. Jimmy and Wavery were beginning their shifts together earlier than usual in preparation for the onslaught of visitors arriving for the Satchmo Fest at the U.S. Mint.

The two chatted as they performed their tasks in a companionable rhythm. Jimmy had stopped to grab breakfast earlier that morning at the Clover Grill further down Bourbon. He mentioned seeing some folks with tool bags pass by the window as he was finishing up his meal. When he had arrived at Laffite's, he noticed the same people going in and out of the house across the street.

Meg asked him if he had noticed a petite, dark-haired woman and a taller, dark-haired man in the crew. She explained how she had seen them before coming and going at the house. Jimmy affirmed seeing the woman but had not seen the man she was describing. The two bartenders mused about what was happening with the house that had stood unoccupied for so long. Not long after, the very woman they had been discussing popped out the door. She crossed the street and walked into the bar.

She smiled up at Wavery who towered over her in height,

"Just a cola for me, please. It is so dusty in that building. I am absolutely parched."

Wavery slid the iced cola toward the women and took her money, saying,

"I guess it wouldn't be a great idea to have anything stronger while you are working with power tools."

That was Wavery's way of trying to find out what was going on so that she could share the info with Jimmy.

Ann took a long sip of the iced drink and said,

"You're right about that. I also have a meeting with clients in a bit, so nothing alcoholic for me."

Wavery looked the woman up and down and hoped she was at least going to shower first.

Wavery decided to cut to the chase and asked,

"Clients? What is it that you do?"

Ann took another sip and began explaining her work in the restoration of old buildings and homes.

"I look at the building and its history, then I try to help the clients bring back the original glory when it's structurally possible."

"So, you're an architect?"

"No, but I work with the architect. I share the design plan per the historical accuracy and the architects ensure that the work can be completed in relation to structural specifications."

Wavery looked at Ann from tip to toe and said in her usual blunt manner,

"Well, you sure are dusty for just sharing plans."

Ann took no offense and laughed aloud,

"Oh, I can do much more than that. I grew up working in my family's construction business. I have no problem jumping in and helping the crew on any job. I am handy with just about any tool and I have no problem getting dirty in the process. It allows me to monitor every step of the process. That way I can ensure that my plan is being carried out with integrity. I'm quite serious about what I do."

With that, Ann placed a tip on the bar and gave a quick wave. Wavery watched the self-assured woman head out the door, turning to walk in the direction of Esplanade.

Wavery picked up the tip and shook her head in admiration. She called over to Jimmy, who had been eavesdropping on the whole conversation,

"Just goes to show, you can't judge a book by its cover. You know when I first noticed her, I thought she was a helpless little debutante type. I was wrong. That woman has some real gumption."

Ann left Lafitte's with a quick stride toward her rental on Frenchman. She only had a short time to shower and dress before jumping in her car to head over to the house on St. Charles. She was excited to be able to show Meg around the house and she was looking forward to having a nice lunch in the back garden area. Thank goodness for the shade of the grand old oak to block the glaring sun.

Ann had checked with the clients, and they were perfectly fine with inviting her friend over to see the completed work. The couple would be bringing the final check by during the afternoon as well. The time had come to move on to the project on Bourbon Street.

Ann loved talking about her work as much as she loved doing it. She was excited to be able to tell Meg about the Bourbon Street plans. The building wasn't too far from Meg's apartment, and she hoped the proximity would allow them to get together more. She had felt an instant connection with Meg since their first encounter. It would be nice to have a new friend in her new city.

Ann was sitting in one of the large white rockers on the front porch of the St. Charles house when she saw Meg hop off the streetcar. Meg was carrying a bag of what promised to be their lunch. The house was mostly furnished now, and the kitchen was complete with all the appliances. Ann opened the door of the large fridge and Meg placed the bag inside before they went on a quick tour of the house.

Ann and her crew had completely restored the beauty of the house. It was clear that great care had been taken in bringing back the original architectural details. Ann told Meg that the owners wanted to keep every room to period as much as possible but had wanted to keep the furnishings simple and minimal. Ann joked that she felt that the wife just didn't want to have to be responsible for dusting a sundry of knickknacks.

"I would think that anyone who could afford such an exquisite property could afford a regular cleaning crew," posed Meg as they returned to the kitchen.

The two women began pulling together paper plates and utensils to use for their luncheon on the outside wrought iron table and chairs.

Ann nodded in agreement but added, "You know, I think they can, but they both strike me as people who like to do things for themselves when possible."

Meg blushed, "Oh, I hope that didn't sound judgmental on my part. While this house isn't as big as many of the homes here in the Garden District, it is just so much bigger than what I am used to for sure. I can't imagine one person doing all the cleaning all the time."

A familiar voice chimed in from the hallway coming into the kitchen,

"Well, darlin', I don't plan to do it by myself, that is why I married John."

Both young women whipped around to see John and Gabby Peabody grinning from ear to ear. Ann felt her cheeks burning in embarrassment regarding the overheard conversation. Meg stood with her mouth wide open.

John walked over and placed a check into Ann's hand and then hugged Meg tightly.

"Okay Ms. Hurley, you better close that mouth before all the flies in south Louisiana make a landing."

Gabby was laughing at the expression on both young women's faces and said,

"Ann, I didn't know you knew our Meg. How did you two meet?"

John made his way over to the fridge and was peering into the bag Meg had brought when Gabby quickly admonished him.

"John, get your hands off the girls' food. Ann, we just came to drop off your check and not horn in on your lunch."

Meg finally pulled herself together enough to let the group know there was plenty to share. Ann seconded the invitation to join the lunch party and they made their way outside for sandwiches and explanations.

Ann and Meg went first. They described their initial meeting and what had ensued since. John went on to tell Ann how they had known Meg since her early days as a student at the college they all worked out now. Neither John nor Gabby knew how much Meg had shared about her new writing career so they both held back that part of the story.

Meg was on the edge of her seat wondering about John and Gabby's new house here in New Orleans. John looked over at Gabby nodding for her to take the story.

"This house isn't really "new" to us. It has been in my family for a while. It was the first house my grandfather purchased for my grandmother after his investments started to return so greatly. He waited to buy it after he was confident that the money he had made was going to stay around a while. Before moving here, they had only lived in small apartments in and around the Quarter. He was a frugal and careful man by nature. Even after making huge returns with his investments, he chose to remain frugal to an extent. He could have afforded one of the grander homes down the street, but he and grandmother chose to live more simply."

"So, your parents didn't inherit this home? I thought they lived in the Garden District area," interjected Meg.

"Well, they do live nearby. My paternal grandparents lived for a very long time and stayed in this house for the length of that time. My parents wanted to stay in the home they bought when they were a young married couple even after my grandparents passed. It might have been easier for them to care for this house, but they loved the place where they had made their own special memories."

"At one time, Father wanted us to move back from Virginia and set up housekeeping here and have my grandparents move in with them. We loved our jobs in Virginia, and we loved to come visit but it just wasn't time for us to come here on a permanent basis. Quite honestly, my grandparents did not want to move out of the house unless they absolutely couldn't live on their own. So, it all worked out in the end. The grandparents had the time of their lives here. John and I visited them often over the years. Now we've inherited the property and we have plans to visit more often, as you know. In between times, we will let friends and colleagues stay here if they want."

The sun had moved across the sky and John looked up at it and back to Gabby.

"Well, Sweety, I think it's time for us to head out. We have a special dinner tonight and we need to let everyone know where we will be meeting. "

John rose from his chair and shook hands with Ann,

"Ann, you did a fantastic job with the house. Gabby can't quit telling everyone we know about it. I am sure you are going to get quite a few calls inquiring about your services."

Gabby went over and gave Ann a hug as if she were welcoming her to the family,

"John is right, you did a perfect job. More importantly, I am so glad that our Meg has a new friend here in New Orleans. We will feel so much better knowing she has someone here when we head back to Virginia."

The young women walked John and Gabby out to their car and waved a final good-bye. Ann turned to Meg and laughed,

"Are you sure they aren't your parents?"

Meg smiled at how lucky she felt and looked at Ann,

"I guess they are surrogate parents to some degree, but both of them are my boss… in different ways." Meg walked back to the house to help Ann tidy up the lunch mess. As they brought the kitchen to rights, Meg filled Ann in on how Gabby and her father, Mr. LeBlanc, had become her publisher during the past week.

Gabby sent a group text to Ben and Meg inviting everyone to meet at the house on St. Charles Avenue at seven that evening. John would meet the three of them at Ben and Jessica's hotel. He would drive them over and back at the conclusion of the evening.

Once they were all in the car for the ride to St. Charles, John told Ben and Jessica the story of the house and offered it to them for future trips to New Orleans. After arriving, John gave Ben and Jessica a tour while Gabby and Meg set out coffee and nibbles in the dining room.

Once everyone was settled around the table with their food and drink, the discussion of the ending of Meg's book and Daniel's journal began in earnest. Since Gabby and John had read Meg's final work thoroughly, they would each take notes as Ben gave a detailed synopsis of the journal. Gabby thoughtfully handed a notebook and pen to Meg so that she could make notes of any new thoughts that might come to her during the evening. Jessica volunteered to keep everyone's drinks refilled as necessary.

Ben began his narration of the third journal written by Daniel Hughes.

"In Daniel's latest journal, he shares more details about how he was able to take Samson on the journey to find his family. Daniel had been very humble about the extent of his woodworking skills in his previous journals. He was actually so talented in his skills that the Reston family, who were the owners of the salt works, commissioned him to build many pieces for their home."

"He was building as fast as he could to provide them with detailed mantles, tables, wardrobes, you name it. It also seems that the varying cousins within the region noticed the artistic pieces of furniture and put in their own orders. It appears that he was able to start making a rather generous living and stepped away from his duties with the church to some degree. In my opinion he only stayed on with the church so that he could ensure Samson would be able to continue living under his protection.

Ben caught himself and promised not to give anymore opinions. He didn't want to influence the story before Meg had a chance to share.

"We do have to remember that Daniel lived a very simple life, so it probably wasn't all that difficult for him to save back money. Money that he would use towards taking Sam southward to find his family.

During this time, the son of the Restons married a daughter of a prominent general down south. The couple received a rather grand wedding present from the bride's family, a home on the Mississippi River just north of New Orleans. Not to be outdone, the Restons of Virginia would ensure that their son's new home had the finest furnishings made to order from the wood of his home state. So, they commissioned Daniel once again to build and deliver a few pieces to their son for his approval. If he and his bride liked the craftmanship, they would pay Daniel to remain nearby to build anything the couple wanted for their home."

Jessica paused her husband to inquire how they got the few pieces that Daniel had already made all the way to Louisiana and Ben answered,

"The very same way they had been sending salt down to Florence, Muscle Shoals, Natchez, and even into New Orleans... by barge. The Restons had their own barge builders and they had two barges specifically built to take Daniel, the already finished pieces of wood, and extra Virginia wood to build anything else that their son wanted to remind him of his home state."

"The barges traveled the Holston River down to the Tennessee River and then eventually connected to the Mississippi. According to Daniel's journal, the barges made it all the way to Natchez where the cargo was unloaded for transfer to a steamboat heading toward New Orleans. The Restons paid well for the boat to stop on the river near their son and daughter-in-law's plantation home."

"Of course, the Reston's were so enamored with Daniel's work and their pride in being able to send the very craftsman to their son's home, they agreed to let Daniel take Sam with him. They assumed that Sam would be there to see to Daniel's needs and assist him with the more mundane tasks associated with building the furniture. What they didn't know was that Sam could turn out pieces of furniture as well made as Daniel's. In fact, he was the one who drew the plans and carved the intricate scrolls and designs added to each piece."

Meg felt the need to ask a question.

"Did Daniel not give Sam the credit for his work?"

"According to Daniel's writings, he wanted to do so, but Sam asked him to hold back. It seems that Sam felt it best to be as inconspicuous as possible. Given the happenings of the time period, it probably was the wisest plan."

Meg understood and yet the unfairness of it all simply amplified her need to share the truths that had long been hidden. Ben continued sharing from the journal.

"When the two men reached Natchez, the weather was turning quite bad. It was the end of summer and as we all know, that means hurricane season. The crews were glad to be off the barges and on dry land while they waited to see what the ensuing storm might bring. According to Daniel, the storm passed by New Orleans and to the east."

"Natchez was saved from anything too devastating, but the storm had slowed the arrival of any boats coming up from New Orleans. The plan had been for Daniel and Samson to board a boat sent from New Orleans that would turn around and take them, the furniture, and supplies to the designated delivery point."

"The few days they had to wait came in handy for Daniel. While they were waiting, Daniel was able to search out and find information that indicated the arrival of Sam's family to Natchez. Daniel assumed that the family had been picked up by the cousins from New Orleans. He found out differently. He had to break it to Sam that the family had been separated in Natchez. Ironically, the twins had been sold and were taken to the very plantation that Sam and Daniel were heading to the next day."

John, Gabby, and Meg were scribbling fiercely in their notebooks. Ben decided to take a quick break and help Jessica make another pot of coffee. When the coffee had been poured, Ben continued.

"When Daniel and Sam arrived at the plantation, they quickly decided it was in everyone's interest to keep Sam's identity undercover until they could find the whereabouts of Henry and Louisa. Sam wanted his brother and sister to be kept safe. He worried that for some reason their relationship might put them in some type of harm. Sam did not trust anyone, except perhaps Daniel and Emil."

"Daniel was given lodging in a house that one of the overseers had once occupied. That overseer was no longer at the plantation."

At that point, Meg had to wonder if that was the home of Hiram, but she did not voice her question aloud.

"Daniel requested that Sam be allowed to stay with him in the house. Again, it was wrongly assumed that this request was because Daniel required some type of service."

"It seems that the pieces of furniture they had brought from Virginia met the approval of both the husband and wife. The plantation home was already outfitted with furnishings, so the couple wanted the rest of the wood to be made into additional furniture for a home they kept in New Orleans."

"Basically, it all worked out that Daniel would be paid to go to New Orleans to live and build furniture to completely re-outfit the house there. He would use the Virginia wood and be given any other wood and supplies he would need to complete the project. The younger Reston couple would pay for his services and arrange for a small living and working space. Sam could accompany him, but Daniel would be responsible for providing Sam with food and clothing."

This time, Ben interjected his own viewpoint.

"In a way, that sounds prestigious on Daniel's behalf, but my gut tells me it was more of a brag for the Restons to say they had an artistic craftsman on site from Virginia."

Jessica gave him a look that said, "Remember, we aren't supposed to add anything until everything is shared."

Ben continued,

"Daniel and Sam had to wait a few days for yet another boat to take them and the remaining wood to New Orleans. While they were waiting, Daniel was able to poke around on Sam's behalf. He doesn't say how he started the conversation, but he writes of speaking with an older lady who worked in the kitchen area. She seemed to know everything that happened on the plantation. Once he was sure he could trust her and that he had Sam's permission to tell her about Sam and his family, he found out some truly disheartening news."

"The woman, that everyone referred to as Miss Tassy, shared that Henry had died on a night of a new moon. The talk was that he had gotten too close to the water and an alligator had taken him under. His body has never been found but blood was found on the shore. Strangely enough, his sister disappeared not long after and has never been found. Several personal items were missing from her quarters and the talk was that she had somehow made a run for it. The boss put out a lookout for her in all the local papers, especially places further north."

Ben looked up and saw a look of surprise on everyone but Meg's face. He wondered just how closely the journal and Meg's story were aligned. He thumbed back through the pages of Daniel's journal before continuing.

"Daniel wrote of how it pained him to return to Sam with such dreadful news. He recalled watching as an eerie calmness came over Sam when he heard Daniel's words. Daniel looked into Sam's eyes. He saw them harden into ice.

Daniel wrote that they sat in silence for almost an hour before Sam spoke aloud. Sam asked if they would be able to search for his parents and little sister once they arrived in New Orleans. He felt it was best that he shared the news with his parents if they could be found."

"Within the week, the boat going to New Orleans stopped near the plantation. The cargo of wood and supplies was loaded by workers from the plantation. Daniel and Sam boarded and soon found themselves on their way to a city that they would call home until the following spring. Or at least Daniel would be there only for that length of time. Daniel was planning on giving Sam his papers of freedom, once the two men located what was left of Sam's family.

Meg shifted in the high back dining room chair to try and get more comfortable. The group had been sitting there for a while. She was grateful when Gabby suggested they all move to the softer furniture in the front living room. Meg and Jessica carried the cups and plates to the kitchen, promising to do a wash-up before they left. Gabby went into the room facing St. Charles and turned on the lights but pulled the drapes for privacy. The men took a quick stretch on the back veranda. Once they all had settled in the living room, Ben continued with the information from the journal.

"Basically, Daniel and Sam settled into a small property in what we know as the French Quarter. Daniel didn't write an address, but he described the property as being near a few rowdy locations. He was also surprised that the Reston family allotted them such nice property. Later he found that the property was a foreclosure that Reston had taken over from someone who owed him a substantial amount of money."

"The entire building had been left in rough shape, so it was a good place for them to do the woodworking in the back rooms and outside area. Not long after settling in, Reston let Daniel know he would also be paid for any improvements he could make to the property before leaving to head back to Virginia in the spring."

Daniel wrote of conversations that he had with Sam regarding finding his father, mother, and baby sister. The good thing was that they knew the names of the cousins of the family that had taken Nelson, Sarah and Dibby. It wasn't hard for Daniel to locate the Dupuys. Ironically, their home was very near the large home that belonged to the Restons."

"This offered a chance for Daniel and Sam to covertly look around the neighborhood hoping to catch a glimpse of Sam's family. Sam told Daniel that he felt he would recognize his mother and father even though it had been a few years since they had parted back in Virginia. He was sure that Dibby had grown so much he wouldn't recognize her. He could only hope she would remember him."

"Neither of the men wanted to cause a problem for what remained of Sam's family. They had no idea what the family who took them from Natchez was like and how they were treating the three. Sam and Daniel decided it was not in the best interest of anyone to boldly walk up to the front door inquiring about the family. So, they waited weeks before trying to plan to attempt to see Nelson, Sarah, and Dibby."

"During those weeks, Daniel and Sam began their woodworking in earnest. The long days were spent working in unison to produce some of their best work. Daniel watched in awe as Sam carved and formed the decorative additions that would enhance the functional pieces of furniture. One night after they had finished their evening meal, Sam pulled out paper and a piece of charcoal to work on a delicate design for a scroll that incorporated the flowers of the dogwood tree that grew so prolifically back in Virginia."

Daniel wrote that he absentmindedly remarked to Sam that hands that could draw like that surely could produce beautiful handwriting, if only he could write. Daniel was taken aback when Sam told him quietly that he could write *and* read. In the three years that they had known each other, Daniel had never been aware of this information about Sam. Of course, Daniel knew that in many states, it was illegal for anyone to teach an enslaved person to read and write, so he was aghast that Sam had told him of his skills. He asked Sam why he was sharing it now."

"Sam told him he knew the danger Daniel faced for trying to help him. He said if he couldn't trust Daniel, there was no one else left to trust."

Sam explained that his former owner was aware of the penalties he would face for allowing any enslaved person to learn to read and write but his wife had insisted upon teaching Sam and his brother Moses. She was a godly woman who believed that everyone should be able to read the Bible. She told her husband that writing was just a natural product of reading."

"So, she taught both Sam and his brother Moses, hoping they would in turn teach their brother and sisters. She gave a stern warning to the older brothers telling to not let her husband know she was encouraging them to teach the others. Sam told Daniel how eager Louisa was to learn from her brothers, but that Henry couldn't stay away from the horses long enough to settle down for a lesson. Dibby was too young at the time. Sam had hoped when she got older, if they were all still together, that one of them could teach her. He knew that his mother couldn't read and refused to learn. She was against learning the skill because it could put them all in danger. Yet she never tried to stop the lessons given to her children. She said she knew her place with the lady of the house. His father, Nelson, never said a word either way. This left Sam to wonder if perhaps he could already read and was hiding the fact."

"Daniel promised Sam that he would never mention it again unless Sam wanted to talk about it. After that, however, Daniel purposely left books near Sam's workbench. They would disappear for several days before showing up in the exact spot where they had been left."

"Life in New Orleans was very different for the two men in both climate and culture. Both agreed they were looking forward to wintering without snow and ice. It would be nice to be able to take care of daily chores without the cumbersome addition of heavy clothes."

"The difference between living in the mountains and now in a growing city shocked them both, especially the behaviors of the residents. Daniel had never witnessed so many well-to-do people or so many businesses that provided so much fodder for the vices. He reckoned that had to do with both his upbringing in the mountains of Virginia and his calling to serve the church."

"Sam shared his shock at seeing people who shared the same skin color as he had walking around free. Serving no one. Both men learned that many had once been enslaved but had worked to purchase their freedom. Sam bluntly told Daniel that he wasn't trusting of that situation.

How could they trust their freedom would not be taken away once again?"

"Not many weeks after that conversation, Daniel was able to share another bit of wonderous information with Sam. He described an event that was held on Sundays across New Orleans. On Sundays, those who were enslaved were permitted a day to gather and they did so at several green spaces around the city."

"One gathering was not far from the house they were occupying. Daniel suggested that Sam attend and look for his parents. Sam told Daniel he was not sure he trusted the people here enough to go out on his own. Daniel said he would walk as far as the entrance to the area and wait for him to return. Daniel would carry Sam's papers with him in case something did happen, and they had to prove who Sam was and where he belonged."

"They made their way to the event for two weeks in a row with no sighting. Finally on the third week, Sam recognized his father standing across the way under the shade of some large trees. Sam later described to Daniel how he carefully approached his father, who looked much older than he had the last time he saw him. When Sam returned to where Daniel waited, he was smiling and seemed happier than Daniel had seen him in a very long time. Daniel wrote that his smile dimmed when he explained that although he also got to see his mother and sister, too, he decided to hold off telling them about the stop in Natchez. He felt the shock would be too much all at once. They agreed to meet there every Sunday."

Ben stopped to take a breath, and said,

"I know this seems to be taking a while to tell, but honestly, Sam and Daniel experienced a lot of living in the months they were in New Orleans."

Ben told the group he needed a stretch and went to the kitchen for some water before coming back to share the last part of the journal.

"During the week after Sam's first meeting with his family, Daniel encouraged Sam to tell his parents about Louisa and Henry on the next Sunday. Daniel wrote that he brought a pen, ink, and an empty journal and handed it to Sam. He told him that sometimes writing things down helped when it came time to handle a difficult task. He did suggest that Sam not use names in his writing. That way no one could tie the journal back to Sam. Daniel wrote in his own journal that Sam asked for two more before the return to Virginia the next spring. Daniel never saw them and did not know what Sam had done with them. He wondered if he had burned them when Daniel wasn't around."

"The winter months in New Orleans proved to be profitable for Daniel. Many of the Reston family's friends also commissioned pieces of furniture. The work that he and Sam did on the building they were staying in was very satisfying to Mr. Reston and he was generous with his payment. Daniel knew that he would have more than enough money to use for his return to the mountains. There would be no problem leaving some with Sam to use for himself and his family."

"Daniel began inquiring about work for Sam as he was planning on signing the papers that would give Sam his freedom. Sam had finally broken the news of Louisa and Henry to his parents and Dibby. It was more important than

337

ever to Daniel to try and help the remainder of the family to stay near each other. Daniel hoped to help Sam find work to help pay for their freedom papers as well."

"Sam always glowed with such happiness after spending his Sundays with his family. He had even gained enough trust to make his way to and from the park on his own. So, it was upsetting to see Sam return to their shared house one Sunday with a look of utter despair on his face. Daniel waited until later in the evening before mentioning his concern to Sam."

"According to Daniel's journal, Sam didn't hesitate to share what had upset him. He had spoken with his parents about helping to secure their freedom, but they had refused. They told him they were too old to do anything but what they were doing now. They felt they had a place in the household that gave them some degree of safety."

"His parents did agree that all three could use the money they had saved to purchase Dibby's freedom papers. Sam's parents remembered all too well the sorrows of being split away from Sam, Moses, Louisa, and Henry. Knowing that they would never see Henry or Louisa again had made them want more for Dibby. She was still young enough to find a way to live in the city as a free woman or make her way north, if that was her choice."

"Daniel felt this was a good time to share his plan for signing over the freedom papers for Sam before returning to Virginia alone. Daniel told Sam that he had promised Emil that they would go into furniture building business together in the upcoming summer. Emil wanted to leave the saltworks behind."

"Daniel was stunned when Sam asked him not to sign the papers. He explained that he may return to New Orleans one day as a free man but for now he wanted to leave in the spring as well. He asked to work for Sam and Emil and promised to help them farm as well. Daniel asked Sam to help him understand why he didn't want his freedom now."

"Sam was clear in that he could do nothing more for Henry and he would probably never know where Louisa had gone. He did know that his parents would probably always be in New Orleans and hopefully he would see them again. Dibby had to make her own mind up about what she wanted and that only left Moses. He was hoping that Sam would take him back to Virginia and they could find Moses. Sam promised he would work hard for Daniel and Emil. He vowed to pay off any debt for finding Moses.

Ben looked at the journal lying in his lap and then over to Meg,

"Basically, that was all the most important parts of the journal, except for the last page where he writes about the tearful good-bye between Sam and his family on their final Sunday in New Orleans. They sailed upriver the next day heading back to Virginia."

Chapter 25

The entire group sat in stunned silence for a moment and then Jessica broke the unsettled hush by quietly asking,

"That's all? We don't know what happened after they left to go back to Virginia?"

John answered, "Well, maybe this is where Meg's intuition kicks in and allows her to present an ending that is logical."

"Oh," Jessica turned to Meg, "How close was this to the ending that you have already written?"

Meg looked over to John and Gabby, who nodded toward her, and she answered Jessica.

"Pretty darn close. I included their stop in Natchez, but not with the same details. In fact, I have a narrative that was shared with me that gives more explanation about Louisa and Henry than was shared with Daniel. The narrative shared with me has no documentation. It was more folklore of the area. Readers might even consider it a ghost story. But... it is as believable as any other documented information I have gathered so far."

Meg stood, stretched, and walked over to the window to peek through the drapes. She looked out into the night before continuing,

"I noted that Daniel and Sam stayed in Nola for the winter but mostly because of the weather conditions they would face trying to travel north before spring. They could only take a steamboat so far before they would have to begin traveling over land back to the mountains. The idea of taking a barge back upriver was out of the question. Barges of that period didn't have the ability to maneuver back upriver. So, once they reached their southern destinations, they were torn apart, and the wood was used for other things."

"Honestly, it just made good sense for them to stay in New Orleans for the winter. I did create a story around how they found Nelson, Sarah, and Dibby. It didn't match the story we heard tonight but I can make revisions so that it matches Daniel's journal. I also included the lack of safety Sam would feel in New Orleans for various reasons and that coupled with the fact that he wanted to find Moses was foremost in Sam's decision to return to Virginia with Daniel."

"If there are no more journals that we know of, I think I should end the story just as abruptly as it feels Daniel's journal ends. A simple return to Virginia. Maybe if we find more journals or information about Moses later then that becomes a book as well."

Gabby smiled at the thought of Meg already thinking of the next book. She suggested they share all of this with her father on Saturday night at dinner. She was sure he would love the idea of a second book.

An idea popped into Gabby's head. She asked Ben and Meg if the surname of the New Orleans cousins who held Sam's family had been revealed.

"It was documented in the papers found in Virginia and Natchez."

Gabby told John to make a note of that for editing purposes and turned to Meg once more,

"What was the name of the family here in New Orleans?"

Meg answered without hesitation,

"Devereux. I know they had a large house here in the area of the Garden District but no plantation ownership that I can find."

Meg looked over at Gabby, who had suddenly turned pale and was staring at John. Gabby turned back to Meg,

"The Devereux line are cousins on my mother's side." Gabby shook her head in disbelief and continued,

"We still have some distant cousins left on that side. I believe they still own that original house but if mother was right, they were leasing it out to a company that operates wedding and party venues. Maybe you do have a lead on a second book, but we need to get this one finished first."

Meg looked at Gabby and then the rest of her little group.

"You're right; I need to finish this book first. I'll use everything we've uncovered now. Anything else that comes to us, well, we will see how that falls into the next book. But there is something just as important to me as the book that I need to finish."

John looked over to his former student and now colleague. He thought he might know where she was going with this.

"This whole adventure began with my own disappointment. I was upset when I realized that my hometown had shied away from telling the whole story of the history of our town. A history that deserves to share the truth about *all* the people who made the town what it was, what it is, and what it could be."

"While I was busy researching the facts about the Slave Trail of Tears and Sam's journey, I learned more than I anticipated. I quickly discovered that my little town wasn't the only place to have done this. It's happened all over the south and more than likely all over this country. I think I've also come to an understanding that while I am disappointed in myself for not coming to this knowledge sooner, there is nothing I can change about that. There is nothing to gain by being angry with myself or with others."

"Anger won't change the past and I personally don't believe it can change the future. The only hope we have is in understanding. It is so important to try and understand everything that has gone on before us so that we don't make the same horrible actions ever again."

"All I can hope for is that just one person reads the story about Sam and his family and comes to an understanding that sharing the whole truth is the right thing going forward. If that were to happen, then I would feel that I have done what I could.

Meg walked back to the sofa and sat down again,

"I've also decided to go back home in a few weeks. I need to do more than write a story. I need to share the facts with certain people back home to see if we can work together to make a few changes. We need a location dedicated to the *whole* story of the saltworks. Various sites around town need placards that explain exactly who did what jobs at the saltworks among other bits of information."

John asked, "Are you staying in Virginia permanently? Or will you be taking the deal to work between Byars Creed and here at Tulane?"

Meg grinned, "Oh, I'm most assuredly taking the deal. I'm trusting my own intuition from now on. My gut tells me that even if I can't find anything else about Sam's family, there are other stories to be told… and I know just the place to try out future writing sessions."

John smiled knowingly,

"Back at Lafitte's? Is it the ambience or the purple drinks? Gabby and I wouldn't want you to take Hemingway's route."

John, Gabby, and Meg all laughed heartily but Jessica was confused and asked for clarification.

"What? Hemmingway wrote at Lafitte's?"

Gabby, the English and Literature expert answered,

"Hmm, not that I know of but that could be some good research as well. No, what we are laughing about is an old quote attributed to Ernest Hemingway. I have even seen it printed on key chains at a little boutique store in the Quarter. It reads, 'Write drunk, edit sober.'"

Meg assured them all that the drinks had nothing to do with the flow of writing she could accomplish at the bar.

"No, I promise you that I won't be using the famous purple drink as my muse when I can use the other spirits floating around the place."

Jessica was enthralled at the idea.

"Do you mean that you see ghosts there inside the bar?"

Meg's eyes softened as she remembered her new acquaintance Wavery. Nope, make that new friend. Meg was determined they would one day be on good terms. Wavery was the one who could see what was going on, but Meg was beginning to understand that she herself "heard" what was going on around her and it had nothing to do with the physical realm.

Meg trusted the four people who were sitting with her as much as she trusted her own parents. Her parents knew and understood the special gifts that members of her family had been given. She looked at the four people sitting with her at this moment ready to include them in on the family secrets.

She explained to Jessica about her grandmother and the special gifts that the women in her family carried. Thankfully, Jessica wasn't flustered by what Meg had shared. In fact, she seemed in awe. Meg also looked over to see John and Gabby exchange a strange look. Meg wondered suddenly if the two of them thought Meg had lost her mind and was both relieved and surprised when John shared a bit of personal information.

"You know folks, women from the mountains aren't the only ones that can have such experiences. Sometimes, we men are blessed or cursed, depending on how you look at it, with the same type of gifts."

Meg looked at her former professor with her jaw open wide,

"What do you mean, who do you know that has such gifts?"

John blushed a bit and quietly replied,

"Me, but only sometimes. For me, it has only been when I am in certain circumstances or locations. Mostly when I am in the building where our offices are located and a few other places around campus."

It was Meg's turn to have a look of wonderment on her face.

"You see things… people…?"

John shrugged his shoulders,

"Yes. I see people. I hear them when they speak. Dang it, with a few, I can sometimes have a back-and-forth conversation. I try to keep the radio playing soft and low in my office when I am alone. That way if anyone passes by and hears a conversation, I can blame it on whatever is being broadcast. I wouldn't share this information with just anyone and I am going to ask you folks to keep it to yourself. I don't want the college president to have me hauled away to the loony bin and lose my retirement."

For a moment, Meg thought John was serious about the last part until she remembered that John was known for his quaint idiosyncrasies. Still, it was a very personal share, and she would never betray his trust.

The evening had been very productive, but it had also been mentally and emotionally taxing. The group decided to call it a night. Jessica and Meg offered to help with cleaning up, but Gabby said that she would take care of it while John drove the three of them back to the Quarter.

Meg assured Gabby that John could just drop her off at the hotel and not attempt to find a way to get her to her apartment on the lower end of Bourbon Street. Gabby's protective instincts had her trying to argue but John assured her that Meg knew what was right for her. Of course, John knew that there was always someone walking just behind Meg, and he knew she would be just fine. He looked forward to the day he could tell Gabby all about it. He hated keeping a secret from his sweet wife, but he had made a promise. A promise that would keep Meg safe. John still had Meg give him a call when she was inside her apartment safe and sound.

Meg made the conscious decision to put a hold on her writing for the weekend. Instead, she spent it with her friends who had come from Virginia. The days were filled with great music and fabulous food on the grounds of the U.S. Mint.

On Saturday night, Ben and Jessica joined in at the dinner held at the LeBlanc's home. It was a casual barbecue, and the evening temperatures had uncharacteristically cooled down creating the perfect setting on the huge porch that surrounded the entire house.

Meg tried not to pre-judge but if she were being honest, she expected that the luxurious façade of the home might indicate the LeBlancs were really "fancy" people, as her granny would have described them. However, Meg had never met two people that were more down to earth. It was clear how Gabby had grown into the kind and authentic person she had become.

After a few hours of conversation, she recognized that both Mr. and Mrs. Leblanc didn't care a whit about what others thought of them. If they were too low key for folks in their neighborhood, those folks were left to go about their own business. These two people cared about two things: their family and helping others. It was refreshing to say the least.

The couples shared their plans for returning to Virginia. Ben and Jessica were flying back home on Tuesday, so they had brought the journal for Mr. LeBlanc to look over. Ben did his best to get Meg to keep it with her until she returned to Virginia.

Meg would only agree to take it with her that night for a read over so she could make additional notes. She would return it to them before their flight out. She had promised herself the weekend away from her work, so she would spend all day Monday reading and taking the additional notes she needed.

The Peabody's plans were to leave the following Sunday as they had an anniversary party to attend on the upcoming weekend. Meg didn't want to get anyone's hopes up, but she felt she could very possibly have her edited finale of the story completed by Wednesday. Meg kept that information to herself in case it didn't work out.

Monday turned out to be wet and stormy all day long, so Meg cracked open the French doors to listen to the rhythm of the rain and the interspersed thunder. She sat on her sofa pouring through the last journal of Daniel Hughes, making copious notes. She compared the notes to the additions she had scribbled on a notepad the past week. She smiled in satisfaction.

That night, Meg hurried over to Ben and Jessica's hotel to return the journal and say good-bye. Meg's passion for the work came on full force the next morning and she was able to easily complete the final edit by Tuesday evening.

Meg texted Gabby to let her know she would be receiving an email with the manuscript in its entirety within the hour. Meg gave the file a final look, then pushed the send button. Meg wasn't sure how she felt now that the book was out of her hands and in her publishers' domain. It was like she had just sent her smiling child off to summer camp. She was proud of the child, but she suddenly felt lonely.

Meg decided to take a walk and see what was happening in the Quarter. She headed to Jackson Square to see who was playing street music. She watched as folks gathered for the variety of ghost and vampire tours leaving from the center of the Quarter. Meg had gotten used to the slowness of Tuesday evening when visitors were booked on outgoing flights back home.

This week was an exception. Even though the Satchmo Summer Fest had ended and White Linen night at Julia Street art galleries was over, some of the visitors remained in the city. They would be joined by others waiting on the next set of events for the upcoming weekend.

The LeBlancs had tried to prepare Meg for the craziness she would be witnessing right outside her door. Saturday morning, the Quarter would be filled to the gills with men and women outfitted in a variety of red attire. Most would be wearing sneakers, but more foolhardy souls would be showing off in stilettos as they all attempted the Red Dress Run. Later that night, folks would gather in the art galleries on Royal Street for Dirty Linen Night. Meg laughed at herself for not understanding the background of the name. Dirty Linen night had been established for the patrons of art galleries on Royal Street. Supposedly they were to wear the same garments they had sported the previous week at White Linen night on Julia Street.

After living a quiet existence in the mountains for most of her life, Meg had decided that living in the Quarter was exactly what she needed now. She was filled with such gratitude for the opportunities she had been given by the LeBlancs. Just last night she had spoken with her parents to tell them that she would be heading back to Virginia in a couple of weeks, but it wasn't a permanent move. She explained all that had transpired and that she would be traveling and living between both places. She half expected her parents to be sad, but they were truly thrilled for her. They promised to come down and visit. Her parents assured her that she would always have a place to stay when she was back home in Virginia.

Meg placed a tip in the bucket sitting in front of one of the local brass ensembles and turned to head up Chartres. When she hit the crossing at Chartres and Saint Phillip, she decided she would see if she could squeeze in at Lafitte's. She rarely went there in the evenings because of the throng of people, but tonight she was craving being lost in the crowd.

It had been days since she had spent an afternoon at Lafitte's writing. She wondered if Meg would still be on shift. When she arrived, there were two bartenders she had never seen before and no sighting of either Meg or Jimmy.

Meg decided to order a different drink rather than her usual and carried it with her to find a table. Her favorite table was already taken but there was a small one by one of the front windows next to the juke box. The table legs were a bit uneven but if she nudged her knee just right against one of the legs it was fine. Actually, it had to be fine because it was basically the only table left.

The sun was beginning to set low in the sky. The busser for Lafitte's moved around the room lighting the candles that sat in the center of each table. Meg was staring into the flame of the candle on her table when she heard her name.

Meg looked up to see Wavery with her bartending apron in one hand and her purse slung over her shoulder.

"Meg, what are you doing here? This isn't your usual time and that's not your usual drink. Are you meeting someone?"

Meg smiled and pointed to the chair sitting on the other side of the table,

"No, not meeting anyone. Just changing up my routine a bit. Looks like you are off shift, want to join me?"

Wavery made it a practice not to spend evenings in the bar where she worked but she could see nothing wrong with grabbing a soft drink and chatting with Meg for a few minutes. A few weeks ago, the very idea would have appalled her for a variety of reasons. Instead of making her way back to her solitary apartment, she chose to hang her purse and apron on the chair across from Meg. She tried not to think too much about the reason why she felt comfortable enough with Meg to change her routine, even for a bit. She asked Meg to watch her stuff and went back to the bar for a soda.

When Wavery returned to the table, she took a sip and said,

"I have to be honest with you Meg, it is really odd to see you here without a notebook."

Meg laughed and replied, "You have no idea how odd it feels. How odd everything feels."

Meg went on to tell Wavery about everything that had happened since they last saw each other, including the last journal that had helped her complete and turn in her book to LeBlanc Publishing. Meg was about to ask Wavery what had been going on with her when they both looked over to Ann walking up to the building across the street. Ann was dressed in a cute cotton summer dress and did not carry any tools for once. Instead, she held a cardboard roll container like the ones architects use to store their plans.

Wavery and Meg continued to watch as two men came out of the front door of the building. They both recognized the same dark-haired man they had seen there before but the shorter, slightly older fellow was new to them both. Ann handed off the container to the shorter man

352

who was smiling from ear to ear. The three spoke for a few moments before the two men walked away.

Meg called out to Ann and waved her over. Wavery winced to herself, feeling a dread at having to make small talk. She suddenly wished she had left earlier for her apartment. It had been a long time since she had to be social with anyone longer than it took to serve them a drink.

Ann walked up to the window to say hello. She was so petite that she had to stand on her tiptoes to look inside at the two other women. Wavery decided that had to be uncomfortable and told her to come inside and join them. She had shocked herself with the invitation and wondered where it had come from. Wavery looked around to see who or what might be floating around trying to influence her actions. She saw nothing, not even Meg's friend who always seemed to be nearby.

Ann agreed, stopped by the bar to grab a drink for herself before joining the other women. Meg had already grabbed an extra chair from one of the larger tables and Ann settled in smiling at both women. The personalities of all three women were so different. Meg was quiet and observant until she was comfortable, Wavery was always guarded, but Ann appeared to always be smiling and open in every situation. Unbeknownst to the other two, Ann had a knack for getting people to open up and feel comfortable. It was like she had a magic key that fit everyone's lock.

Ann's magic began working immediately. It wasn't long before all three women were sharing general information of how they came to be in New Orleans and how they had met each other at different times. Both Ann and Meg saw how hard it was for Wavery to share even the simplest day-to-day details. Wavery didn't understand how the other two could do it so naturally.

Wavery almost choked on her drink when she heard Meg tell Ann how she could write with a better flow here in Lafitte's because she had found out that she had a special muse floating around whispering in her ear. Wavery looked over to see if Ann was going to be shocked or laugh at the suggestion of a ghost assisting Meg with her writing. She was neither. Instead, she leaned over the table closer to Meg and asked her to tell her more.

Wavery interrupted,

"You mean you don't find that strange, even preposterous?"

Ann looked at Wavery with a very matter of fact expression and said,

"Of course not. Everyone has gifts if they are open to them. I can't hear or see people but that doesn't mean that I don't think others can."

Gifts. Wavery still felt a bit skeptical about that kind of respect, especially remembering how she had been made to feel the odd one out during her teenage years.

"Everyone?" asked Wavery, "You really believe that?"

Ann saw that she had struck some kind of nerve and replied gently,

"Everyone that *wants* to recognize them. Not all people are comfortable with the responsibility of having such gifts. Some people, for a variety of reasons, just can't or don't want to believe. Some even run from them."

That last sentence cut deeply and Wavery decided to step away from the conversation. She excused herself to go to the ladies' room while she tried to recenter herself. She hoped the other two wouldn't discuss her while she was gone from the table. Neither of them did. When she returned to the table, there seemed to be a silent agreement to chat about more mundane topics.

Ann took her own turn going to the ladies' room. While she was gone, Wavery ventured back to the subject of Meg's muse.

"Thank you for not telling Ann that it was me who could see your shadow man. I appreciate it."

Meg's response was sincere.

"That part of the story is not mine to tell. You'll know when it's time to go deeper."

Just as Ann returned to the table and sat down, a couple of EMS trucks rolled and rumbled by in the street outside the bar. All three women placed their hands on the rickety table to hold it steady. Ann, who favored her left hand reached out to steady the candle in the center of the table.

In the illumination from the candle, Meg saw something familiar on Ann's left hand. She had the exact same scar on her middle finger that Meg carried on her own. Wavery noticed that Meg was staring down and looked to see where her gaze had landed. The trucks with their blaring sirens moved away from the Quarter. Wavery reached over to push the candle away from the center of the table. She took Ann's left hand and placed it where the wood had been warmed by the burning candle. She then placed her left hand on the table and looked over at Ann.

"How in the world…" she began but was interrupted by movement from Meg. Meg had placed her left hand on the table as well. All three women looked down and saw the exact same scar in the exact same placement on each of their left hands.

They sat there speechless, staring at the three different hands for what felt like hours but was only a few seconds. One of Wavery's co-workers walked past and she brought herself around long enough to request another round of drinks for the table,

"And make mine a whiskey, a double. "

"Mine, too," said the other two in unison.

After the drinks had been served and they all took a large gulp, the logistical side of Meg's nature came to the top.

"I think it's safe to say that while we are all three very different, we obviously have something oddly in common. Who wants to go first and tell the rest of us how you got that scar?"

It was clear that Wavery wasn't ready and even Ann had been taken aback so much that she needed time to pull her thoughts together. Before Meg began her story, she requested they all be honest and forthright and that anything they shared stayed among the three of them.

Meg had no qualms that Ann would be okay to share once she had grounded herself, but she wanted

Wavery to feel safe in a way that she may not have felt before. She was proud of Wavery when she immediately began telling the story of her own grandmother after Meg was complete. Ann finished up with how she had received the scar.

Once the women had shared their stories, they sat in silence for a moment, contemplating what all of this meant for them. They recognized the gifts that had been bestowed on each of them. Their respective grandmothers had taught them the skills needed for healing through plants and herbs native to their region. They had that in common. Individually, they brought something different to the table. Meg could intuit or at times even "hear" information being given to her. Wavery could "see" people who had passed, and she could use her glass pieces to interpret situations. Tonight, they learned that Ann had a gift for "feeling" out the spirit of place or objects. They believed they had been brought together for a reason, but they just couldn't figure out what or why.

Ann, back to her upbeat self, said simply,

"Well, we have time to figure that out. I am here for the eventual future. Wavery still has her graduate program to complete and Meg, you have your work at Tulane. So, we can get on this mystical mystery right away."

Meg had not told the girls that she was returning to Virginia for a while, so she broke the news to them now. She explained she wanted to hopefully help guide folks back home in sharing the whole truth of the story behind their hometown. She would volunteer to help set up a display dedicated to the work and history of the enslaved who had toiled in the salt works operation. She wanted to find a way to add the much-needed information to the various placards at the historical sites around town.

Wavery had a sudden feeling of loss wash over her. She would miss Meg, the writer girl. How strange that felt. When she had awakened this morning, she never dreamed she would be sitting here with two other women who in a split moment had found they had an unexplained connection.

Meg saw a new kind of sadness in Wavery's eyes and even a touch of it on Ann's face. She looked at each one of them and reassured them.

"Ladies, my plans had been to stay back home in the mountains until late fall, but I am going to take care of what I need to do as quickly as I can. I don't think I can be away for that length of time. Something is going on here that none of us understand…yet. There has to be reason this is happening."

Ann agreed wholeheartedly and her smile was back, already anticipating Meg's return. Wavery still sat quietly contemplating everything that had happened during the summer and the links between their lives.

"It seems we have more in common than any of us ever thought," Ann said.

Wavery looked at the other women and said,

"And we share something that has yet to be revealed."

Meg nodded solemnly in agreement, hearing the words whispered in her ear,

"You share it all… all but the blood."

Epilogue

The drive back to Virginia was going quickly for Meg. Using the interstate highways instead of ambling back up the Trace was making all the difference in the world. The eleven hour drive back to Virginia was providing time and space to contemplate everything that had happened since Meg had last been in her beloved mountains.

So many things had changed for Meg personally and professionally. She had made two new friendships that promised great adventures ahead. She had a new pathway in her career, and she was already anticipating writing a second book.

Most of all, she had stopped looking for gifts that weren't meant for her. Meg had found gratitude for the ones she did have. She had been sad that her grandmother's voice appeared to have faded from her after Natchez, but she still had all the memories and all of her grandmother's teachings that would never fade. Meg reached up to touch the necklace that her grandmother had given her. She remembered the love with which it had been given.

Meg looked forward to reviving those memories with her mother when she was back home. She was sure her mom would be able to share more stories of her grandmother that had happened before Meg was born. She looked forward to writing those down.

"Grandmother stories are the best," she said aloud to wind blowing through her open window.

"Well, of course they are," said a recognizable voice.

Meg almost ran off the side of the road and looked around. Still no visual but that voice was clear and familiar as if the person was sitting in the passenger seat.

"Granny, where on earth have you been," asked Meg incredulously.

"Youngin, don't you speak to me with that kind of sass," her grandmother's voice replied and then she heard her grandmother's laugh.

"You should be wise enough by now to know I can always get to you if you *really* need me."

Meg laughed at her grandmother's own brand of sassiness and started to tell her everything that had happened since Natchez.

"Hold on girl, don't waste your breath. I know exactly what has been happening. I told you once, I shouldn't have to tell you twice, I am always with you. Always. Especially when you call on me. Just because you don't always hear me doesn't mean I am not there. Sometimes it's better that you hear other voices that need to come through to you."

Meg was amazed and asked,

"You mean you know about the whisperings in my ear that helped me with my book? Did you have something to do with that?"

"I knew it was happening, but I had nothing to do with it. That came from... some other source. I have no

control over others, just me. That's the way it should be…
with the living as well," and she laughed her feisty laugh.

Her grandmother's voice continued,

"I will tell you this. This first book of yours might
be finished but the story you are looking for isn't over. I am
so proud of what you are doing. You know, telling the
truth, much less seeing the truth, ain't always easy. Most of
all, I am thankful you are finally understanding that you
don't need to see me to know that I am with you. Seems
like you finally have the gumption to trust in what you
feel."

Meg nodded her head and Granny's voice
continued,

"And another thing, don't you forget… faith is
believing in something or someone else. Trust is believing
in yourself. You put those two things together, well, there's
nothing you can't set your mind to…"

A few moments of silence passed as the words
landed in Meg's heart. Granny's voice softly broke through
once more,

"After all this, do you finally believe I will always
be with you?"

Again, Meg reached up and fingered the chain
around her neck, "Yes, Granny, I do. I really, really do."

All But The Blood

References

Debord, A. L. (2013). *Slavery in Smyth County, Virginia 1832-1865*. Emory, Va: Emory & Henry College.

Feldblum, S. (2022, May 11). The Slave Trail of Tears: Recreation or Reckoning. Scalawag Magazine.

Humence, B. E. (1989). *Before Freedon, When I Just Can Remember*. Durham NC: Blair.

Shannon, K. M. (2021). *Antoine of Oak Alley*. New Orleans: Pelican Publishing.

Stevenson, G. J. (1963). *Increase in Excellence: A History of Emory & Henry College 1863-1963*. New York: Appleton Century Crofts.

Sutcliffe, A. (2000). *Mighty Rough Times I Tell You*. Winston-Salem NC: John F. Blair.